Prologue	4
Chapter 1	6
Chapter 2	18
Chapter 3	24
Chapter 4	33
Chapter 5	49
Chapter 6	64
Chapter 7	68
Chapter 8	84
Chapter 9	95
Chapter 10	103
Chapter 11	111
Chapter 12	117
Chapter 13	129
Chapter 14	137
Chapter 15	149

Chapter 16	162
Chapter 17	180
Chapter 18	190
Chapter 19	196
Chapter 20	204
Chapter 21	216
Chapter 22	232
Chapter 23	241
Chapter 24	247
Chapter 25	256
Chapter 26	263
Chapter 27	274
Chapter 28	282
Chapter 29	287
Chapter 30	292
Chapter 31	303
Chapter 32	308
Chapter 33	316
Chapter 34	319
Chapter 35	323
Chapter 36	329
Chapter 37	333
Chapter 38	341
Chapter 39	343

Chapter 40	356
Chapter 41	358
Chapter 42	372
Chapter 43	375
Chapter 44	379
Chapter 45	381
Chapter 46	384
Chapter 47	389
Chapter 48	392
Chapter 49	396
Chapter 50	402
Chapter 51	407
Chapter 52	413
Chapter 53	420
Chapter 54	425
Chapter 55	435
Chapter 56	437

AN IMMORAL MURDER

By
Will Cameron

An Immoral Murder

Copyright © 2021 Will Cameron

The right of Will Cameron to be identified as the author of this work has been asserted in accordance with the Copyright, Design and Patents Act 1988.

All rights reserved. No part of this book shall be reproduced in any form or by any electronic or mechanical means, including information storage and retrieval systems, without written permission from the author, except for the use of a brief quotation in a book review.

This book is a work of fiction. Any resemblance to actual persons, living or dead, is entirely coincidental.

WILL CAMERON

For Karen

Prologue

The man stands perfectly still in the kitchen darkness. He tries to control his breathing as he glances back at the open window and listens to the almost silence. A murmuring fridge. A ticking clock. A slowly dripping tap. The distant, lazy acceleration of a car.

Little sounds of insignificance and nothingness.

The man switches on the pen torch and the searchlight darts along the wall. Menial objects come into view before passing into darkness once again. A calendar for 2008. July's image, a couple of big-eyed kittens looking forlornly out of a paper bag. He scans down and around. Kitchen roll. The wooden slants of a bread bin. Cups. He gently pulls open the fridge door. Eggs sit on an inside tray. Orange juice. Cheese. Yoghurt. Other shit. He shuts the fridge door and looks down at the lino floor. The whole place smells of lemon.

The man walks into the hallway and stops, trying to get his bearings. Doors. One. Two.

Three. The first one open. He sees into the living room. Shadows. TV. Settee. Windows. Half-closed curtains. He sees a sign and image on the closed second door. A Victorian lady holding a parasol. Bathroom, it says. The third door is half-open. Another sign – a little rectangular one with pale blue flowers around the writing. Susan's bedroom, it says.

The man gently pushes the door open, and there she is, the young woman lying on the bed just as he imagined her, turning her head, sighing, still asleep. The curtains are open, the orange streetlight streaming in and shading the girl's tousled blonde hair, tanning her innocent face. He smiles. Excited. Aroused. Angry. The covers are half over her naked body now, and he's quickly sitting astride her, pushing down, grabbing, squeezing, tighter, harder, tighter, as tight and as hard as he can till his hands ache with the pressure, the pleasure. He loves the way her delicious eyes bulge. Then he notices a book on the bedside table: The Big Book of Dolphins. That does it. From then on, he completely loses it.

Chapter 1

Normal Service Resumed

Detective Chief Inspector Michael Patterson made his way up the steep, stone stairs of the close in Glasgow's West End. He squinted against the early morning sunlight cascading through the first-floor stained-glass window. Sunbeams reflected off art deco tiles and lit up motes of dust suspended in mid-air. It only added to the overall sense of calm within the well-kept Partick tenement that Sunday morning, belying the fact a brutal murder had not long taken place in the top-floor flat.

As Patterson reached the third floor, a fellow officer in white coveralls was kneeling, storing samples into a case while another was scanning the oak front door for marks and fingerprints. On entering the flat, the first thing Patterson noticed was its high, elaborate corniced ceilings and the thick cream carpet underneath his feet. The overall air of tidiness and touches of decor, such as the framed black-and-white pictures of Paris on the walls, gave the impression of a home rather than simple accommodation. Not always the case nowadays, where flats across the city were being split up into practical bedsits for migrating workers.

Noticing Patterson at the door, the head of crime scene, Tom Doolan, motioned him to come forward.

'Morning, Mike, looks like it's going to be another cracking day, eh?' he said cheerily.

Patterson replied with an unsure move of the head, something between a nod and a shrug before he added in a lacklustre voice, 'I see normal service has been resumed for a Sunday morning.'

'Aye,' Doolan said. 'A bad one, I'm afraid. A young woman in the bedroom to the right there.'

Patterson headed to the room indicated and looked inside. As always, the crime scene was filled with a variety of useful and useless people. Detective Constable Brian McKinnon could have fallen into either category depending on which day of the week it was. Noticing Patterson come in the door, McKinnon walked apprehensively towards his boss, his slightly dishevelled hair complementing his somewhat lacklustre manner.

'Morning, Brian. So what can you tell us?' Patterson looked around, still unable to see the victim because so many others were in the way.

'Can't tell you much, sir – just got here myself.' McKinnon then moved to one side, which gave Patterson a better view of the victim.

A young woman lay naked in the centre of the bed. She appeared peaceful at first, calmly looking up towards the ceiling with her mouth slightly open, in no discomfort. It was only on further inspection – the open eyes staying open, the paleness of the skin, the purple-tinged lips – that it was clear she was no longer alive. She looked in her early twenties with a bright blonde bob cut, the clear blue eyes apparent even from a distance, her well-toned body indicating she cared about her fitness.

As Patterson looked over the body, his gaze was instinctively drawn to look for injuries and marks that could give a clue as to how she'd died. He soon noticed the bruising around her neck in the shape of irregular dark pressure points as well as some bruising on the outside of her waist and the tops of her hips. Signs of a sexual assault perhaps, yet on the inside of the legs, around her dark and neat pubic hair and around the slightly parted inner thighs, there appeared no bruising at all. Her arms had been crossed over her chest, covering her breasts, placed there by her killer, knowing she would be found like this.

'For fuck's sake.' It was unclear if Patterson was saying this in response to seeing yet another victim of this callous city or if it was in response to the fact this was a young woman who had been killed in the prime of her life.

Focused as he was on the victim, it was only now that Patterson took full notice of the pathologist, Tasmina Rana, who kneeled by the side of the bed, shaking a test tube with some liquid in it, holding it between thumb and forefinger, while dictating some thoughts to her assistant, who was writing those thoughts down.

For the moment, Patterson knew it was best to let Tasmina get on with what she had to do instead of asking questions she probably couldn't answer yet. Turning his gaze away from the body, Patterson observed Detective Sergeant Jack Simpson approaching him. Simpson raised his eyebrows to Patterson, correctly knowing there wasn't much he could say in response to the scene before them.

'Morning, Jack,' Patterson said. 'What have you got so far?'

Simpson looked down at his notes. 'Her name's Susan McLaughlin. Twenty-two years of age. A friend arrived this morning. They went jogging every Sunday. The friend came upstairs, found the door open, and the victim lying there as you see her now.'

'What time?'

'Just after nine this morning.'

'Anyone hear anything?'

'No one we've talked to so far.'

'Any ideas of how the murderer got in the flat?'

'None so far,' Simpson replied. 'There's no sign of forced entry, but the main door is broken downstairs. It has been for some time, apparently.'

'The friend still here, I take it?'

'Yes, living room.'

'What's her name?'

'Shona Anderson. Not sure you'll be able to get much out of her though; as you can imagine, she's still in shock at seeing her friend like that.'

'Aye, that's as maybe, but it's worth a go. I'll have a word with her in a minute.' Patterson was still trying to take everything in while attempting to ignore the bustle of the people around him. He hated being in a crowded scene like this when a body was found; he hated having to wear the restrictive white polythene suit, immediately looking for clues and signs to solve a crime that could end up taking days, weeks, months to solve – if it ever got solved, that is.

'So with no forced entry, the killer could have been let in by the victim?' Patterson asked.

'Possible,' Simpson said. 'Then again, as I said, the security lock is broken on the main door downstairs. The murderer could have easily walked up and knocked on the door. Susan opened the door and—'

'Aye,' Patterson quietly said as he returned to the front door. There was just one reasonably strong-looking lock with no splintered wood around, no evident scrapes or marks whatsoever.

'Anyone else live with her?'

'Nope, not according to her friend Shona —'

'She lived here alone?' Patterson interrupted before scanning the flat once more. 'Big flat for just one person, is it no'? Did she work?'

'She was a student at the university. Training to be a vet.'

'Student loans must have gone up since I was at uni,' Patterson said. The flat wasn't the height of luxury, but he knew the price of accommodation around here wasn't that cheap.

Tasmina finally stood up, putting items away into a case as she looked down at the body with a sadness in her usually more objective gaze. Patterson walked across to her.

'Morning, Tasmina. Any thoughts so far?'

'Aye, there's too many bloody psychos in this city.' 'I'm with ye there,' Patterson agreed. 'But what happened here? Any ideas?'

'Well, you probably noticed the severe bruising around the neck. First impressions, I'd say we're looking at asphyxiation – strangulation, manual. Then there's that concentrated bruising around the outside of the waist.'

'Any ideas on that?'

'It's possible the killer was on top of her, sitting astride. Overpowered her, strangled her. Having said that, it's all conjecture at this stage, I'm afraid. As per usual, the sooner I can get her down the slab house, the better.'

'Aye,' Patterson concurred.

As the room started to empty, Patterson turned his attention away from the body to the surrounding bedroom. Nothing seemed disturbed; no overturned furniture or sign of a struggle. However, Patterson noticed a book on the floor, face down, its pages spread, as if it too had been the victim of violence. Patterson twisted his head round to see its title better: *The Big Book of Dolphins*.

Turning his attention back to the room, he noted some, but not many, feminine touches. An orangutan teddy bear sat on top of the cupboard with an expression of complete innocence Patterson had seen all too many times before on the faces of Glasgow hard men. There were framed photos of animals on the walls: tigers, polar bears, elephants.

He looked back towards the bed. The duvet with its pink rose cover had been pulled off and was lying in a small gap between the bed and the far-side wall. Naturally, Patterson had dealt with many dead bodies in his time. As with all of them, this battered corpse simply looked empty. As if all that had made this woman who she was had been roughly snatched from inside of her and casually tossed aside.

Feeling anger and despair rise within him, Patterson quickly shut these emotions down. He knew he had to be the professional, logical and objective copper who would simply do everything he could to find this murderer. Yet, try as he might, Patterson's humane, emotional side couldn't help but be deeply saddened that another young life had been prematurely stopped in this all too often violent city. He now had to find out who had killed this woman, and that was what he was determined to do, no matter what. He went through to see Susan's friend, Shona.

Shona was a tall, athletic, healthy-looking woman in her early twenties. She sat on the settee with her head bowed, wearing a grey hooded sweatshirt with pink jogging trousers. Her long dark hair was tied back in a ponytail. She looked up at Patterson as he came into the room, and her red-rimmed eyes followed him intently as he sat down on a chair opposite her.

'Shona? My name's Detective Chief Inspector Mike Patterson. I understand this is all a shock to you and upsetting, but I need to ask you some questions if that's all right?'

Shona nodded with a look of incomprehension that usually accompanied all relatives and friends of a murder victim.

'I believe,' Patterson continued, 'that you were good friends with Susan, is that right?'

'Aye, since school,' Shona said quietly. 'We'd always known each other, looked out for each other ever since we were kids.' Shona was well-spoken, not posh, but well-spoken.

'Did Susan have a boyfriend, partner?'

Shona shook her head. 'No, she didn't. Last time she knew someone steady was over a year back. It was never that serious, though. She always said she'd meet the right man when the time was right. She wasn't going to rush it. God almighty—'

'What about a flatmate?' Patterson asked.

'No, she lived here alone; two years,

roundabout. She loved this flat; it was her pride and joy.'

'Did Susan mention anyone causing her trouble recently? Anything unusual or anyone bothering her?'

Shona shook her head and, for the first time, tried to smile as she thought of Susan alive. 'Susan didn't have an enemy in the world. God's honest truth, I know they always say that after someone's... she really was the nicest person you could ever wish to meet. Everyone loved her. I swear you couldn't not like her. Everyone liked her. Everyone.'

Patterson indeed knew that everyone thought the best of those who had just died. Shona seemed genuine in her thoughts, mind you. 'Was Susan out this weekend, do you know?'

'Not that I'm aware. Susan wasn't one for going out. She preferred to stay in, get on with her studies; she was studying to be a vet. I mean, we went for the odd night out 'n' that but not a lot. Susan really only knew me well, I'd say; a couple of other mates we knew as well back from our school days. She was just... what's the word? Conscientious. She was determined to pass her exams, and she was dead close to her mum. God, her mum! This will destroy her.' Shona sighed, gulping back inevitable tears that were sure to engulf her later on. 'Susan didn't really have any hobbies, apart from reading. She loved animals, of course; travel, she loved to travel, and, oh, she was also into fitness like me. That's what we were doing this morning. We always go for a jog around Kelvingrove Park every Sunday.'

Susan gulped in air, clenching her hands, still fighting to keep the tears back so she could help the police as best she could. Yet, even now, as she spoke, it would suddenly hit her that Susan was dead and make her realise this was all real; that her best friend since her schooldays was dead.

Patterson realised it was best to leave Shona for now and stood up. 'Thanks, Shona. We'll make sure we get who did this. I promise.' Patterson looked over at a female police officer waiting by the door and nodded to her. 'We'll get you home for now.'

Shona rose unsteadily from the chair and made towards the door. 'One last question, Shona. You mentioned she was close to her mum. Do you know where her mum lives?'

Shona finally broke down at the thought of Susan's mum hearing the news. 'Aye, Drumchapel. Kinfauns Drive – 285 Kinfauns Drive.' The WPC put her arm around Shona and led her out the door. As Patterson was writing down the address, Simpson came into the room.

'Sir, got some news. Might be a bit of luck.'

'What?'

Simpson walked towards his superior and said quietly, 'We may have a witness.'

Chapter 2

Long Time Coming

'Where were you last night, anyway?' The question took Daniel McLeod by surprise. He was the one who had just woken up to find Deborah packing her things, and yet he was the one on the defensive. Aye, well, there was no way Daniel was standing for that! Although he thought it best to answer his girlfriend's question first.

'What do you mean where was I last night? I went for a drink, OK? In case you've forgotten, I lost my job on Friday. I needed to get pished, and since you were nowhere to be found, I went to get pished alone! Anyway, how come you're the one leaving, and you're having a go at me?'

Deborah was about to defend herself in turn when she realised Daniel may have a point. If she'd explained earlier, maybe it wouldn't have come to this. Yet, it had come to this. It was Sunday morning, and she just had to leave now.

This very minute. So instead of trying to explain herself to him, she returned to the bedroom and continued packing her things.

Meanwhile, Daniel was still completely surprised by Deborah's actions. Yes, he'd stayed out late the night before; he was bang to rights on that score, but was that really a reason for Deborah to leave? He had to say something, do something; he walked to the bedroom to see Deborah packing a large suitcase.

'Oh, for Christ's sake, don't be so daft, Deborah. You can't leave just like that...'

Deborah didn't answer but just continued to pack her things.

Daniel tried again. 'Listen, the kettle's boiling; just calm down for a minute. I'll make you a cup of tea.'

Deborah acknowledged this with a look to the ceiling and another shake of the head. She began to pack her underwear into a large, brown leather holdall lying beside the suitcase.

Daniel returned to the kitchen where, after taking some loud gulps of orange juice from a carton in the fridge, he retrieved two mugs from the dish rack and placed a teabag inside each one as the noisy kettle rumbled, clicked and settled down. After pouring the boiling water into the two cups, Daniel stirred the tea, squeezing the teabags against the side of the mugs with the teaspoon as hard as he could.

He still couldn't understand it. What the hell was Deborah doing? Did she suspect something? Did she know? He scooped the teabags out of the cups and dropped them into the rubbish bin. You can't just leave someone after three years in a relationship on a Sunday morning, he thought. He could hear a suitcase being zipped up. Buckles being tightened. Other bags being closed. Then silence again before Deborah finally appeared in the kitchen doorway, slightly out of breath.

Her perfume smelled nice.

She stood with her arms crossed and leaned against the kitchen door frame with her coat on. Daniel stuck to his keep calm and carry on plan and handed her the cup of tea as if everything was completely normal. 'Do you want some more milk in it?' he asked. Deborah took the cup of tea and didn't answer.

'You still haven't told me where you were last night,' Deborah asked.

'I told you: the pub.'

'Till three in the morning?'

'There was a lock-in.' Deborah sighed as if she was severely disappointed with Daniel's answer. 'You were in some state last night.'

'I'd been drinking – that's what happens.'

She paused before asking the next question but still didn't drink the tea. 'Why were you so angry?'

Daniel straightened up with a look of surprise. 'Angry? Was I? I honestly can't remember. Then again, I've just lost my job; what do you expect?'

Instead of answering, Deborah took a mobile phone out of her coat pocket and dialled a number, tossing back her long black hair and putting the phone to her ear. 'Hello, could I have a taxi for Shawlands, please? Pollokshaws Road. I'm at 42 Crow Road. McKendrick. OK. Thanks.' She closed the phone and put it back in her pocket.

'Shawlands?' Daniel said with some interest. 'So you're going to stay with your mum?'

Deborah looked up. 'Yes. I thought I'd stay there until I got somewhere else to live.'

'Why do you need somewhere else to live? Why can't you stay here?'

Again, she didn't answer – just looked up at him. 'You do know you'll have to get another job.'

'Yes, I do realise that. Thanks for the advice.' For the first time, Daniel looked directly back at Deborah, meeting her gaze. 'Could you at least tell me why you're leaving?'

'I just can't stay here any longer.' 'I gathered that. But why? Why are you leaving all of a sudden?'

'Don't, Daniel! Don't make this any more difficult than it already is.'

'What? Don't I deserve an explanation? You're leaving just like that. After three years?'

'It's been a long time coming.'

'A long time coming?' Daniel repeated quietly. He didn't want to ask the next question but knew he had to. 'Is there someone else? Is that it? At least tell me that.'

Deborah threw her head back and laughed. 'Someone else? Of course not! Please, at least give me credit for that. 'No, there's no one else. I just have to get away, that's all. I'm really sorry I—' A taxi horn sounded from the street. Deborah turned as if someone she knew was calling her. 'Listen, I've got to go. You look after yourself, OK?' Daniel suddenly felt very frightened. It wasn't all an act, a bluff. Deborah really was leaving him. 'Don't leave, Deborah... please....' He said it quietly, his voice now almost a whisper to himself.

'I have to – the taxi's waiting.'

Deborah turned and went into the hallway. She opened the front door before picking up the suitcase and a couple of holdalls and placed them on the close landing. Deborah re-entered the kitchen and, seeing Daniel still leaning against the cooker with a look of complete despair, she went over and gently kissed him on the cheek.

She cupped his face in her hands. 'I'm sorry – really I am.' She held his arm. 'Oh, I nearly forgot.' She took a bunch of keys out of her pocket and placed them in Daniel's hand, closing his fingers around them.

Daniel remained silent. An overwhelming sadness made him unable to say anything more.

Deborah looked at Daniel for one last time before quickly turning and walking out the front door. He listened to her struggling down the stairs, the suitcase and bags scraping and bumping on each step.

For a moment, Daniel's sadness turned to anger once again. Against himself as much as Deborah. Why didn't he say something more? Why didn't he tell her how much he loved her? Why did he just let her leave?

Through misty eyes, he opened his fingers, looked down at the keys in his hand, and threw them onto the wooden kitchen table. They landed with a loud clunk, like a prison door closing for the first time.

Chapter 3

Witness

'What do you mean we have a witness?'

Simpson answered the question from Patterson by turning towards the hidden hallway and beckoning a figure forward.

'Would you come in here for a minute, Mr Melrose?'

An overweight, unshaven and slightly grubby man sheepishly appeared from behind the door, glanced at Patterson and smiled before looking back at Simpson as if waiting for his next instructions. They duly came.

'Take a seat, Mr Melrose,' Simpson said politely, and Melrose awkwardly shuffled forward before sitting opposite Patterson.

'Mr Melrose, this is DCI Patterson,' Simpson continued. 'If you'd just like to tell him what you've just told me.'

Melrose rubbed his eyes in a quite childlike fashion and coughed self-consciously before beginning to speak. 'I saw who did it.'

At this, Patterson looked up at Simpson with a half-smile, not bothering to hide his scepticism, then back at Melrose, waiting for him to expand on his rather dramatic statement. Yet Melrose said nothing more, and it was up to Patterson to prompt him.

'You think you saw who did what?'

'Killed the lassie. I got telt a lassie was killed here last night.'

It was Patterson's turn to rub his eyes. How he now longed to be home on this Sunday morning, pottering around the house doing nothing instead of listening to this nonsense. Melrose coughed once more before continuing; he didn't appear to be in the best of health. In artistic terms, his skin tone would be Prussian Fucked. 'I was out last night, you know, for a drink. Well, a few drinks as it happens. See, I live across the backcourt. Right across from here, in fact. Except I'm on the second floor across, no' the third like here and well, anyway, I came home absolutely blootered. I mean, like I still knew what was going on and stuff, and anyways I looks out the windae, and I swear I sees this guy, well it was mair like this shape, to be honest, climbing up the drainpipe up this building, right towards this flat.'

'You saw someone climbing up the drainpipe last night towards this flat?' Patterson asked, trying to clarify the waffle.

'Aye, right towards this flat – a guy. I mean, Ah couldnae see much about him, just this dark shape like I said, climbing up the drainpipe.'

'What time was this exactly?'

'Ah cannae mind exactly.'

'At a rough guess.'

'Rough guess, I'd say it was about midnight, just after, maybe just after.'

Patterson was still sceptical. The man was an obvious drinker who had no doubt suffered from the odd Glaswegian mirage or two. However, in the name of optimism, he gave the ill-looking neighbour the benefit of the doubt. 'Go on.'

'I didnae think much of it at the time, like. I just thought some guy had lost his keys or something.'

'Really? You see a man climbing a drainpipe around midnight, and you assume somebody had lost their keys? You didn't think it could be something more serious, like a burglary perhaps?'

'Oh aye, after a bit I did, so I said to masel'

I better call the police, cos even if it's innocent like you said it could be some guy breaking in or something, so that's what I did: I went to call the police.'

'So you called the police?'

'Oh no,' Melrose said, shaking his head. 'I didnae call the police.'

Patterson looked down at his fingernails, surprised once again at how fast his nails seemed to grow. He looked up at Melrose again. 'But you just said you went to call the police,' Patterson asked patiently.

'Oh aye, that's right. Ah went tae call the police, but I didnae make it.'

'You didn't make it, how exactly?' Melrose looked even more sheepish than before. 'Well, I sat down for a sec on the couch to catch my breath – see I'm not actually the fittest guy in the world – and that's the last thing I remember. Next thing I wakes up this morning and at first had forgotten all about it. Then I looked out the windae and seen all yous coppers about, and it was then I remembered about the guy climbing the drainpipe. I came down intae the backcourt, and your colleague here was telling me a young lassie had been done in.'

'Are you sure you're not imagining all this?' Patterson said. 'I mean, by your own admission, you say you were very drunk. Is it not possible you just thought you saw someone climbing up a drainpipe?'

'How could I imagine all that? Naw, no way – I swear it, man. God's honest. Aye, fair dos I wis dead drunk I said that, but that's what I saw. It was like a dark shape, a figure, a man – I'm sure it was a man – climbing up that drainpipe outside.'

'What about clothes? Height? Can you tell us anything about this man?'

'Naw, that's the thing – Ah cannae. It was so dark. Ah mean, I'm trying to remember, but I couldnae see his face or anything. Except one thing. I'm sure he had like a beanie on, you know, like a fucking commando—'

'But you're fairly sure it was a man?'

'Fairly sure, aye.' Patterson nodded. 'OK, Mr Melrose, you'll have to come down the station later to make a statement. If you remember anything else in the meantime, make a note of it if you could or just give us a call. My DS here will give you our number.'

Melrose rubbed his forehead and then looked at the floor. 'I feel so fucking guilty, scuse my French. If only I called then maybe—'

'There's no use beating yourself up about it. We appreciate you coming forward now. Like I said, just try and remember what you can, and we'll be in touch later.' Melrose rose unsteadily from the chair and was led out of the room by Simpson. After a couple of minutes, Simpson came back in.

'Well, what do you think?' Simpson asked.

'He may be telling the truth, but he wouldn't be the first drunk in Glasgow to have hallucinations, no matter how real they seem at the time.'

'Maybe, but he came across as sound to me,' Simpson said in his Mancunian drawl. 'Besides, I checked the drainpipe he was talking about, and it does go up right past the kitchen window.'

'Mind you, when we arrived, all the windows were shut, including the one in the kitchen.'

'That doesn't mean owt,' Simpson countered once more in defence of his witness. 'The murderer could easily have shut it once inside.'

'I guess. Here, that's a thing. Did you have your windows open last night, Jack?'

'I did; it was stifling.'

'Aye, so did I. I would guess most people did. So maybe you're right – how come the windows here are all closed?'

Patterson got up, walked through to the kitchen and studied the window. It was a standard PVC window which opened up halfway via two handles. Easy enough to push it open further if it was already open.

Patterson went up to one of the officers who was dusting for fingerprints. 'Make sure you get all around these window frames, especially the kitchen window – there's a good chance our intruder entered that way.'

The fingerprint woman looked back at Patterson with annoyance. 'Will do, Sherlock.' She was still waiting for the day she could go to a crime scene and not be told the bleedin' obvious by one of the detectives.

Patterson and Simpson then walked through the flat, room to room, seeing if there was anything else that could have been significant in Susan's murder. On initial inspection, there was nothing of note. Everything was neat and tidy and in place. Hopefully, forensics would come up with some good news later.

'OK,' Patterson said, 'I guess I better get to The Drum and break the news to the mother.'

'She'll have already been told.'

'How's that?' Patterson asked, genuinely mystified.

'The new procedure in place,' Simpson replied, equally mystified why his superior wouldn't know this. 'Do you never read memos?'

'What memo?'

'Remember Becky McDonald's murder a few weeks back?'

'The jogger? Great Western Road?'

'Yeah, well, apparently, the mother learned of her death via a condolence message on Facebook. You must have heard. There was a big stink about it at the time.'

Patterson shrugged. He vaguely remembered something about the station being in the papers. Parents complaining about social media or something or the police being incompetent, but that was nothing new.

Simpson explained further. 'Well, since that happened, Dunard has been looking at ways to inform the family ASAP. So, we now have a family liaison officer on call 24/7. As soon as we can be fairly sure of a victim's identity, the FLO is sent immediately with a uniform to give the dreaded news instead of waiting for us to do it. It means we can keep on investigating the crime scene without having to rush away to inform the parents. It's a trial thing.'

'Fairly sure of a victim's identity? That's reassuring. Right, so you're saying there's an FLO with Mrs McLaughlin now?'

'Should be, yeah.'

'Sounds daft to me,' Patterson said. Every week his boss Dunard seemed to come up with some new initiative which ended up being dropped as quickly as it had started. 'I mean, we've just got here. What if it isn't Susan. Or what if...' Patterson shook his head. 'OK, you stay here and see if there's anything else you can find. Get McKinnon to make himself useful. And find out where Pettigrew is. I'm still heading up to see Susan's mum. She could have vital information we need to know about directly, not via an FLO. I'll meet you back at the station later.'

With that, Patterson went to leave the flat, but before he did so, he had one last look at Susan as she was being lifted to be taken away. Her eyes had been closed. A few hours earlier, she would have been going to bed, thinking about another day, thinking about her life ahead. Someone had suddenly stopped that life, and Patterson was determined to find out who was responsible. Apart from anything else, he knew there was always the possibility that if the murderer wasn't caught quickly, they could kill again.

Chapter 4

The Drive

Kinfauns Drive curved through the heart of Drumchapel in a never-ending loop, ideal if ever a demand for a Drumchapel sightseeing tour arose. That, however, seemed an unlikely prospect since the main attraction of The Drum, as the housing scheme was known locally, was the severe poverty you could find in any one of a dozen such schemes across the city.

Susan McLaughlin's mum lived in one of the better parts of this deprived area, in the second-floor flat of a neat, three-storey pebble-dashed block which lined part of Kinfauns Drive going towards Great Western Road. Patterson parked on the other side of the street, next to some wide-open green space which reminded visitors they were on the north-western edge of the city.

PC John Henderson was standing guard outside the close. Henderson had not long graduated from the Scottish Police College at

Tulliallan. Still, Patterson's first impressions of the young man were that he would go far if he stuck it out.

'Everything all right, John?'

'Fine, sir, thanks.' Henderson was pleased to see Patterson. He seemed to be less of an idiot than some of the other senior officers he had so far come across.

'How is Mrs McLaughlin?'

'Bearing up; quiet when I left her. I guess she's still trying to take it in.'

'No doubt. Is the liaison officer with her?'

'Aye, been in there about an hour now.'

'Who is it?'

'Emma Booth.'

'Right,' Patterson said, wondering who the hell Emma Booth was. He'd been expecting Laura White or Davie Forsyth.

'And were you the one who accompanied Booth when she broke the news to Mrs McLaughlin?'

'Aye.' Henderson glanced momentarily over Patterson's shoulder, avoiding his superior's gaze and betraying the difficulty of the situation. It prompted Patterson's next question.

'Your first time doing that?'

'No, sir, done it once before. Joyrider – he and his two mates were killed in Yoker. Just seventeen, he was. Parents were completely distraught, as you can imagine.'

'Aye, all part of the job, unfortunately.'

'I know, sir,' Henderson said firmly, still avoiding Patterson's gaze.

In a way, Patterson was glad that the procedure for informing the death of a family member was now down to an FLO. Maybe an officer specially trained to deal with this highly sensitive task would be far better than, say, a couple of inexperienced police officers who happened to be in the area by chance or a couple of dyed-in-the-wool DIs who could inadvertently let their matter-of-fact attitude get in the way of their compassion. Having an FLO break the news first also meant that when Patterson arrived later, the initial shock, crying, screaming or whatever else happened on hearing the news may have lessened to some degree, giving Patterson more opportunity to get the answers to the questions he needed to ask sooner rather than later. Yet he still wasn't convinced.

'Has any other family been called?'

'Aye, Mrs McLaughlin's sister should be arriving soon,' Henderson answered. 'Driving up from Motherwell.'

'Right,' Patterson said. He awkwardly

patted Henderson's shoulder as he passed as a way of saying 'well done' without actually having to say the words.

On the second floor, a tartan nameplate indicated Sandra McLaughlin's heavily painted dark red door was the one he was looking for. Patterson pushed the door open and walked inside.

He found himself in a narrow hallway. A gallery of family photos lined the walls on either side. He could identify Susan in most of them, the pictures detailing her life from childhood to short-lived adulthood. Many photos were of mother and daughter together, and it showed there was a noticeable absence of an older man who could have been Susan's father. It was also clear from the photos that Susan wasn't only the pride and joy of her mother's life; she was her mother's life.

Patterson edged further forward and passed an open doorway to the left, which, on looking inside, he saw was a large, empty front room that had the smell of fading carpet and Polaroid family get-togethers. Walking on, he could hear a murmuring female voice holding a one-way conversation. Lightly tapping on the half-closed door, Patterson pushed it open, the bottom of the door making a whooshing sound as it brushed against the carpet. Patterson immediately recognised Sandra from the hallway photos and, through a process of elimination, worked out that the other young, dark-haired woman beside her must be the family liaison officer.

Although he still didn't recognise the FLO, there was something familiar about this Emma Booth. When she looked up at him, their gaze held as if she recognised him too. She then stood up as Patterson lingered awkwardly in the doorway.

'Hello, I'm DCI Patterson – Michael – Partick CID, Mrs McLaughlin. I know this is a difficult time, but I wanted to talk to you for a few moments.'

Sandra continued to look at him with a vague, uncomprehending look he'd not long experienced with Shona.

'Sir, I was just going to make a cup of tea for Mrs McLaughlin; would you like a cup?' Booth smiled a bright, natural smile, and for some reason, Patterson liked her immediately.

'Aye, thanks. That would be great. Two sugars, milk, ta.'

As Booth made her way to the kitchenette, Patterson looked around the room and saw he was in a comfortable sitting room with a large brown leather settee filled to the brim with cushions. Sandra sat leaning forward on a matching armchair. In the corner of the room was a large TV turned off, and still more photos on the walls and mantlepiece detailing additional aspects of Susan McLaughlin's short-lived life. To the back, there was a small kitchenette where bright, early morning sunshine streamed in through the windows. He found himself watching Booth busying herself, making the tea.

She suddenly glanced up and caught him staring at her. He looked away as if he'd been caught doing something he shouldn't have been. He turned and looked at Mrs McLaughlin, who stared back at him.

'Is it true then?' Mrs McLaughlin asked.

'Is what true?'

'That Susan was murdered?'

'Yes, we believe so.'

'How? How did she die?'

Patterson hesitated before answering, wondering for a moment what he should say. In the end, he opted for the truth. 'We believe she was murdered while she slept. Strangled by an intruder. That's all we know at this time. As soon as we know more, I promise you'll be informed.'

Mrs McLaughlin didn't answer, and Patterson wondered how to break the awkward silence. Eventually, he decided the best way would be to do a runner. 'Actually, Mrs

McLaughlin, I'm just going to have a word with my colleague. I won't be a minute.'

Patterson stood up and went through to the kitchenette, closing the door slightly behind him. Both officers walked to the back of the kitchenette, where there was a small alcove. It was such a small space they found themselves close to one another, whispering as if they were having an illicit conversation.

'Pleased to meet you, sir. I'm the FLO, as you may have gathered.'

'Yes, likewise. I take it you're assigned to this case permanently, Emma?'

'As far as I'm aware. Superintendent Dunard called earlier and told me to get down here. Said you were going to be the SIO. He didn't tell me much, in fact. Just that a woman had been murdered in Partick, and I had to break the news to the mother.'

'Aye, so have you learned anything of interest so far?'

'No, not really; it's just been a case of looking after Mrs McLaughlin and learning about the family. She was very close to Susan; she was her only child. There's no father – he buggered off when Susan was a kid. Sandra has an older brother who's in the US – the west coast – and a younger sister in Motherwell. She should be here anytime.'

Patterson nodded. 'Are you new to this division? I don't think I've seen you before.'

'Aye, I've not long been transferred down from North East Division, Aberdeen; this is my first case for Partick. I've worked on a couple of cases in Glasgow, Central Division; still getting to know the ropes down here.'

Patterson thought he could detect a slight Aberdonian tinge to Booth's voice. 'Right. Well, I'm sure you'll get used to our ways soon enough.' Patterson had this strange feeling talking to Booth. What the hell was it? Attraction? He was a married man, for Christ's sake. Besides, this woman was at least ten years younger than him.

Patterson felt himself looking a little too long at Booth and quickly thought of the case again.

'So, Mrs McLaughlin hasn't said anything of interest so far?'

'Not really, sir.'

'Right,' Patterson said as he manoeuvred away from her and made towards the living room. Patterson sat down on a dark brown settee, moving half a dozen cushions like he was clearing away a rockfall.

'I know this is a difficult time, Mrs McLaughlin, but I need to find out as much as

I can about your daughter's last movements as soon as possible so we can hopefully find out who did this to her.'

'My name's Sandra – you can call me Sandra.'

It was always nice, thought Patterson, that no matter how much suffering people went through, some still went out of their way to be friendly and polite. They would never lose their dignity, no matter what.

Patterson nodded and took out his notebook and pen. 'Sandra, could you tell me when was the last time you saw Susan?'

'The last time?' Sandra repeated the question, realising its new added meaning. After thinking for a moment, she whispered, 'It was on Friday. Susan came up after work, Friday – two days ago that was... the last time I saw her.'

'How did she seem?'

'Seem?'

'I mean, how did Susan appear? Happy? Nervous? Did she seem all right? Was there anything unusual about her behaviour?'

Sandra shook her head. 'No, nothing unusual She seemed happy, just her usual self.'

'So, nothing seemed to be troubling her?'

'No, if anything, she seemed—' Sandra

stopped, remembering something.

'Seemed what, Sandra?'

'I don't know, excited, I would say. If anything, I noticed she seemed excited for some reason. Mind you, I think it was just because it was the weekend.'

'Did she say if she was going to do anything on Saturday, anything special? Why would she seem excited?'

'No. In fact, she just said she was going to have a boring weekend, staying in on the Saturday, catching up on the housework, said she was doing some studying as well. She's training to be a vet, ye see.' Sandra smiled with pride. 'Glasgow University. One year to go.'

As quickly as the smile appeared, it disappeared. 'Susan said she would see me today. I was saying to your colleague Emma. Susan always came up on Sunday for her tea. She was here most days, in fact.' Sandra continued to talk as if this was all just a bad dream.

'But you say she seemed excited even though she was going to have a boring weekend? Excited in what way?'

'I don't know, she just seemed happy; I felt she was excited for some reason. Maybe I was imagining it.'

'Did Susan ever mention anything unusual

recently – if there was anything she was worried about, or if anyone was threatening her?'

'Threatening her? Why would anyone want to threaten Susan? Everyone loved Susan. She was an angel. Susan didn't have an enemy in the world.' Large tears were slowly falling from her eyes, but Sandra still talked in a kind of daze.

'So, you can't think of any reason someone would want to do this to Susan?'

Sandra shook her head, trying to think. 'No, I can't; I really can't. Everyone loved Susan; they really did. If you met her, you would understand. I remember her going out that door on Friday, that's all. She turned to me and said, "Love you, Mum." She always did that. Always told me that. That was the last thing she said to me.' Sandra had that confused look again as if she was trying to fully understand what was happening.

Booth came in with the tea and put it on a side table, which she pulled over to the side of Patterson.

'Did Susan have a boyfriend?' Patterson continued.

'No. I think she had seen one or two lads from uni, but that's all, no one steady.'

'And Susan didn't phone you or get in touch yesterday?'

'No, she didn't, actually. Funnily enough, that was something unusual. We usually talked every day, but she didn't phone yesterday. Don't know why.'

Patterson nodded and took a sip of the tea, which was still too hot, but he wanted to show Booth he appreciated her making it. 'Does Susan still have her room here, a place where she would sleep over?'

'Aye, why?'

'Do you mind if I have a quick look? Just in case there's something that could be helpful.'

'Of course. It's just to the right there, through the hall.'

Patterson got up with some difficulty from the large couch – it was like pushing down on a huge marshmallow – and walked through to the room indicated. It was the room of a teenager. Patterson quickly realised it had been kept the same way since Susan had left years ago and no doubt would be kept the same from now on. Initially, he was looking for a diary, notes, anything that might suggest where Susan had been at the weekend, if any place at all. Patterson was already curious whether she had stayed in on Saturday or had gone anywhere. He wondered why Susan had seemed excited if she hadn't been planning anything special.

Everything in the room was neat and tidy.

Even in the drawers, nothing seemed of interest, apart from indicating Susan as an everyday person, a girl with a love of music and animals. He decided he would come back at a later date when he had more time and walked back into the living room. Booth was still at Sandra's side, crouched down with a hand lightly placed on her back. Patterson sat down again and took another sip of the tea, which, now cooler, tasted very nice.

Sandra suddenly looked up at Patterson, her eyes wide, excited, as if a thought had occurred to her.

'Are you sure it is Susan? I mean, you do know it's her, for certain, do ye?'

'Yes, we're quite certain. You know Shona – you do know Shona, Susan's friend?'

'Aye, course.'

'Well, she was the one who found Susan.'

'My God, Shona, that must have been terrible for her. They've known each other since school.'

'Nevertheless, we will still need someone else to formally identify Susan. For instance, you or a family member would need to come down to the mortuary. Not right now, but sometime soon if possible.'

Just then, a dark-haired woman in her forties rushed into the room crying and immediately went over to Sandra, bending down to hug her. Booth moved out of the way as Sandra now burst into loud sobs, letting out the grief she had mostly been holding back until now. Patterson knew there was probably no use trying to get anything else out of her for the moment. He stood up and made to head out.

'I'll leave you for now.' Patterson nodded to the sister as well as Sandra. 'Emma here will look after you, and if there's anything at all you need, just let her know.' Patterson looked at the sister. 'I was just saying to Sandra we'll need someone to come down and identify Susan formally.' He wasn't sure if Sandra would be up to it.

The woman didn't reply, too occupied in trying to comfort her sister. Patterson made to leave but stopped in the doorway. 'One last thing, Sandra: would you know if Susan was in the habit of keeping her window open or closed at night. Or did she always keep them closed?'

'How did you know about that?' Sandra asked.

'Know about what?'

'Susan always had a thing about keeping her windows open. She always kept her bedroom window open like when she stayed here. She always said she felt claustrophobic if the windows were ever shut. She—' Sandra broke down again, crying.

Patterson left it at that and walked out into the narrow hallway, followed by Booth.

'What did you want to know about the window for?' she asked. 'Do you think that's how the murderer got in the flat? Bit high up, is it not?'

'You'd think so, but it's possible. We have a witness from across the backcourt who says he saw someone climbing a drainpipe around the time the murder took place. Thing is, as you say, it's one hell of a climb. You'd be risking your life to climb that high. Plus, the windows in the flat were all shut when the body was found. Still, if what Mrs McLaughlin says is true, then it's more a sign that whoever killed her must have shut the windows before or after the actual murder took place.'

'Right,' Booth said.

'Anyway, I'm heading back to the station,' Patterson said. 'You know what to do: find out what you can, anything that'll help our enquiries. Also, arrange as soon as is appropriate either for Sandra or her sister to get down the mortuary for identification. I'll try and get down there myself. No doubt, I'll see you sometime. Bye, for now, Emma.'

'Bye, sir,' she replied and closed the door quietly as he went onto a landing which now echoed with the sound of children's voices.

Patterson made his way back to his car, saying bye to Henderson on the way. When someone was murdered, it wasn't just the victim but close friends and family who were killed to some degree. They're the ones who had to live with the cruelness of a needless death. Once again, that was the case here, and Patterson was once again reminded he needed to find the murderer of Susan McLaughlin.

Chapter 5

DCI Michael Patterson

Just after eight the next morning, Patterson looked down from the window on the second floor of Partick police station. The station resembled a quiet health centre, as if the building itself was trying to keep a low profile. It stood just to the west of the busyness of Central Partick in one of those in-between areas people mostly passed through as much as lived in.

It was here, in this in-between area and in this understated Glasgow police station, that Patterson spent most of his days. Patterson had a kind of understated appearance too. Anyone who saw him looking out of that second-floor window would have seen a tall man of slim build with short, tidy grey hair. He wore thin silver-rimmed glasses with clothes that always gave him a kind of old-fashioned look. If anyone had to guess Patterson's profession by appearance alone, school teacher would have come near the top of the list.

Patterson was so tired these days, he seemed to be fighting tiredness as much as crime. It wasn't until past eleven on Sunday night that he'd got home. Thankfully Stephanie had been fast asleep, and Patterson had lain down beside her, racing thoughts and adrenalin keeping him awake till after two. Eventually, though, he'd dropped into a troubled sleep only to wake up again at six, bleary-eyed and only slightly less exhausted than before.

So far at the station, Monday morning had been taken up with paperwork about the previous day's activities – reports to be processed as well as organising the outline logistics of the upcoming investigation that would now take place into the murder of Susan McLaughlin. At a meeting with Superintendent Dunard, Patterson was informed that instead of the two investigating teams that would usually be assigned for a murder enquiry like Susan's, there would only be one, with Patterson confirmed as the senior investigating officer. Cutbacks, Dunard said. Patterson couldn't remember the last time he'd had a conversation with Dunard where cutbacks hadn't been mentioned.

Like most senior investigating officers, Patterson liked a close-knit team around him, hard-working colleagues he could depend upon to do a good job. So, as he looked out the window, eventually, three of his first-choice colleagues sat down at a table with coffees and teas in front of them in the small temporary office made available until a proper incident room was set up. Those three officers were DS Jack Simpson, DI Claire Pettigrew and DC Brian McKinnon.

DI Claire Pettigrew was an intense figure, always determined to be the very best at her job. In her late twenties, she clearly had ambitions for promotion and saw every day as an opportunity to take a step closer to reaching that goal.

In contrast to the clear confidence she had in her investigating and general policing skills, Patterson sensed an insecurity she had about herself. She would always dress down instead of up, never wearing anything that could be described as stylish or revealing, only practical. She also had a habit of making self-deprecating jokes, more often than not, about her weight which, in reality, was nowhere near as evident to those around her as it appeared to be to herself.

In striving to be the very best, her competitive streak brought some tension with other team members. It was quite hard to get to know this very capable officer, and it seemed to Patterson she often used her police work as a kind of barrier towards others getting to know her more. Trying to have a personal conversation with her would inevitably turn into a discussion about work. However, she was as dedicated to

Patterson as he was to her. A result of them arriving at Partick CID around the same time and being a great help to one another when they were both still trying to settle in. Patterson liked Pettigrew a lot and would trust her with his life if need be, and that had already happened more than once.

In contrast, DC Brian McKinnon was an easy-going individual who everyone got on with. Tall and gangly, his limbs never seeming to be in sync with one another, he gave the impression of having a haphazard approach to anything he did, including police work. Similarly, he gave the impression that the job was nothing more than that, just a job he did to get by and that he could just as happily leave the force as try to get a promotion.

His real passion was for his family, his wife and two kids, his be-all and end-all, and for all his apparently careless attitude, Patterson could still see his usefulness. McKinnon may take the scenic route occasionally, but he invariably got answers to questions that would stump his fellow officers. Patterson also felt at ease in his company. McKinnon never tried to pressure him into being the leader he was supposed to be. Patterson needed that leeway within the team, another reason he simply liked McKinnon.

DS Jack Simpson, meanwhile, was a naturally talented investigator who could instinctively come up with solutions to any problem that arose in an enquiry. Originally from Manchester, he had only been in Glasgow for three years, but in that time had got to know the city and its shady workings more than many of the local officers. Simpson made things happen and seemed to attract information and people towards him. It was typical, for instance, that Mr Melrose had picked out Simpson at the crime scene and told him what he saw. This natural attraction was perhaps due to his open, handsome face and calm demeanour. People trusted him, even some of the bad guys, and it made Simpson seem even more the good guy with a heart of gold – which, in fact, wasn't that far off the truth.

As Patterson walked from the window to address the three fellow officers he usually worked closely with, he suddenly felt a little light-headed, his breathing shallow, his heart beating just a little faster. Perhaps it was the lack of sleep or what was going on with Stephanie, or maybe it was just the realisation of knowing he was once again the senior investigating officer in another emotive murder enquiry. Whatever the reason, Patterson stopped and turned back to the window once again to look down on the passing traffic. He continued to take longer, deeper breaths, clenching his fists, until the anxiety faded – and it did, almost as quickly as it had arrived.

Patterson glanced back at his colleagues; the others hadn't noticed or, as was often the case, didn't show they had. Another reason he wanted these three on his team.

Patterson now successfully walked back across to the main Perspex incident board, where all the details known so far about the murder of Susan McLaughlin were written in black marker pen. Pride of place went to a photo of Susan smiling shyly into the camera, her blue eyes sparkling and full of life. In time, many connections would be drawn from this photo, different coloured lines going off in different directions, indicating various suspects and leads. At the same time, there would be far more detailed information going into computers and specialist software used to decipher these connections between people and places. At the end of it all, hopefully, there would be someone. A name, the name of whoever had murdered Susan McLaughlin.

'OK, what do we know?' Patterson said loudly as a sign this initial briefing had begun.

Before waiting for a response, Patterson proceeded to answer his own question. 'Susan McLaughlin. Twenty-two years old. Born and brought up in Drumchapel, she moved to Partick two years ago when she began her studies at

Glasgow University, where she was studying to be a vet. According to those we've talked to so far, her mum, best friend, neighbours, etc. Susan was a quiet girl, well-liked by all, who didn't have an enemy in the world. So far, so normal. She was dedicated to her studies and animal welfare; other interests include keeping fit, veganism, and travel. You spoke to the landlord, did you not, Brian? What did he say again?'

'He said Susan was the perfect tenant,' McKinnon replied. 'Never any trouble. Always very polite and quiet. He even kept her rent down because he liked her so much.'

'That's good of him. What's his name again?'

'Zach Papadakis. Has a few properties around the West End; quite a respectable businessman by all accounts.'

'OK. So, we have a young woman with her whole life ahead of her who everyone liked. A good person who didn't deserve to die so young or in the manner she did. Any thoughts so far?'

'She must have had a life outside her studies and fitness?' Simpson said.

Patterson nodded. 'Of course, and that's what we intend to find out. We know she occasionally went for a night out, but not often. She was close to her mum and worked part-time in a local vet surgery. Now, I want you, or should

I say us, to check out three avenues of her life further.

'Jack, I want you to go to the university and find out all you can about her. Talk to her friends and tutors – you know the score. Claire, if you could head to the gym and find out if she was close to anyone. Apparently, she went there on an almost daily basis. Find out what you can about her visits recently, especially if she was there on Friday and Saturday. I'll head down to the vets where she worked.'

'What about me?' McKinnon asked.

'You'll be checking on her personal life, bank details, etc. Go through the documents that were found at her flat. Find out if she was talking to anyone online regularly who could be of interest. I want us to use our resources wisely. As you've probably heard, we're the only team on this case, and we must be extra hard-working in solving it. Getting back to the actual murder, let's start with the basics. Claire, what do we need to find out?'

Pettigrew sat straight in her chair, enthusiastically writing down notes and thoughts. She stopped to answer Patterson's question with her ever-serious demeanour. 'We need to find the motive. Why would someone want to kill Susan? We also need to find out about her movements in the time previous to when she was killed.'

'As always,' Patterson concurred, 'we need to find out about her movements, not just for the day previous but for the week previous and beyond. As far back as is necessary. I want every detail of her life – what she was doing, who she was seeing, talking to, thinking about – noted and recorded.'

'She didn't have a partner, no boyfriend?' McKinnon asked. 'Is that correct?'

'As far as we know, no boyfriend. Her last regular partner was just over a year ago. Gary McKenzie, who we have an address for in Edinburgh. Our Lothian colleagues are contacting him today.'

'And Susan wasn't involved with anyone else?' Simpson asked.

'According to her friend Shona and her mum, no. Of course, they may not know everything. That's why I want you, Jack, to head up to the university and check out her fellow students and teachers – Come up with as much info on Susan as you can.'

Pettigrew interrupted. 'What about how she was murdered? Can we go over what we know so far?'

Patterson nodded and took a sip of his coffee. 'Preliminary findings indicate Susan was manually strangled, most likely while lying in bed. There were no signs of a disturbance elsewhere in the flat. Tasmina believes, going by the bruising to her hips, the killer sat astride Susan, strangling her until she died. For now, we're also presuming our killer climbed the drainpipe in the backcourt and entered through the kitchen window. We presume this because we actually have a witness of sorts from across the way – a Mr Melrose, who says he saw a man, or at least he thinks it was a man, climb a drainpipe, which leads to the side of Susan's kitchen window at just after midnight. This would certainly tie in with the pathologist's time of death. We're still waiting on forensics to give us something more. We've found many fingerprints in the flat but nothing so far from the drainpipe. Most probably, he or she was wearing gloves, and these fingerprints from inside the flat will belong to friends and family, but you never know. Apart from some scuff marks found around the drainpipe and on the wall leading up to the window, there's been nothing else to go on up till now.'

'What about CCTV?' asked Simpson.

'DCs Forsyth and Broughton are checking CCTV from the area as we speak. Other footage will be gathered today and in the following days. The area was bustling during the time of the murder, which has been preliminarily put at just after midnight. A lot of pubs were emptying at the time, which could be a positive – or not, as the case may be. As you know, we've got an incident van set up in Gardner Street, and we're having a press conference this afternoon to formally announce Susan's identity and ask for more information.'

'What time's the press conference?'

'Three, here in conference room C. A press release has already been sent to the usual mob. Before the press conference, as I said, I'm heading down to the vets, where Susan worked part-time as a volunteer. Jack, I want you to return to her mother's house after you go to the university. I was there yesterday but didn't ask too much, so you may get something I didn't. Another thing to follow up on is that Susan seemed unusually excited by this weekend. Yet, she said she was just going to have a quiet weekend studying and doing some housework. It's possible Susan was keeping something from her mum. Get in touch with the family liaison officer as well beforehand. Emma Booth. I'll be bringing her in more often as part of the team. She's new to the division but seems competent enough. Oh, and Brian, I also want you to review all the recent crimes in the area over the past year. Needless to say, particularly those with a resemblance to Susan's murder. Who knows, maybe it could still be a burglary gone wrong?

Seems unlikely but nevertheless, get a list of any previous crimes and suspects that could be of interest.

'OK, so what else do we want to find out?'

'There were no signs of sexual assault?' Simpson asked.

'We'll know for definite after the autopsy this afternoon, but at this stage, Tasmina doesn't believe there's any indication of sexual assault, no.'

'What I want to know,' Pettigrew said, 'is why he chose that flat? That wasn't the only window open that night; it was a warm night. There could have been anyone in that flat. Why did the killer choose that particular flat which just happened to have a young woman living there? What are the chances of that? I doubt it was simply chance. I think he probably knew Susan was in that flat.'

'So do I, Claire,' Patterson said. 'So do I. In all likelihood, our killer knew Susan was alone in that flat, which, in turn, means that our killer probably knew Susan.'

'Or it could be he maybe just saw Susan at the window earlier,' McKinnon said.

'How's that?' Simpson asked.

'Well, maybe he was hanging around,' McKinnon expanded. 'Her killer was looking for an opportunity to do a place, noticed Susan at the window, waited till night and then—'

Simpson shook his head. 'You really think he was hanging around, looked up, saw her and decided to kill her?'

'No,' McKinnon answered defensively, not liking Simpson's dismissive attitude. 'I didn't say that. I mean, he could have been watching her for days. Like Claire says, it's most probably not luck he entered the flat of a young woman.'

'It's what we still have to find out, and our murderer could still be a female; you never know,' Patterson said. 'Brian, make sure all the CCTV is properly checked. That includes the streets leading back towards Hyndland Road as well. The murderer could have come from that direction and not Dumbarton Road. However, from what we know so far, we can say that the killer climbed up the drainpipe, entered the kitchen window, closed it behind him, strangled Susan while she was in bed and then left.'

Simpson tapped a pen on his notepad as if tapping a question he'd written down. 'Why risk your life climbing 30 feet up a drainpipe when the main door downstairs was open. He could have just walked up the stairs and knocked on Susan's door. He's either right stupid or crazy.'

'Perhaps our killer didn't know the downstairs door was broken,' McKinnon said.

'Wouldn't he have at least looked, checked, tried the door?' replied Simpson. 'And if he somehow knew Susan, would he not try the buzzer, simply say hello?'

'One other thing we can assume at this stage,' Pettigrew added, 'from the murderer climbing that drainpipe, it means whoever did this is fit. I mean very fit. I certainly couldn't have done it with the extra pounds I'm carrying, but I don't know many people who could have climbed that high. It takes some effort on the arms and legs. Especially pulling yourself across from the drainpipe to the window. We're definitely talking about someone who looks after themselves physically.'

Patterson nodded. 'Which is another reason I want you to go to the gym as soon as, Claire. It's possible our fit friend went to the same one as Susan and met her there. Naturally, we'll have officers going round the doors again to see what we can pick up.'

'OK, does everyone know what they have to do?' Patterson took the silence as a yes. 'OK, let's get on with it then.'

As his fellow officers left the room, Patterson took a deep breath and then looked at his mobile phone. There was a message from Billy. Got some info for you, the message said. Billy was one of his most useful contacts but strictly for small-time stuff.

'Not today, Billy,' Patterson whispered to himself. 'I've got bigger fish to catch.'

As Patterson put the phone back in his pocket, he noticed his left hand was shaking. He took another deep breath and walked back across to the window. In a case like this, it was a race against time. He needed to find Susan's murderer before the case drifted into yet another unsolved and soon forgotten crime – or worse, another murder took place. Patterson also knew that, in recent weeks, his anxiety had been getting worse. It was another reason he needed to find Susan's killer quickly before his stress levels increased to such an extent he was no longer able to do his job.

Chapter 6

Stone Investments

Wearing a blue-and-green-chequered scarf tucked inside an old cream-coloured raincoat, Bob Mackintosh entered Stone Investments on Dumbarton Road and was ushered straight through to Stone's office by Jenny, the receptionist.

Bob continued to shuffle towards Stone's desk. Thin red hair lightly covered his whitish/blue pate as if the top of his head was a long-forgotten mushroom in the back of the fridge. He held a brown and yellow tartan cap in his left hand, and with his right hand, he leaned at a steep angle on what, Stone assumed, was supposed to be some kind of walking stick.

'Bob, good to see you! How you been keeping?' Stone had a beaming smile for his elderly investor.

Bob gradually sat down with a loud sigh, like a bus arriving at a stop and letting out air pressure. Once seated and having recovered his breath, Bob spoke for the first time.

'Thanks, Stone. It's my bones, not what they used to be.'

'Och, no need to apologise – I know the feeling. I need to phone a taxi to get out of bed. So tell me, why do I have the pleasure?'

'Well, ye see, I have this wee problem.'

'Yes? Oh, excuse my manners, would you like a cup of tea?'

'Naw, ye're aw right, thanks.'

'So, what's this wee problem, then?'

'Well ye see, it's ma telly. The other day it just conked out there and then.'

'Right. Did it not have a guarantee?'

'Aye, but that ran out ages ago, and I was wanting to buy a new one, you know, flat screen and all that, but I hivnae got much spare cash at the moment.'

'Well, we'll soon sort that. How much would you like – £100, £200?'

'Well, I was hoping for a bit more, but oh, £200 would be fine. I knew I could depend on you.'

'And I'm glad you did. My door is always open to yourself – you know that.'

After some more informalities, Bob made to leave. As he went out the door, he turned to Stone and said in a sincere, quiet voice, 'You know, you're such a good man, Stone. I wish everyone was like you, I really do – the world would be a much better place.'

Stone waved away the compliment, embarrassed but touched by the elderly man's sentiment. 'No worries, Bob. I'll have the money transferred to your account in a couple of days.'

Stone walked back to his office and sat down at his desk. Giving Bob £200 was a pain, but considering how much Bob had invested, it was a small price to pay and keep him off Stone's back for a while longer. The phone rang. It was Greg, his agent.

'Stone, listen, I've got some great news. Great news!'

Stone raised his eyebrows. 'Go on.'

His agent could hardly contain his excitement. 'Well, I had a meeting with Peter Webb from the BBC this lunchtime.'

'The BBC? You didn't tell me you were talking to the BBC?'

'I didn't want to get your hopes up. Given the present credit crunch, they're developing a new financial show and thinking of you as the presenter.'

Stone's face lit up. 'You're kidding!'

'I am not. What's more, the BBC want it up and running as soon as so they're having a meeting down at Pacific Quay tomorrow morning, and they want both of us to be there to go over some ideas.'

'What time?'

'Eleven o'clock. I'll pick you up at your office around ten. Sound good?'

'Sounds excellent. Cheers, Greg, you're a star.'

'You're the star, Stone. Remember that. I'll see you tomorrow.'

Stone put the phone down. The BBC. The Beeb. National television. The whole of Scotland. No more presenting a financial segment on some regional lunchtime news programmes on some crappy cable TV news channel. He nodded to himself. This was the break he'd been waiting for.

Stone then thought back to Bob's parting words. 'You're such a good man, Stone.' The thing was, Stone knew he wasn't a good man. In fact, Stone knew he was a bad man, a very bad man. How long could he get away with it? How long would it be before the police came knocking on his door?

Chapter 7

River View

It was with some relief that Patterson was able to escape the confinements of the police station and head out to the veterinary surgery where Susan worked part-time. He'd been feeling anxious all morning and, as ever, couldn't quite pinpoint why that was. Panic attacks and being overcome by nerves and stress seemed so random yet were an ever more regular occurrence for Patterson nowadays.

He pulled out of the police station car park and onto Dumbarton Road. He was soon observing the daily bustle of Partick, and from the security of the car interior, he felt a little calmer.

Anxiety was something Patterson had lived with most of his adult life. There was no telling when or where this crippling fear would happen; it seemed to take pleasure in creeping up with the most silent of steps. Oh, for a time when he didn't have to deal with the daily hell of social interaction, a time when he could relax and feel at peace. Yet nowadays, it was as if the anxiety was always there, simply stepping back into the shadows for a moment to recharge its batteries, waiting for tomorrow or the next day or the day after that to launch another full-scale assault on his senses.

Patterson had suffered from anxiety even when he'd first joined the police force back in the early eighties. Even then, he couldn't quite explain why dealing with the public and his colleagues was a daily nightmare. As much as he'd tried to be logical about everything and fight fear with reason, the anxiety was always stronger. It meant every day, in addition to the natural pressures of the job, everything was that little bit harder. However, back in the day, somehow, the quiet, reserved, but constantly sweating Patterson managed to survive.

The problem was that surviving was the only thing Patterson had done in those early days. After nearly two years in the job, his police career prospects hadn't improved – he'd simply been running in order to stand still, nothing more. With every day that passed, he'd become increasingly convinced he'd made the wrong career choice – that he should have been an accountant, a storeman, a car parking attendant – and he'd just been waiting for the right moment to hand in his resignation. Then he'd heard they were looking for police officers to relocate from Glasgow to Campbeltown. With a problem recruiting police officers in Argyll and Bute, they had turned to Glasgow to tackle the shortage.

The image Patterson had of Campbeltown was a small, backwater coastal port where he could have a slightly quieter, and therefore easier, time than he'd had on the dark streets of Glasgow. The more he'd thought about the move to the smaller town, the more it had appealed to him, so he'd applied for a position in Campbeltown and was accepted. It turned out to be the best decision he could have made.

He started to feel more at ease with himself and more relaxed, which meant he was able to demonstrate his talent for problem solving. This meant, in turn, that he became a standout, professional police officer, respected by his colleagues and much admired by his superiors. In a very short time, he'd made rapid progress as a police officer but also as a functioning human being.

It was also in Campbeltown that he'd first met Stephanie. Confident, outgoing and up for anything, Stephanie was the life and soul of any party. It was truly a meeting of opposites, with Stephanie encountering quiet, down-to-earth Patterson. To everyone's surprise – no more so than for Stephanie and Patterson– they were married within the year. Stephanie embraced the calmness and stability of being a wife and then a mother. Their two children, Calum and Aisling, were born within a couple of years of each other and brought, for the most part, even more joy into the lives of the quiet, hard-working copper and his adoring, contented wife.

Meanwhile, Patterson's crime-solving success rate continued to impress those with influence, and he was encouraged to apply to CID. It meant moving back to Glasgow, but then Patterson had to admit that despite his new-found love of Campbeltown, he had always missed the familiar buzz of his hometown. So, he transferred back to Partick, where he'd soon been promoted to detective inspector, then detective chief inspector. He then settled down to down what he did best – solving crimes.

Recently, however, things hadn't been so easy. His anxiety, which he'd managed to generally keep in check in Campbeltown and those first few years back in Glasgow, was worsening. Glasgow was doing his nerves no favours at all, and he soon remembered why he'd deserted the city in the first place. Glasgow had reinvented itself as a city of culture. However, Patterson had to deal with the real Glasgow, his Glasgow, where no sooner was one assault, one robbery or one murder solved than another would take place.

In addition, Stephanie's drink problem had grown worse in recent times – much worse. It had started back in Campbeltown when the novelty of being a housewife and looking after the home and kids soon wore off. Patterson being dedicated to his work meant he was away from home for longer and longer periods. So Stephanie started drinking during the day, which soon became a habit and an addiction. She did have short periods of sobriety, but sooner or later, the drink would send another invitation she couldn't refuse.

Now Calum and Aisling had left home, Stephanie had been drinking more heavily than ever. She would try to hide the evidence, concealing bottles around the house. She was seemingly oblivious that being pissed most days was the clearest evidence she had become an alcoholic. Now, when Patterson came home, he didn't know what would be awaiting him. That, too, had been a big part of why his nerves were even more frayed of late.

Patterson drove under the bridge at Partick railway station and along to where Dumbarton Road met Byres Road. Glasgow's West End had a reputation for being a little bit more upmarket than some other areas of the city. In some ways, it was, but in other ways, it was still part of the same metropolis that churned up the badness that seemed to lie within everyone.

It was a short drive to River View Veterinary Surgery on Dunaskin Road, where Susan had worked part-time. Nevertheless, it took a while for Patterson to find the place, as it was situated within an anonymous-looking small industrial unit made up of grey Portakabin-type properties.

Once in the portable cabin that housed the veterinary surgery, Patterson found it as anonymous inside as it was outside. There were no pictures on the walls; no effort had been made at all in regard to decor. It was merely a rectangular space with some plastic chairs placed along the walls with a few more positioned in the centre. It was also curiously quiet for a veterinary surgery – no barking dogs or birds squawking, the only noise a polite cough from one of the waiting clients, an elderly gentleman holding a cat basket. This gentleman looked at Patterson with some curiosity, as did the one other customer, a woman holding a small oval birdcage which, in turn, held a placid-looking parrot.

Patterson walked up to the reception window, where he was met with a welcoming smile by a young woman who, in appearance, reminded him of Susan McLaughlin. Her equally bright manner gave him the impression the surgery hadn't yet sussed that the Partick woman murdered at the weekend was their work colleague.

'Can I help you?'

'I'm from Partick CID; I'd like to see the manager if possible.'

The girl stood up and walked through an open door to her left. She returned a minute later and asked Patterson to follow her through a side door she'd opened next to the reception window.

Patterson duly followed her along a small, fusty corridor to a room where he anticipated seeing a vet standing over a restless dog or cat being examined on a table. Instead, he was greeted by a man playing a video game on a computer. Seeing Patterson at the door, the man paused the game, stood up and held out his hand.

'Andrew Williams – I'm the manager. How can I help you?'

Patterson held out his identification. 'DCI Patterson, Partick CID. I just need a word, if you don't mind.'

The receptionist – Becci, according to her name tag – went to leave, but Patterson called her back. 'If you wouldn't mind staying as well, this is for the both of you, and anyone else working in the surgery for that matter.'

'No, there are just the two of us here today,' Williams answered.

'Good. This won't take long,' Patterson

answered. 'I believe Susan McLaughlin works here?'

'Yes,' Williams replied.

'Well, I'm afraid I have some very bad news. Susan was found murdered at the weekend. You may have heard about it on the news. There will be a press conference later to release her identity to the public and appeal for information. Still, I thought it best you know beforehand.'

Becci let out a gasp, putting her hands to her mouth. Williams said, 'Christ, Susan!' and walked over to Becci, putting his arms around her.

'Becci, go and tell whoever's in the waiting room we're closing. Write out a note and put it on the door. We can't work today.'

Becci turned as in a daze and walked out the door. Williams sat back down at his desk and bent over, putting his head in his hands.

'How long did Susan work here, Mr Williams?'

'A year – just over a year, I think,' he said quietly as he sat up again.

'Had everything been all right recently?'

'In what way?'

'Did Susan say she had any problems –

trouble at home or anything?'

Williams shook his head. 'Not that I know of. You'd be better off asking one of the girls that work here, especially Becci or Deena – they were closer to her than I was.'

'How many others work here then?'

'There's six altogether. Mostly veterinary students plus another full-time vet and part-time receptionist.'

'We'll need to interview them all – either myself or a colleague will be down during the week. So, you're the manager?'

'Yes, and the owner. I set it up a few years ago. It's quite a popular surgery.'

'Seems quiet today.'

'Yes, we have days like this too.'

Patterson looked at the vet manager again. He was what you would call a clean-cut young man and gave the impression of being public school educated. Tall, dark, well-spoken, with boyish good looks. He was in his mid-thirties but could have passed for someone much younger. Now and then, he would put his hand through his thick dark hair, and Patterson had the impression that Williams possibly spent more on grooming products for himself than some of the poodles he dealt with.

'How well did you know Susan exactly?'

'As I said, not that well at all. Don't get me wrong, Susan was friendly but quite a private individual. What I can tell you was that she was excellent at her job and will— would have been, I should say, an excellent vet. Can't believe she's dead. Are you really sure it's her? I mean, I'm sure you are; it's just that—'

'We're sure. So did you never go for a drink after work together, things like that?'

'No, I can't say I ever went for a drink with Susan. Like I say, she was closer to Becci and Deena, and Lorraine too. She would come into work, do her job and then go home.'

'When was the last time you saw her?'

'Must have been last Thursday, I think. Yes, she had a long weekend off – she was due back tomorrow. She just did a few hours a day, two or three times a week, but she was an invaluable help. I don't know how we'll cope without her, to be honest. God, I still can't believe… Have you no idea who did it yet?'

'No, it's early days. We're still trying to put a picture together of Susan and her last movements. She didn't mention to yourself what she would be doing at the weekend?'

Williams looked directly at Patterson. 'To me? No. No idea. I—'

Becci came back in, her eyes and nose red,

and she held some tissues in her hand. 'I've sent everyone away, well there were only two customers, and I've put a note on the front door. We're fine to leave.'

'If you don't mind, Mr Williams, could I have a word with Becci alone?'

'Yes, of course. I'll go and make sure everything is switched off.'

Once Williams had left the room, Patterson turned his attention to Becci. 'So you and Susan were close, I believe?'

Becci nodded, continually dabbing at her eyes with a hankie. 'Aye, Susan was lovely. Was! God help us. She had a heart of gold. Do anything for anyone so she would.'

'Did she say anything about what she was doing this weekend?'

'No, can't think. I hadn't really seen her much of late. We were always working at different times in the past few days.'

'And she hadn't mentioned anything to you recently about any problems she was having or anything – anyone she was worried about?'

Becci shook her head. 'No, nothing I can think of...' But then she stared at Patterson, her eyes widening as she suddenly remembered something. 'Oh my God, hang on, aye, she did 'n' all. Oh my God! She told me this guy had been hassling her after she left work, I remember now. She thought this guy, this same guy, I mean, was following her home as well.'

'When was this?'

'Just a couple of weeks back. I'd been meaning to ask her about it again, but like I said, we were always on different shifts recently. She seemed quite upset about it at the time. Worried. Said this guy was hassling her outside when she left work.'

'Hassling her how?'

'Like he was following her, asking her questions, trying to chat her up, and one time she was sure he'd followed her all the way home. She was worried he knew where she lived. One time, she said she looked back when she was near her flat, and the guy was still behind her. Freaked her out. See, she usually walked back home – it's no' that far to her flat. Mind you, sometimes she would still get the bus, or otherwise, she would walk up to the gym around the corner before heading home.'

'Did she say what this guy looked like?'

Becci furrowed her brow. 'Just said it was a young guy.'

'How young?'

'Teens. Bout nineteen or something. Skinny 'n' all, she said, but she said he was kind of trendy like. No' a ned if you know what I mean. Cos, that's what I said to her. Is it an addict? A wee ned or something, and she said naw. Said he was quite smart, as it happens. I don't know if it stopped or no'…

' 'Would you be able to come down the station now? Make a statement? This could be important.'

'Aye, of course. If it might help.'

'Excellent. I'll give you a lift to the station if you like.'

Becci nodded as Williams came back into the room.

Patterson informed him Becci was going to the station with him, that she had some information that could be useful. Williams nodded and proceeded to turn everything in the vet's office off, including the computer game still on pause.

As they walked outside, Patterson asked another question. 'Did Susan mention anything to yourself, Mr Williams, about someone hassling her after work?'

'Hassling her? No, not that I can remember?' Williams looked at Becci. 'How did Susan say that to you?'

'Aye,' Becci answered. 'Couple of weeks back, some guy after work, following her home.'

Williams shook his head. 'You should have told me. I could have paid a taxi for her.'

Becci looked even more upset, as if she could have done something. 'I know, but—'

Patterson interrupted. 'Do you have any CCTV here?' He was looking around, but he couldn't see any cameras.

Williams confirmed there wasn't. 'No, there's none at this place. It's supposed to happen soon, all the businesses are chipping in, but it's taken ages being organised.'

'OK,' Patterson said as he beeped open his car for Becci to get in. 'Thanks for your help, Mr Williams. We'll probably be in touch again to ask some more questions.'

Williams nodded and then went over to Becci and hugged her. 'I'll phone you later,' he said.

As Patterson drove Becci back to the station, he remembered he had the press conference at three, and a cold shiver ran down his back. He tried to take his mind off it and turned to Becci, who was quietly crying beside him.

'I'm sorry about this, Becci. I know how difficult this must be for you.'

'Aye. It's just hard to take in. I'm not saying I knew her really well, but Susan was like…

genuine. A good person. She was an angel, so she was. You know how you can just tell some people are good people? Well, she was one.'

Patterson did know there were people you could just tell were good deep down, just as there were others you could tell straight from the off they were right evil bastards.

'How did Susan get on with your manager?'

'They got on well. To be honest…'

Patterson turned to her. Becci had hesitated as if she was thinking twice about saying something.

'Go on.'

'It's nothing, just that I think they were quite close. Susan told me she'd gone for a drink with him a couple of times. I dunno, I sometimes thought they were even a lot closer than she let on.'

'Mr Williams,' Patterson asked of Becci, 'is he a good manager?'

Becci gave a half-hearted laugh through her sniffles and tears. 'Wouldn't say good. You've seen the state of the place. We're no' even doing good business. Think it's in trouble myself. So did Susan. Andrew treats it like a hobby, no' a business. He's got money through his family. He seems more interested in video games than animals.'

As he drove back to Partick police station, Patterson couldn't help but be pleased with the new information he'd uncovered. Someone had been hassling Susan, following her home, and he also wanted to look further into Andrew Williams. Patterson sensed there was something not quite right with him. For one thing, there was more to the relationship with Susan than he was letting on. Hopefully, CCTV would show who'd been hassling Susan. There were plenty of cameras along Dumbarton Road – one must have picked him up.

Then Patterson took a deep breath again as he thought once more of the press conference later that afternoon.

Chapter 8

The Crow and Crown

After a difficult few days, it was pleasing for Daniel McLeod to answer the phone on Monday morning and hear his best mate Jamie asking if he'd like to go for a drink. Daniel readily agreed, and Jamie said he would meet him in the Crow and Crown at three. Daniel had to ask where the Crow and Crown was since he didn't know it and was surprised to learn it was on Dumbarton Road, not far from Partick station bridge.

So it was that just before three, Daniel walked along Dumbarton Road towards the Crow and Crown, which he now realised he'd seen many times before. It was just one of those pubs he always walked past and never went in.

Upon entering, and to his surprise, Daniel found that not only was Jamie not there but that the pub was completely empty. Finding any pub in Glasgow completely empty was quite rare.

As Daniel pondered whether this was

indeed the right pub, he surveyed its interior. Small lights in the high ceiling bathed the whole place in a pale-yellow glow. A dark wooden semi-circular bar stood in the centre of the premises, a large oblong mirror behind the counter describing the delights of a particular malt whisky in elegant writing. Glamorous bottles of varying sizes stood on glass shelves, bottles filled with all sorts of liquids – yellow and green and blue and red. A faded brass copper rail ran around the bottom length of the highly polished counter. Around the pub, here and there stood rather grand, imposing columns carved in the same ornate fashion as the counter. They rose high up into the ceiling, painted in thick white, gold and blue paint, a reminder of a more prosperous age.

As Daniel walked towards the bar, behind him, stained-glass windows mostly blocked out the view of the non-moving traffic outside, although the tops of tenement buildings could still be seen across the street. Around the walls of the pub sat round wooden tables, scarred by time and experience, in front of red leather seats. Photographs of dark trams and charcoal people hung here and there on the pale white walls. Photographs of an old Glasgow long since gone.

Out of nowhere, an elderly man in a yellow shirt appeared behind the counter, a white cloth hung over his left shoulder. 'Can I help you?' The old man's voice was soft with a slight Hebridean lilt to it, pleasant to the ear.

'Are you open?' Daniel said in an apologetic tone of voice.

'We are indeed,' the old man replied, seemingly half-bemused at Daniel's question.

For a moment, Daniel wondered if the man took the question as an insult, an uncomfortable reminder that the pub was empty, so he was glad to see the straight lines of the barman's face eventually curve into a smile.

The elderly man walked quickly behind the bar, flicking a few switches that immediately filled the gloomy pub with a bright white light. He then strode up behind the bar counter, opposite to where Daniel was standing.

'Now, what can I get ye?'

Daniel ordered a pint of lager and looked around him once again. Under the brighter light, he could now see that the whole pub was like a well-preserved museum. A Wurlitzer jukebox stood next to the far wall, sparkling but silent in keeping with the rest of the pub. The only noise was still the muffled sound of car engines, the shrieks of buses braking, horns and footsteps from the traffic of vehicles and people outside. Now Daniel noticed a gas fire, which gently burned with a modest hiss in the middle of the bright red carpeted floor.

Once he'd poured Daniel's pint, the grey-haired barman picked up a remote and pointed it towards a small TV in the corner. It clicked on with an old-fashioned blinking before the sound of animated voices slowly filled the air.

Daniel liked the pub and wondered why he'd never thought to come here before. It had the air of original nostalgia that many more modern pubs in the city were now trying to replicate. However, whereas they were destined to remain shining brass-and-wood imitations, the Crow and Crown was the real deal.

With the barman continuing to pour him a pint, Daniel turned and looked over his shoulder to watch the small television in the corner. A well-groomed but serious-looking young man with exaggerated pointy hair and chubby cheeks appeared on the screen and started talking.

'Police today appealed for information regarding the murder of a 22-year-old woman in the Partick area of Glasgow. Detectives are still trying to find a motive for the killing, which, they say at this stage, seems to be a completely random attack. Lorna Turnbull reports.

' A passport-sized photograph of a smiling Susan filled the screen.

'It was in the early hours of last Sunday that Susan McLaughlin, a 22-year-old veterinary student at Glasgow University, was murdered in

Gardner St in Partick. Police believe her killer climbed thirty feet up a backcourt drainpipe before entering the flat via an open kitchen window. Susan was then strangled while she lay in her bed. Today, at a press conference, DCI Michael Patterson appealed for anyone with any information to come forward.'

Patterson appeared on screen with a noticeably sweaty forehead.

'We're particularly asking for anyone who was in the vicinity of Gardner Street and Dumbarton Road around midnight on July the 19th. If you saw anyone acting suspiciously or seen anything which could be of interest to the investigation, no matter how trivial it may seem, please contact Partick police station or the Crimestoppers number, which is on the board behind me. All calls, of course, will be treated in confidence. Thank you.'

The barman turned to Daniel shaking his head. 'This town's getting worse, int'it?'

Daniel nodded and was about to say something in reply when the pub door squeaked open, and in walked Jamie Campbell. Daniel had known Jamie since their shared schooldays. Over time, the differences between the two young men had grown. However, they stayed in touch because they were friends, and they were friends because they had stayed in touch.

Apart from that, they had little in common. Whereas Daniel had worked at Campbell and Hill's Insurance for seven years, Jamie had been in countless jobs over that period. Currently, Jamie mainly worked in a call centre but had been a chef, carpet fitter, decorator, steward and waiter in the last two years alone. He also had less mainstream work and considered himself an artist, dancer, actor and writer.

It was because of this that when they met, Daniel inevitably waited for Jamie to say he had lost his job. It was also because of this that Daniel waited with some pleasure to say that he had lost his job.

After ordering a pint of cider, Jamie turned his full attention to Daniel. 'So, how you doing?'

'Good,' Daniel lied, not wanting to get into everything that had been going on in recent days straight away.

'How's the call centre?' Daniel asked. Jamie shook his head. 'Please, let's not talk about the call centre.'

'That bad, eh?'

'Honest to God, I don't know why I stick it. Remember I told you about that mad supervisor we got, Helen?'

'Aye, the one that shouts at you all the

time?'

'Aye, her. Well, the other day, two days running, in fact, she had us standing up, and we weren't allowed to sit down till we got a lead.'

'Seriously?'

'Aye, seriously. I'm tellin' ye, I'm so pissed off man, it's doing my head in.' 'Why don't ye have a word to the bosses about her?'

'Ye're kidding. That's like complaining to the SS about Hitler. Nah, I just have to keep my head down and get on with it. That's all I can do; I need the money.'

'What about everything else? Any luck?' Daniel was referring to the other jobs Jamie was invariably doing.

'I'd rather not talk about it.' Jamie replied.

'That bad, eh?'

'Let's just say I've had better weeks.'

'Well, guess what. You're not the only one who's having a hard time of it. I lost my job at Campbell and Hill's.'

'Seriously?'

'Seriously. Late Friday afternoon, the manager, Steve Pritchard, calls me in, says he wants a word. So I go into his office, and he starts giving me this gumph about the financial crisis and how he needs to lay off staff, and he's so sorry and all the rest of it. Says I can leave there and then, if I take my holidays and I'll be given a redundancy settlement. So just like that I'm out on the street.'

'Wow. Sorry to hear that, mate. Then again, out on the street? Getting sacked from there could be the best thing that could have happened to ye.'

'You think?'

'They treated you like shite. So, anyway, what are you going to do now?'

'What do you think? Look for another job. Oh, and guess what else?

' 'What'

'Deborah's left me.'

Jamie looked at Daniel with a fixed smile on his face waiting for the punchline, which didn't come. 'Away ye go! Deborah hasn't left you. Deborah would never leave you. You've been together like forever. '

'Not forever, exactly. Three years. It does seem like forever, I'll give you that. I woke up on Sunday morning, and she's packing her things. Left me just like that.'

Jamie shook his head. 'Wow. Honest mate, I'm really sorry. So she left you cos you lost your job? That's a bit shitty, is it no?'

Daniel looked back at his friend. The thought that Deborah could have left him because he had lost his job had never occurred to him. 'No, I don't think she left cos of that,' said Daniel. 'She said she just had to leave. Don't know why.'

'Fuck's sake,' said Jamie. 'You really have had better weeks. Ach, anyway, I wouldn't worry about it; you're probably better off without her.'

'You think?'

'Not really, no.'

Jamie laughed, and Daniel joined in. They then talked about the usual. That's to say anything and everything. For the next couple of hours, Daniel forgot about his troubles. As Jamie finished his latest pint, Daniel stood up to take the empty glasses back to the bar, but Jamie put his hand up. 'Not for me, Daniel. Got to be up early the morra and hit them phones bright and breezy.'

'Ye no' staying?'

'Naw, honest ah cannae, you staying?'

'Aye,' Daniel said, 'may as well. I'll have one more, then head up the road.'

'OK, listen, I'll see ye when I see ye and cheer up – ye'll get another job soon and another girlfriend for that matter. Just think yourself lucky ye're no' working in the call centre from

Hell.'

'Aye.' Once his mate had left, Daniel went up to the bar to order one last pint.

*

It was now nearing 10 p.m. Daniel sat at the bar, squeezed by a crowd bunched up all around him. Music was blaring from the jukebox, and everyone seemed to be having a whale of a time. Daniel still felt a little better. Alcohol had numbed his woes and cloaked reality in a soothing haze of a couldn't-care-less/fuck-it attitude.

'Are ye all right then?' said the elderly barman, coming over to Daniel in a rare free moment.

'Fine, thanks,' answered Daniel in a tired voice.

'Good. I'm glad to hear it. Ye looked as if ye had the world on yer shoulders when ye came in here.'

'Aye, well…' said Daniel, swaying and taking another gulp of his beer. A customer on the far side of the bar had an erect twenty-pound note pointing in the air and was calling the barman over. The barman shook his head. 'Ah'm telling ye, I've no' seen this place so busy in such a long time. Ye bring luck to other people, so ye do…'

The barman then patted Daniel on the shoulder, and Daniel nodded, slightly confused by the comment, suddenly realising it was probably time he headed home. Yet, Daniel felt better in a way now. Maybe Jamie was right. Losing his job could be a lucky break – the new start he was looking for. He turned and headed for the pub exit, squeezing past the people around the door, and stepped outside.

An unusually cold wind blew along the pavement, causing Daniel to instinctively button up his jacket. He was semi-paralysed by the sudden unexpected reality into which he now found himself plunged. Within the turn of a second, the warm embrace of alcohol and hope and a possible new beginning had been flipped over by the chilled outside air of inescapable reality. He was just another number amongst the unknown throng. An intense anger rose within him. He heard laughter. Were people laughing at him? Life was completely shit. That was the truth of it. He needed to do something. So much anger. He really needed to do something.

He turned around and started walking along the road, not quite sure where he was going.

Chapter 9

Angel

On Tuesday morning, Patterson was standing in front of the bathroom mirror brushing his teeth, thinking about the press conference the day before. He'd hated every second as per usual, but he thought it had gone all right. Patterson thought of himself as a background kind of guy. That's how he preferred to do his job. Unlike some of his colleagues, who loved any chance to appear on the local news. Simpson, for instance. Aye, he was only a DS, but next time Patterson would get Simpson to do the press conference. He loved all that stuff. He even watched Crimewatch, for Christ's sake.

Patterson realised he was thinking about the job again, and that was the problem with his line of work. You could never really switch off. Sooner or later, no matter what he was doing, Patterson's mind always drifted back to his work, and that was especially the case now with the murder of Susan McLaughlin.

Patterson tried to treat every murder

investigation with equal thoroughness. With some enquiries, however, you couldn't help but get more involved than others. This was one of them. Susan McLaughlin was as innocent as anyone could be. Murdered while lying in her own bed in her own flat.

She wasn't an addict or a dealer who'd got on the wrong side of a Mr Big. She wasn't involved in a fight with another drunk or drugged-up woman. On the face of it, she just happened to be in the wrong place at the wrong time. And that was in her own bed, in her own flat.

Patterson knew that every murder was wrong. Yet, Patterson also knew some murders were worse than others, and the murder of Susan McLaughlin was a particularly immoral murder.

The response so far from the press conference had been poor. Nevertheless, there was still that new and potentially very promising lead that had surfaced through Patterson's visit to the vet and talking to Susan's colleague Becci. That young man in his teens following Susan home after work could be very interesting indeed. He had already been dubbed the vet guy by the investigation team, and CCTV was being checked along with further enquiries to identify who this guy really was.

Patterson wiped the toothpaste from the

side of his mouth with a blue towel, which he then placed neatly on the side of the bath. He walked out of the bathroom, past the bedroom where Stephanie lay sleeping. As Patterson passed her room, he pulled the bedroom door slightly closed before gently making his way down the narrow carpeted stairs. His skin nice and smooth after the shave, his teeth clean, and with a welcome fresh shirt on, Patterson was starting to feel a little better than he had on waking up.

He went into the kitchen for breakfast, finding some sliced sausage and a couple of not-too-stale rolls. He crushed them down with his fist to make them softer and buttered them as he waited for the sausage to cook. For a moment, he thought about calling up to Stephanie to see if she wanted one, but then thought twice about it. Best leave her be.

His thoughts turned once again to yesterday's press conference. It was good that no one seemed to have noticed how anxious he was. He could always tell when his own unease made others unsettled. Yet it had seemed to go all right. He'd answered the usual questions with the usual answers and found the correct words to say. It was a minefield nowadays giving statements because he knew one lapse of concentration, one wrong word, and upstairs would be demanding he issue an apology.

Why had Susan been killed? It was the question he kept coming back to. Why? It was confirmed there had been no sexual assault. No signs of a burglary. Had it really just been the fact that she'd left a window open that night that had cost Susan her life? Or did the killer know who'd lived in that flat, as Patterson suspected?

Another promising lead had come to light on Monday afternoon when Pettigrew had visited Susan's gym. According to one staff member, as so many others had said, Susan was a quiet girl who mostly kept herself to herself. Still, apparently, there was one guy she talked to regularly, a man called Markus Sepp. Pettigrew had immediately gone to his address, which was just around the corner from the gym on Gilbert Street, but there had been no answer. That was what made this guy particularly interesting – he hadn't been back to the gym since Susan's murder, whereas beforehand, he'd been there almost every day without fail for over a month. Granted, there was nothing else to connect this Markus Sepp to Susan or the murder apart from seeming to be good friends at the gym.

Further enquiries revealed Sepp was from Estonia, but a call to the Border Agency hadn't revealed anything of interest. He had no previous convictions apart from a drink-driving offence in his home country five years ago. Still, Patterson was keen to talk to Sepp sooner rather than later. He had a feeling Sepp was worth talking to, and, besides, Patterson would unashamedly grab at any straw right now.

He sat down at the kitchen table and drank his tea before moving to turn the sausage over, watching the fat drip onto the silver foil beneath.

Looking around the kitchen, he pictured Calum and Aisling sitting at the same table, getting ready for school. How many years ago was that now? The radio playing. The rush. The happiness. The love. Patterson an eager young police sergeant; Stephanie all energy and life. Now there was only the sound of sizzling sausage as Patterson took it off the grill and placed a slice in each roll. The fat immediately oozed into the dough.

Calum and Aisling had long since gone; Stephanie, too, in her own way. Things had deteriorated so fast, despite the fact that Patterson had worked his way up to detective chief inspector through hard graft and hidden anxiety. He sat back down at the kitchen table, biting into his roll, alone, conscious of the space around him, the silence.

Patterson knew Susan might have had a private life away from her mother, neighbours, and friends. It was strange she hadn't mentioned to her mum or Shona about the man following her home from work. Maybe she liked secrets. He knew some – many – people did.

And, again, he came back to the question of why the murderer climbed up to that particular window? More than one neighbour had left their window open that night. Yet the killer had climbed past other windows below to reach that of Susan McLaughlin. Why? There must have been a reason. It was three floors up. A fall of sixty feet. Yet the killer had risked his own life to take another. Was it purely for the thrill of murder? No, the more Patterson thought about it, the more he was convinced this wasn't a random killing. Susan had been murdered for a reason. Patterson just had to find out what that reason was, and that would lead him to the killer.

Patterson looked up at the clock; it was coming up to seven. He wiped the melted butter and fat off his hands with a tea towel, got up and switched on the radio to listen to the news. The headlines, though, hadn't changed for weeks. The credit crunch. Cutbacks. Scotland losing at football. The usual, just the usual.

Patterson downed the rest of his tea, made sure everything was switched off and walked into the hallway. He put his jacket on, picked up his papers and car keys, and opened the front door. The early morning air was crisp, but light blue skies above indicated another warm, sunny day lay ahead.

As Patterson shut the front door and walked across the gravel path to his car, his mobile phone rang. He flipped it open and took the call. It was Billy again. Patterson's irritation was clear in his voice. 'Listen, Billy, I haven't time right now, I've—'

Billy interrupted him. 'Aye, I know, sorry, but I've got some info for ye, it's about the murder of that lassie Susan McLaughlin.'

*

Upstairs in the bedroom, Stephanie lay on the bed. Her eyes open. Her head thumping. She felt terrible. Even though she felt so ill, she still wanted to go downstairs and talk to her husband. Apologise for what she said last night. Did last night. Once again. She was scared. How long would it be before he cracked? Before he simply left her?

The thought of that happening terrified her. She needed to talk to him. Go downstairs and say how sorry she was. Say that she would make an effort. That she wouldn't drink that day.

But she didn't get up. She didn't go downstairs. Instead, she just lay in bed, staring ahead, listening to the odd sounds rising from downstairs. The grill getting taken off the stove. The kettle boiling. A chair scraping across the tiled floor. The radio being turned on, then off.

She waited. Eventually, the sound of the

front door shutting reverberated around the house. Then silence. A tear rolled down her cheek. She still had hours to wait before the off-licence opened.

Chapter 10

Complications

Patterson's agreed meeting point with Billy was down by the Clyde, on the walkway opposite the Glasgow Science Centre. Patterson remembered when he used to come down to this riverside area many years ago in search of peace and quiet. Back then, it was just a derelict waste ground, nothing more than wooden docks covered in dirty green moss and the scent of damp and decay hanging in the air. With the dark, imposing Finnieston Crane towering above the empty wasteland, the area gave the impression of having been abandoned in a hurry, as if someone hadn't paid the rent and done a runner.

Now, as Patterson cut between the Scottish Exhibition and Conference Centre and the Clyde Auditorium – or the Armadillo as it was better known – the whole area resembled a technological theme park with glass and silver buildings of impressive shape and sparkle on either side of the river. On this particular day, with the blue sky above and well-dressed conference attendees passing in and out of the SECC, with joggers and those just out for a stroll, it seemed to be the vision of a computer-generated architect's illustration brought to life. The impressive but impassive River Clyde constantly flowed slowly past, as if consciously ignoring its ever-changing surroundings.

Patterson looked west along the Clyde Walkway and could see Billy sitting on the usual bench just beyond the Millennium Bridge.

Patterson had known Billy Anderson for some time. He still seemed to be wearing the same clothes he'd worn when Patterson had first met him all those years ago – a faded grey tracksuit top and bottoms with expensive white thick-soled trainers. No matter how hot or cold, Billy would be dressed the same as a jogger who never jogged in summer or winter.

Billy was in his mid-thirties now. Never into anything serious, he just skimmed a few rules now and then. Sold things he shouldn't have sold. Fake DVDs, CDs, perfumes, etc. Looks like, sounds like, smells like. Not something Patterson approved of, but Billy was harmless enough, and besides, he had his uses now and then. Billy looked up and saw Patterson's tall, thin, slightly self-conscious frame striding towards him. He rubbed the top of his balding round head, which no amount of tactical shaving could hide, then looked back at the Clyde, where a mother duck determinedly led three ducklings along the dark grey choppy waters of the river.

Patterson sat down next to Billy without saying anything at first. Across the water was the large glass box of the BBC building and the sloping glass front of the Science Centre. The Glasgow Tower, part of the Science Centre, was impressive for its ability to fully turn on its axis and for never working. A breeze began to pick up, and as Patterson sat beside Billy, he could hear the soothing sound of fresh water lapping against the moss-covered stonewall sides of the riverbank.

'Hi, Billy, how are you? All right?'

'Hello, Mr Patterson. Aye, I'm fine, thanks – getting by.'

Patterson nodded as both men's attention was again drawn by the ducks making slow progress along the river.

'So you said you know something about the Susan McLaughlin murder which might be of interest?' Patterson said this, still not expecting that much in return.

'Aye, Ah do,' Billy said firmly, sensing Patterson's scepticism.

Patterson turned to look at Billy, waiting for him to explain further, yet Billy's attention still seemed focused on the ducks.

'So, what is it?' Patterson enquired further with just a hint of annoyance apparent.

'Well, you know this lassie, Susan; it seems she was involved with somebody she shouldnae have been involved with.'

'Meaning?'

'Meaning' – Billy took a cigarette out of his tracksuit pocket and, after putting it to his lips, brought out a lighter but then lowered both – 'she was seeing some guy who's no' a hundred per cent legit.'

Patterson leaned back on the bench, always seeing in his mind images of the empty, neglected dockside of the past rather than the developed present.

'Who?'

Billy cupped his hands together and skilfully lit the cigarette. He took a couple of quick draws before continuing. 'Like Ah said, it's just to let ye know that there's this guy she shouldnae have been involved with, and the word is he's no' too happy.'

'Not happy about what exactly?'

'Well, let's just say this guy, he had a liking for this Susan bird, and now some cunt's killed her.'

'Aye, it can be terrible that.' Patterson turned his head towards Billy again to see if his part-time informant was seriously thinking that Patterson would let him go without naming who he meant. 'So what are you telling me?'

'Just this man, this bad man, is no' a happy bunny. He's looking to hurt someone. Looking to get whoever murdered this Susan bird and do him big time.'

That was all Patterson needed. Complications. One of Glasgow's high-life lowlifes interfering in his investigation.

'I need to know who it is, Billy,' Patterson said, just in case Billy happened to really think otherwise.

'All Ah can say is he's after whoever killed Susan, and if the toerag that done it is caught by this guy, believe me, the last thing he'll be getting is life.'

Patterson heard a low intermittent chugging noise begin from downriver. He looked to his right to see a small, narrow waste-carrying barge sailing up towards town. As he thought about what to do with Billy and his half-hearted information, Patterson looked at the tall cranes of the Govan shipyard. Heavy-duty hammering could be heard. Thumping. He could make out the grey metal hulk of a warship being built, its square backside hanging out over the Clyde.

Maybe Patterson could just dangle Billy over the Clyde. Enough was enough.

'OK, Billy. Stop with the shite. If you don't tell me who this guy is in the next few seconds, everyone from Govan Cross to the fucking Moon will know you're a grass. I haven't got time to fuck about. We're talking about the murder of a young lassie here, remember? I need a name.'

A thought suddenly occurred to Patterson. 'For fuck's sake, is it you? Don't tell me it's you.'

Billy turned to Patterson, smoke drifting out his open mouth and blanketing his face. 'Me? Course it isnae me! What are you oan aboot?'

'Then name!'

It didn't take much for Billy to give in. 'McGregor. Davy fucking McGregor.'

'Chuckles?'

'Aye, Chuckles.'

Patterson looked at Billy to see if he was legit in what he was saying. Why would Davy McGregor be bothered about Susan McLaughlin? Yet, if it really was McGregor, then he could understand Billy's reluctance to name him. Billy needed McGregor's nod to punt a few DVDs and other stuff around the pubs in his patch. The thing was, Billy had never given info on McGregor before. Far too dodgy. But McGregor? Susan didn't seem the type of girl to be involved in any way with a scumbag like him.

'Are you sure about this?'

'Aye. McGregor put the word out he wants to know who did her. To be honest, I thought ye might have heard already.'

Patterson thought he should have known as well. At least he knew now and was intrigued to find out more. 'OK, fair enough. If you're not bullshitting me, thanks for the info. Let us know if you hear anything else.'

'Mr Patterson, I'm gonnae be at the market on Saturday. I was just wondering if there's anything happening—'

'You'll be all right. I'll have a word.'

Billy was savvy enough to know there would be a raid now and then at the market. If not this week, then next. A blind eye to his activities wouldn't hurt as long as it was discreet.

'Thanks, Mr Patterson. Say hello to yer wife for me as well now.'

Patterson didn't respond. Instead, he looked upriver towards the Squinty Bridge. He still couldn't figure out why Susan would be connected to McGregor in any way.

Patterson left Billy and walked along the walkway, retracing his route back to his car. If McGregor was connected to this enquiry, could he have had anything to do with Susan's murder?

McGregor putting the word out that he wanted to find Susan's killer could be a bluff. He could be a bad man when he wanted to be. That included having people killed, though it was usually other psychos trying to take some of his business. Killing young lassies didn't seem his style. One thing was certain: it was definitely a new lead that had to be investigated. Patterson would have to pay McGregor a visit ASAP.

Chapter 11

The Big Glass Box

As Stone Johnson and his agent, Greg Ross, walked towards the main entrance of the BBC Scotland building on Pacific Quay, there was no doubt in Stone's mind that Stone Investments belonged to his past and his future belonged on the telly.

He'd been the financial expert on Caledonia Television's lunchtime news programme for two years now. The small but popular cable TV company had brought in Stone to shore up their flagging news programme. To the producer's delight, audiences had indeed risen significantly since his arrival.

The main news presenter there was Abigail Andrews, a bright and bubbly blonde who, at the launch of her career, had the original feature of reading the news standing up. However, with her confidence dented by disappointing viewing figures, she went back to sitting down again.

Stone didn't like working with Abigail; he found her too self-obsessed, and she thought the same of Stone. However, their mutual animosity was interpreted as chemistry by the viewers, with added hints their relationship was more than just professional.

Although Stone didn't like Abigail, he loved working in television, and now it was towards the big glass box of BBC Scotland that he and his agent walked. Stone and Greg strode through the sliding glass front doors and up to the main reception desk.

'Stone Johnson and Greg Ross to see Peter Webb,' announced Greg.

The young male receptionist checked a list before calling a number on the phone. 'Someone will be right down to see you. If you'd just like to take a seat over there.'

Stone and his agent sat waiting in the foyer, admiring the big glass box. Inside, it looked like a forward-thinking prison. Massive stairs led to different floors, with the well-coiffured heads of media types scurrying along silver and glass balconies on each side, like fashion-conscious screws dealing with multiple disturbances.

Zoe Young, a young, smiling assistant something, came down to meet the two men and take them to the meeting room. The meeting room was bright and airy, its vast plate-glass windows from ceiling to floor giving a clear view of Glasgow to the north. Stone and Greg stood in the doorway and looked on as four serious-looking men and two even more serious-looking women were chattering with each other.

Once formally introduced by Zoe, the two men sat down. It was Peter Webb in his Home Counties accent who broke the silence. Peter was a large man with a shaved round head and rimless glasses. He looked important but relaxed, wearing a cream-coloured jacket and an open-necked blue shirt.

'Right, as you know, this is just an initial meeting to inform you of our ideas for the finance show we're planning and also, of course, to get some ideas from yourselves – hear how, if we do decide to go ahead with the programme, you and we see the programme developing. We've been really impressed by your work on Lunchtime Live, by the way. We understand since Stone started' – Peter directed this comment towards Greg – 'that the viewing figures have gone through the roof?'

Greg nodded. 'Indeed. If it wasn't for Stone, Lunchtime Live would have been dead in the water months ago.'

Stone nodded, suddenly a little more nervous, afraid of saying the wrong thing and blowing this massive opportunity. These were important people he was surrounded by – bona fide grown-ups.

Peter turned to one of his colleagues. 'Jake, tell Stone and Greg about our current thinking.'

Jake, the business editor, nodded, and they talked about ideas, plans, possible scenarios and schedules for the next hour or so. It all went well, and Stone loved it. They were obviously gagging for him.

Peter took over once again. 'A slot has opened up six weeks from now. We know it's short notice, but we plan to go for it. We should have a lot more meetings before then, of course. We can discuss contracts at a later date, but if you're happy – and, well, I think we're all happy – then it's all systems go.'

Stone looked at Greg and nodded. 'Yes, everything sounds fine. Excellent.'

There were murmurings and movements around the table meant to indicate happiness and satisfaction.

Peter put his finger in the air. 'Oh, but one other thing we're excited about is for you to have a co-presenter.'

'A co-presenter?' Stone asked, trying to hide his disappointment. He was under the impression this was to be his show and his show alone.

Noticing Stone's doubtful expression, Julia explained further. 'We mean someone who can do outside reports. Someone prepared to stand in the rain in Argyle Street for a couple of hours and ask the punters what they think of the latest rise in the price of eggs, etc.'

Stone nodded. 'Sounds good. What sort of person had you in mind?'

'What we were thinking is trying to create a kind of dynamic like you have with Abigail at Lunchtime Live,' Peter said.

Stone didn't like that idea at all, but still, he knew to keep quiet.

'Actually,' Peter continued, 'we weren't thinking of Abigail in particular; what we meant was just someone in that mould. You know, someone you could work off.'

David, the ideas man, chimed in. 'Actually, we're looking for brand new talent like yourself. A completely new team that would bring a freshness to the show instead of the same tired old faces. The one person we did think of is Geneva. Geneva Scott? You know, out of Castle Dangerous? Have you had a chance to see her? She would certainly add another dimension to the programme.'

Stone did know Geneva. 'I just did a radio

show two weeks ago with her as it happens. I was quite impressed. Seems a nice person. I suppose it's an idea we could run with for now.'

'Great,' Peter said. 'Now we're getting somewhere. Julia, call Geneva's agent this afternoon and arrange a meeting.'

Looking around and then at his watch, Peter clapped his hands. 'Right, I think that's enough work for now. Why don't we all have some fresh coffee and biccies before we talk some more and get round to some kind of timetable we can work with?'

There was a further murmur of agreement as a trolley of sandwiches, biscuits, and large pots of tea and coffee arrived.

Stone stretched, stood up and walked over to the window. He looked down on the slow-rolling waters of the Clyde, over the spires and towers of old Glasgow in the background and the shiny new Glasgow in the foreground.

Stone's eye drifted down to the river again. He could see a barge carrying waste up the river. Cyclists and joggers moving smoothly along the walkway. Taxi drivers standing and chatting with each other outside a hotel. Two men talking to each other on a bench. They were all just characters in the world of Stone Johnson. A world in which Stone was the real star of the show.

Chapter 12

Chuckles

The Emerald pub was similar to many others on London Road. The colour scheme was predominately green and white, and when you entered, 'The Fields of Athenry' would invariably be playing in the background. On the walls, in-between photos of Billy McNeill and Henrik Larson, paper three-leaf clovers hung here and there. Behind the bar, they had Guinness, Kilkenny's and O'Reilly's on tap. In front of the bar, the talk was always about Glasgow Celtic and about the problems they were having. Because no matter how well they did, like Rangers, Celtic always appeared to have problems.

Patterson entered the large wood-panelled pub, which trying to keep up with the times, had decided to go open plan. The Emerald was Davy McGregor's office. Patterson immediately spotted him sitting at his usual table in the corner, surrounded by three of his wannabes. The job of the wannabees was to laugh at Davy's jokes, go next door to the bookies for him and do whatever else he expected of them.

Patterson walked across the large spacious floor as all heads turned to watch him move like they were at a fashion show and Patterson was on the catwalk. All strangers in this pub, like many others in Glasgow, were potential coppers and treated as such. Patterson was known, but it was still the done thing to make out he was a stranger and, in doing so, reaffirm the regulars were on the side of the robbers and not the cops.

Patterson went to the bar and ordered a Diet Coke, noticing the faded Gaelic tattoo on the barman's arm. As he took change out of his pocket, Patterson scanned the pub once more. Only McGregor ignored his presence, watching the horse racing on the widescreen TV. A couple of guys at the pool table in the back had also stopped playing to give Patterson an extended gander. All the time, there was a faint smell of weed in the air. Patterson paid for the drink and walked towards McGregor's table.

Davy 'Chuckles' McGregor practically lived in the Emerald. It was here he'd first earned his nickname when the Emerald decided to have a stand-up night, and McGregor decided if all these other fuckers could be stand-up comedians, then he could too. Sure enough, he went down a storm. Although everyone else knew that the punters in the Emerald laughed because it was in their best interests to do so. Heckling certainly wasn't an option. McGregor had then built on this solitary success with surprising speed by performing elsewhere, appearing no less as part of the Glasgow Comedy Festival as one of Glasgow's very own.

However, nowhere did McGregor get the laughs he'd achieved that first time he'd performed, even when he brought his entourage with him. It was perhaps partly because his whole stand-up routine consisted of insulting people with a tagline of a shouty violent threat. Nevertheless, McGregor still thought of himself now as a part-time businessman and part-time stand-up comic. In reality, he was a small-time gangster or an adult ned, depending on your point of view.

Appearance-wise, Davy McGregor was in his late thirties with tousled bleached-blonde hair and designer stubble. He was always dressed in conspicuous designer clothes. No fake rubbish either. He only sold that to the mug punters in the pubs and markets. He was conspicuous in other ways too. He drove a flash car and had countless different wannabee girlfriends who, for a time, replaced his wannabee table mates.

McGregor did have his dangerous side, though, and for all his cartoon clothing and lifestyle, he was someone you'd be a fool to mess with. He ran the local drug trade, the money lending and the money laundering. New foreign gangs were coming in all the time, and McGregor had a hard time trying to keep his territory his, but he was still doing all right. The credit crunch had been good news as far as McGregor was concerned.

For all his scams and cons and robberies and intimidation, counterfeit money was McGregor's first love. Sure, more often than not, the fake tens or twenties would get sussed eventually, and the print shop would get raided. But not before McGregor had made a tidy profit and some other mug had taken the rap. Booze and cigarette runs brought in additional money. There were hundreds of scams and cons, 'operations' as Davy liked to call them, which made up his 'business empire'. Then there were his more 'respectable' earnings. His share in taxi firms and security companies – excuses he could give to call himself a businessman. All in all, it was just different, dodgy ways of making lots of lovely money. And, of course, he now liked to think of himself as one of Glasgow's finest stand-ups.

For all that, though, McGregor was still small-time, first division; everyone knew the big bucks were made by the big boys in the premier league, where you could relax a bit more. Give up the knife fights and the odd shooting and concentrate solely on getting legit deals for non-legit companies. And who knows, down the line, maybe a couple of TV appearances on Channel Five and a book deal thrown in. It was all there for the taking. But Davy wasn't there yet. He was still serving his apprenticeship, still walking that thin line between big-name thug and small-time gangster. That's why the Emerald was where he was likely to be found instead of some little office with a generic name on Dalmarnock Road.

So Davy McGregor was the big man at the moment until the next big man came along. No one sold anything in any market or pub between Glasgow Cross and Bridgeton Cross without McGregor giving his permission. As for some punter coming in the area to sell goods in the big man's patch without him getting a cut? Well, in that case, it would be the punter who got the cut.

McGregor also had friends inside the force. Every dawn raid, every house search, appeared to happen a couple of hours, even a day too late. Nonetheless, Patterson was convinced he'd get McGregor soon. Staying low key was often the savvy thing to do in McGregor's line of business, but McGregor wasn't savvy. Too cocky. It was only a matter of time before he slipped up.

McGregor only looked up as Patterson walked right up to his table. Then he broke into a big smile.

'How's it goan, Mikey? I see you're on the

soft drinks. I suppose yer wife drinks enough for the both of ye, eh?'

The others at the table laughed. Pissed themselves. McGregor was like a breakfast DJ surrounded by his cronies, always convincing him he was the funniest guy on the block.

'Aww man, ye're fuckin' wicked, so ye ur, Davy,' one of the wannabees said, trying to get some more brownie points to move him up the wannabee league.

Patterson ignored McGregor's comment and smiled. 'If only your stand-up routine was as funny as your fucking shirt.'

McGregor could have scored a point by laughing, but he wasn't capable of laughing at himself in any way whatsoever. As McGregor scowled, Patterson continued. 'So anyway, now that the banter is out the way, I'd like a quiet word, McGregor.'

'D'ye hear that, lads? Mr Polisman is wanting a quiet word. Hey, Chesney, move over and let the polisman have a seat.' Chesney muttered a half-hearted, purely for show, 'Aw fuck, why me?' but did as he was told.

'Oh, if it's all right with you, McGregor, I'd rather have a chat alone. I'm sure none of your boys here won't mind missing your repartee for a couple of minutes.' Patterson emphasised the word boys as if to imply they did much more for

McGregor than just putting on bets.

'Ho, what the fuck dae ye mean by "boys"?' A half-stoned eighteen-year-old kid in a Republic of Ireland tracksuit didn't like the implication.

'Leave it, Keiron. Away ye all go and have a fag outside.' McGregor nodded towards the door.

The three boys, no' happy, got up and headed towards the front entrance while Patterson sat opposite McGregor. Patterson took a sip of his warm Coke before getting straight to the point.

'I hear you knew Susan McLaughlin.'

McGregor glanced at Patterson before his attention was drawn back to the large television screen to the right of the pub entrance. The one-thirty at Lingfield had just gone off. He brought a betting slip out of his pocket, looked at it, then called across to the barman. 'Hey, Kenny, what price did Compton Prince go off?'

'Eleven to four,' Kenny shouted.

McGregor kept the betting slip in his hand and remained staring at the big-screen TV as Patterson talked.

Patterson repeated the question. 'I said I hear you knew Susan McLaughlin.'

McGregor took a loud swig of his Guinness and, after a moment, eventually acknowledged the question. 'Susan McLaughlin? Was that no' the name of the lassie killed at the weekend there?'

'Aye.'

'Naw.'

'Naw, what?'

'Naw, Ah didnae know her.'

Patterson leaned forward, firmly tapping McGregor on the shoulder so he'd look at him. 'I can assure ye, McGregor, I didn't come down this Celtic shitehole for the cultural experience. Susan McLaughlin. Aye, that one. Murdered at the weekend. Tell me about her. Otherwise, we can take this down the station.'

'I said Ah didnae know her!'

'OK, your choice.' Patterson stood up, grabbing McGregor by the collar and trying to drag him up. McGregor's pint glass fell off the table and shattered on the floor. Patterson's Coke wobbled but stayed upright.

The horse race was coming to a climax, the commentator's voice rising to a pitch as three horses crossed the line together. Compton Prince wasn't one of them.

McGregor stopped. 'OK. OK. Haud oan.'

Patterson let him go, and they both sat down.

'Bastard. Cunt. Fucking donkey.' McGregor

crumpled up the betting slip and threw it at the table; it bounced off it and landed in the spilled foamy beer on the floor.

Finally, McGregor turned and looked at Patterson. 'You've got fucking beer on ma shoes now.' He motioned to Kenny, the barman, to wait when he saw him getting a brush and shovel. 'Aw right, Susan McLaughlin. Aye, in fact, ye're right indeed. Ah did know her.'

'So how come? Not your usual type.'

'What d'ye mean?'

'I mean, she wasn't a fuckin' desperate tart, that's what I mean.'

'Oh, cheers. Merry Christmas to you too.'

'So?'

'She was a friend of Stevie. Brought her in the Emerald one night. She liked what she saw. You can guess the rest.'

'Who's Stevie?'

'Just one of the lads. Like Ah said, he brought her here one night, and then she met me. End of.'

'Couldn't resist your charms, is that it?'

'You could say that. Ah, cannae help it if the birds find me irresistible.'

'Go on.'

'So, like Ah said, she was a friend of Stevie. And aye, she was a nice lassie. No posh but nicely spoken 'n' that.'

'So how come this Stevie knew her?'

'Dunno. Didnae ask. Stevie just comes in one night with Susie trailing behind. Stevie was out his box. She was all dolled up. Ah, think she thought Stevie was going to take her intae town. A club or sumfin. She obviously didnae know Stevie too well. Could tell she wisnae planning on spending the night in the Emerald, that's for sure. Ah felt sorry for her. Ended up taking her intae town masel.'

'When was this?'

'About six weeks ago.'

'So you went to a club together?'

'Aye, well, gave her a good night, champagne, bit of attention, know?'

'When's the last time you saw her?'

'Bout a week before she was fucking murdered. Couldnae believe it when Ah heard it on the telly. Swear it, man. Bastard, so it is.'

'So how often did you see Susan, average?'

'Average? Twice a week. Seen her about seven, eight times total.'

Patterson nodded and took another sip of the Coke, determined to get his money's worth out of this dive.

'Where were you on the night Susan got killed? Last Saturday night, early hours Sunday.'

'Ho, should Ah be buzzing my lawyer here?'

'It's just an informal chat. Just following up a few leads, that's all.'

'Aye, right. If ye had any leads, ye wouldn't be down the Emerald, noising me up.'

Patterson leaned back. 'Like I said, it's just an informal chat, Davy. No need to get your hair out of joint. So where were you on the night Susan was murdered?'

'Where d'ye think? Here. Ask any of the lads – got plenty of witnesses.'

'Yeah. What time did you leave?'

'How the fuck do Ah know?'

'It was last Saturday. Remember.'

Davy put his hand through his bleached-blonde hair. 'Wait, fair enough. It was later. Bout twelvish.'

'Then?'

'Went home. Listen, don't try and stitch me up, Patterson. No matter what ye think o' me, Ah don't kill young lassies, and you know that, or else you'd have banged me up already. Fact is, Ah hope you catch the fucker before Ah do, for his sake. Get my meaning?'

'Don't even think about it. I hope that CCTV camera up there works, or you're in deep shit.'

'It's working, and Ah can prove Ah was here. You'll just need to stitch up some other poor cunt.'

'Is this Stevie guy here?'

'Naw.'

'Where can I find him?'

'Dunno. He's in here most nights... Otherwise, you might catch him down the snooker hall in Westmuir Street.'

Patterson thought for a moment. He wasn't convinced. McGregor was keeping something from him, but he didn't know what.

'OK, McGregor, I need you to come down the station to make a statement now.'

McGregor threw his hands up in the air. 'What the fuck dae ye mean? Ah just told you the whole score.'

'Aye, right,' Patterson said. 'Get yer coat, yer' pulled.'

Chapter 13

Interrogation

It was a scene that had played out many times over the years. The hardened, embittered cop trying to get a confession out of the sad, small-time crook. It was only a matter of time before the bastard cracked, and this time the interrogator was determined to get his prey to squeal.

'You're nothing but a useless piece of shit. You know that? You're the lowest of the low. I don't even know why I'm wasting my time with you.'

Stephanie's well-educated voice was at odds with the venom which spouted from her mouth. Patterson, meanwhile, was still trying to concentrate on eating his dinner. He carefully picked apart the fish supper he was eating with his fingers as if he was conducting an autopsy on the piece of cod. Above all, he knew, at all costs, it was vital to avoid eye contact with his accuser. It was vital not to react. Vital just to kid on the insults didn't hurt as Stephanie took another large gulp of the clear liquid in her glass.

Earlier, he'd taken Davy McGregor back to the station but couldn't get anything more out of him than a general statement. Patterson had decided to let McGregor go for the moment, even though he knew he was hiding something. It was good enough for now that McGregor knew Patterson was on his tail.

On the way out of the station, Patterson got a call from Stephanie. She wanted a fish supper, and could he also stop by the off-licence? At first, Patterson refused before eventually caving in as he always did. Now, he was home with the couple of fish suppers, one unopened, and the off-licence booty being downed by his wife.

Stephanie now walked behind Patterson and leaned against the kitchen cabinet with the glass of vodka in one hand and a cigarette in the other. She knew that by standing behind Patterson now and again, it would unnerve her husband even more.

Stephanie had the air of a one-time glamorous star. Her natural blonde hair was tied back in a bob, her beauty, even now as it faded day by day, still the first thing most people noticed about her. She brought the cigarette deliberately up to her lips and inhaled slowly before blowing the smoke high into the air, wondering what her next move should be. Then she was on the prowl again, circling, walking round to sit down opposite the lowlife at the table.

She leaned her chin in the palm of her hand, her elbow on the table. 'I mean, look at you. Just look at you! You're pathetic! God knows how I ever ended up married to you.'

Patterson continued to dissect his fish, concentrating as best he could on every cut. Now and then, he managed, albeit self-consciously, to bring a crumbling piece of soggy batter and cod to his mouth before continuing to look down at his dinner. All the time, he was waiting for Stephanie to get bored or get to that drunk turning-point stage, where she wasn't conscious enough to do or say anything at all.

Stephanie, though, for the moment, wasn't going anywhere. Oh no. Patterson had to pay for his crime. How dare he say he wasn't getting her a bottle of vodka when she wanted one? How dare he? Yes, even if he eventually did go to the off-licence like he always did, it didn't matter. The point was he'd initially refused. Patterson treated her like dirt, so he did. And now he had to pay the price for his cheek.

Stephanie herself knew that what she was doing was wrong. She felt it inside, the guilt slipping down her throat along with her unpronounceable vodka. It slightly soured the taste, making her even angrier. Because someone had to pay for the mess she was in, and there was no one else there but Patterson. She wouldn't leave the kitchen until she at least got a reaction from him.

'Enjoying that, are you?' Stephanie laughed, not expecting an answer. Still, she sighed at his lack of response and shook her head. Stubbing out her cigarette and immediately lighting another, Stephanie blew the smoke into Patterson's face and then tilted her head like a puzzled dog, squinting and studying him as if genuinely trying to understand her husband. Her voice was quiet now and confidential, telling him a secret he needed to know.

'You're not fit to be called a husband, you do know that, don't you? And to imagine that you're a detective chief inspector! My God, how ever did that happen? If only they knew down at the station. In fact, I wonder if Philip has any idea what sort of man he has working for him.'

She saw Patterson shift ever so slightly when she mentioned Philip Dunard, his boss. She always called the superintendent by his first name. As if they were intimate friends.

Patterson couldn't help himself and

quickly glanced up at his wife. Stephanie smiled. The little fish was starting to nibble. Good. Now that she'd found her way in, all she had to do was continue in the same calm, understanding voice.

'Yes, when I think about it, that's what I should do. I think I should call Philip. Philip and me have always got on. Think he's got a bit of a thing for me. I really should let him know. He should know what kind of shit is on his police force... don't you think I should phone... darling?'

Patterson was finding it harder and harder to hide his discomfort. They all knew about Patterson's wife at the station, of course. Everyone knew. Even bloody McGregor knew. His boss was sympathetic, but Patterson was aware there was only so much his superior could tolerate.

'Get it sorted, Mike,' Dunard had said the last time Stephanie had phoned up.

Patterson had tried. Caught Stephanie in a rare moment, she was sober. Tried to talk to her. But she wouldn't listen. Still, he had told her. If she didn't at least try and sort herself out, he would have to leave her. It was still the last thing in the world either of them wanted.

Besides, it was his own fault in a way. He should have gone straight to the off-licence. The thought of Stephanie phoning his boss again was too much. Patterson had to say something. Yet he was tired, so tired. This murder case seemed to be draining him so much already – physically, mentally and emotionally. In an almost inaudible whisper, he said, 'Please, Stephanie...'

It was painful even for Stephanie to hear the anguish in his voice. She stood up and started walking towards the phone in the hall.

Patterson rose out of his chair. 'Stephanie, I can't let you phone.'

'What do you mean? You can't let me phone! Who do you think you are? Can't let me! And how are you going to stop me? I told you! Do you think I want to phone? I'm doing this for your own good, Michael. Besides, I haven't spoken to Philip for ages.'

She walked into the hall and picked up the phone. Patterson grabbed her wrist with one hand and, with the other, put the phone back down.

'Please, Stephanie. Stop. You've made your point. For God's sake, just shut up.'

Stephanie laughed and picked up the phone again. 'You're so pathetic, Detective Chief Inspector Patterson, you know that?'

Finally losing his temper, Patterson grabbed her and pulled her through to the living room, where he pushed her down on the settee. He was shaking. Anger. Fear. Exhaustion. Anxiety.

'Listen, I'll get your drink straight away next time you ask. OK? But for God's sake, just calm down – you've made your point.'

'How dare you talk to me like that! How dare you! And how dare you push me!' Stephanie was crying now. Loudly. Becoming hysterical. She was shouting. 'You bastard!' She ran at him, screaming.

He caught her in his arms before struggling to hold her, and they both fell down on the settee. She was trying to claw at his face as he held her wrists, so she tried to headbutt and kick him.

She was getting worse. Patterson had to admit Stephanie was getting worse.

They continued to wrestle on the settee before eventually, exhausted and out of breath, Stephanie gave up struggling.

Breathing heavily, Patterson stood up and went into the kitchen to grab his jacket. He had to get out. Even though all Patterson wanted to do was sleep, he decided to leave. He could stay in a hotel for the night.

As he closed the front door, he could hear Stephanie shouting, 'You wife-beating piece of shit!'

He had to get out. Maybe he had to leave for good. Perhaps Stephanie was too far gone, and he couldn't save her. One thing he knew for sure: at that moment, he just had to get out of that house.

Chapter 14

Turque à la Ronde

When Stone had met Geneva for the first time only a couple of weeks earlier, he'd been a guest on the late-night radio show Walk the Talk, discussing the main news issues of the day while indulging in irreverent banter with the other guests. Those other guests had been Campbell McDonald, the Hebrides grunge poet; Lesley Parkyn, a blogger most associated with the web magazine Skooby; and, of course, Geneva, the runner-up in the reality TV programme Castle Dangerous.

Castle Dangerous was the unsubtle title of a programme which had seen four men and four women living in Invercraig Castle for six weeks. During that time, on limited rations, the contestants had to perform a series of 'dangerous' tasks, such as swimming across a loch or paragliding from a mountain, before one person was voted off each week. It had proved a surprise rating success. Although being the runner-up to the eventual winner, Spam, an alternative juggler from Fort William, Geneva, emerged as the show's real star.

Her accidental witticisms had become a national delight, her lack of intelligence a joy to watch. It was no surprise that, since she'd left Castle Dangerous, Geneva had been in demand for TV and radio appearances from Wick to Wigtown. She had already brought out a music track which had reached number seven in the Scottish download charts. There was talk of her making a guest appearance in the TV soap River City which, although it came to nothing, led to a double-page feature in the Daily Record.

Now considered the new face on the block by the Scottish showbiz circuit, Geneva was determined to make the most of her shot at stardom. It was because of this that she'd decided to permanently leave her small fishing village in the northeast and move down to the bright lights of Glasgow.

Unlike Stone, a regular on Walk the Talk, it had been Geneva's first appearance on the radio show, but she had done well. She was entertaining, and whenever one of the other panellists had floundered for something to say, they were able to make fun of Geneva's lack of intelligence and get a laugh.

Geneva, though, was hiding a secret. She was, in fact, a highly intelligent woman. She had a degree in journalism and an IQ of 124. It was this intelligence which had ironically led to her calculated ploy to play the dumb blonde – a ploy that had nearly paid off in the form of winning the five-grand Castle Dangerous prize. Going into the show, Geneva's thinking had been that she didn't want to be seen as too brainy, as this would be perceived as threatening to the other contestants, as well as alienating many members of the watching public.

Amazingly, everything had gone to plan during the programme, and Geneva's perceived lack of intelligence had won her many fans. She had anticipated that, after the show, she would highlight that she wasn't as dumb as she was making out. Due to public demand, however, she continued to play to type to cash in on her media exposure as much as possible. She had no illusions about her fifteen minutes of fame, only surprised it seemed to be stretching towards the half-hour mark.

The problem for Geneva now was that three months had passed since the end of Castle Dangerous, and she couldn't break out of the simpleton role she'd created for herself. Financially, it was just too lucrative and too tempting to play the dumb blonde just a little bit longer while the offers came in. Finally, she'd made a decision. Now it was time to show the real Geneva, the true Sarah Scott. Not so much make the transition from Jordan to Katie Price but from Katie Price to Kirsty Wark.

So when her agent phoned regarding a possible regular slot on a new finance show for the BBC, she thought it was just what she was looking for. Finally, she had an opportunity to show what she was capable of. To use the degree in journalism she'd worked so hard to achieve. Apparently, all she had to do at this dinner date with Stone Johnson was show him how capable she was. Hence, she now sat nervously at a table in Turque à la Ronde, waiting for Stone to arrive.

Turque à la Ronde was a restaurant situated in a red-bricked oval building on the banks of the Clyde. A one-time grain container, it was now a well-known eatery specialising in Mediterranean cuisine. Its decor had been designed by Colin and Justin, so it was often frequented by those in the public eye, and, as such, Stone loved the place.

Stone handed his black leather jacket to the maître d', all the time glancing around to see if anyone recognised him or if he recognised anyone else. He was disappointed. No one appeared to be looking in his direction, and the only celebrity he could see was an MSP recently cautioned by police for expenses irregularities.

However, Stone cheered up when he saw Geneva dressed casually in jeans and a white V-neck cashmere sweater.

'Hi, Geneva. Sorry, I'm late – had a little business to clear up back at the office.'

Geneva smiled and, being more polite than truthful, said, 'Oh, that's OK; I haven't been here that long myself.'

Stone smiled, still looking around (just in case), and sat down, rubbing his hands. 'I'm so hungry. They do a great couscous here, by the way.'

'Really? I love couscous,' Geneva replied. Geneva didn't love couscous but wanted to be as polite as possible to her potential co-host of a new TV show.

*

Geneva was excited to learn more about the show, but by the time the couscous arrived, all the talk had been about Stone and his plans for the future. Geneva listened quietly, interjecting here and there with the right word to indicate she was impressed by whatever he said. However, there was one thing she couldn't deny.

She didn't like Stone Johnson one little bit.

Geneva sipped at her water as Stone went on about everything he'd accomplished in life. Geneva just wanted to get onto the subject of why they were there, the TV presenter's role, yet every time she brought it up, Stone would change the subject back to him. She tried once again, and finally, Stone was more expansive this time.

'Well,' Stone said, 'it's a financial entertainment show.'

'A financial entertainment show? That sounds interesting. And where do I fit into all this?' Geneva said with renewed optimism, still trying to convince herself she could get over the fact she really, really didn't like Stone.

'We're looking for a co-presenter.'

'Yes, that's what my agent said, but when you say co-presenter, do you mean an actual co-presenter, or do you mean I would have a bit part in the show?'

'I would do the main presenting, and you'd be the voice of the people. With all due respect, you're not known for your intelligence, and that's just what we need.' Stone smiled. 'Sorry, that didn't come out right. You know what I mean.'

Geneva bit her tongue, nodded and tried to eat a little of the couscous. It was like eating chewed-up tissue paper. She now felt as terrible as the couscous tasted. On the one hand, Stone was right about some people liking her because she appeared naïve and unthreatening – yes, a little dumb. She couldn't deny this was why she'd decided to play the dumb blonde in the first place. Yet, suddenly Geneva felt very down. Would she ever escape from being known as the stupid one?

What was also very annoying was that this Stone Johnson appeared to be a real one hundred per cent genuine idiot. There was no acting involved. It was an impression she'd probably formed, if truth be told, when they'd met on the radio show a couple of weeks back. However, then, she'd still decided to give him the benefit of the doubt. Now there was no doubt.

As for the work – no. Geneva had to draw a line in the sand. She had no intention of continuing to play the unintelligent bimbo. She was selling herself short. Yet, despite everything and the real imbecile sitting opposite her, Geneva knew the job would be a regular wage that would be very handy. She wasn't yet in a position to turn down regular employment. Maybe Geneva could do just one more job as the dumb blonde. She was only twenty-three, after all. The main problem now, however, was still Stone. With every minute that passed, Geneva disliked him even more. She was still in two minds about what to do.

Their waiter came over to ask how everything was and took the plates away.

'Ahmed, could you bring me the bill?

Thanks,' Stone said unexpectedly. 'Don't worry,' he told Geneva, 'the Beeb are paying for it.'

'We're leaving?' said Geneva, surprised.

'Yes,' Stone explained. 'I thought we could go back to my place and talk about the show in more detail there.'

Geneva wasn't convinced that was a good idea. As she thought about what she should do, it became more confusing. She didn't want to give up the idea of the show entirely but didn't want to go to Stone's flat. However... She shrugged. 'Well, OK, I guess.'

Stone smiled. After paying the bill, he rose and, after picking up his jacket, led Geneva from the restaurant. As they were walking out, Stone noticed a rather strange-looking man walking towards them. He was holding out a small card towards Geneva.

Stone acted quickly. He put his hand on the man's chest. 'Sorry, mate, no autographs today. We're on personal time here; I'm sure you understand.'

'But—'

'Listen, I said the lady doesn't want to be bothered tonight. Now if you'd kindly like to fuck off, you'll be doing both of us a favour.' Truth be told, part of Stone was miffed that the man was asking Geneva for her autograph and not him.

Stone looked at Geneva and smiled as if to say, 'What can you do, eh?' before turning to see with satisfaction the hate in the little man's eyes.

Ignoring Stone, the young man turned towards Geneva once again. 'Hi, Geneva.'

Shocked at Stone's attitude, with open mouth, Geneva turned to the young man, who was obviously raging he'd been treated so harshly by Stone. 'Crack! How are you? I haven't seen you in ages. Been to any more auditions recently?'

'A couple. Still no luck, I'm afraid.'

Stone stood, just a little embarrassed at having told an apparent friend of Geneva's to fuck off.

Stone held up his hands in apology. 'Hi, Crack, sorry about that; I thought you were someone looking for an autograph.'

Crack, still raging, ignored Stone and continued to hold the card for Geneva. 'I just thought, I... well, I saw you in the restaurant through the window and, to be honest, I didn't want to disturb you, so I waited for you to come out. I wonder if I gave you my card, Geneva, if you could... I mean it's got my details on it and everything in case you hear of any work going which might be suitable for me. It would be much appreciated.'

Geneva took the card. 'Oooh, you've had business cards made. I'm impressed. Yes, of course, Crack. I'll definitely do that. In fact, here – I've got my own somewhere.'

Geneva fumbled around in her handbag for a card which had her own details on it. 'If you ever need anything or even want to go for a drink sometime, just give us a call.'

Crack smiled, obviously grateful. He seemed quite shy. Humble. 'Thanks, Geneva. I'll definitely do that sometime. OK, well...' He started to walk away. 'I just thought... I better go; sorry to trouble you... I didn't mean to... it was nice seeing you again, Geneva. You're doing really well, by the way. We're all really proud of you. Sorry I bothered you—'

Geneva seemed embarrassed. 'Thanks, Crack. You didn't bother me! You take care now. Bye.'

'Bye, Geneva,' Crack wandered away into the darkness of the night, leaving both Stone and Geneva to stand in awkward silence.

Stone tried to explain himself once again. 'Sorry about that. I thought it was another weirdo trying to ask for an autograph. You know how it is. I get them all the time.'

Geneva wasn't happy at all. 'Really, Stone? Really? I'm actually very flattered if someone asks for my autograph, and apart from anything else, I would never, ever talk to anyone the way you did there. Never!'

Stone went on the defensive. 'Well, you can't be too careful in our business. What the hell is he called Crack for anyway? What sort of name is that?'

'Yes, Stone, I wonder what having such a stupid name is like.'

Geneva had had more than enough of Stone by now. She wondered when she'd last felt such hatred for someone. She was actually trembling with anger, something Stone noticed.

'Anyway, best get back to my place,' Stone said. 'It's getting quite chilly, don't you think?' He called a taxicab over to the side of the road.

Geneva shook her head, trying not to say something she would later regret. 'Actually, Stone, I think I'm just going to call it a night. I've got a bit of a headache coming on. You go on by yourself. I'm just going to head home.'

'But I thought we could talk about the show?'

'I've decided I won't be doing the show. You'll have to find someone else. Goodnight, Stone.'

Before Stone could reply, Geneva had entered the black cab, slammed the door shut and sped off into the night.

Stone lit a cigarette as he waited for another taxi to come along. Geneva was even dumber than he'd expected her to be. Ah well, the ungrateful bitch only had herself to blame for what would happen to her.

Chapter 15

Stevie

After Patterson had escaped from a screaming Stephanie the previous night, not for the first time, he'd booked into a small B&B in Kelvingrove. He'd had a restless night but managed to get some sleep simply through sheer exhaustion. Getting up early, only slightly less exhausted, Patterson had breakfast in a local, busy cafe before driving back to Partick Station to continue with the investigation as best he could. The whole morning, Patterson could feel his anxiety poised on the starting blocks, just waiting for the starting gun to go off.

Now it was early afternoon, and Patterson sat in Simpson's car as the rain lashed onto the windscreen, making Westmuir Street look like a Monet during his Glaswegian period. Through the heavy rain, Patterson glimpsed his DS coming out of the snooker club with Stevie by his side. For the benefit of Stevie, Simpson pointed towards the silver Mondeo, and both waited for a gap in the traffic before crossing the road.

Simpson opened the back door for Stevie to get in, then once Stevie had sat down and shut the door, Simpson moved round and sat in the front passenger seat next to Patterson.

Patterson turned round. 'Stevie? I'd like a word if you don't mind. I'm DCI Patterson, Partick CID. We just wanted to ask you a few questions about Susan McLaughlin.'

'What about her?' Stevie, like Simpson, was wet from the rain and wiping the dripping water away from his brow.

'We've been told you may have known her. You did know her, yes?'

'Aye. So fuck, is that a reason tae drag me in the back o' a car?'

'It's nothing to worry about. If you could just tell us how you knew Susan.'

'Shouldn't we be doing this down the station?' Stevie seemed nervous now, apparently thinking he might need a lawyer.

'Is that what you want?' Simpson asked.

Stevie shuffled in the back seat, and his non-answer was an answer in itself. The fringe of his jet-black hair was slightly parted to one side. He was one of the trendier wannabees of the Emerald. His designer clothes were fake, but at least he was making an effort. Today he wore a tight dark green shirt and light blue trousers, a sparkling silver chain dangling around his neck. His style sense was obviously influenced by the fashion house of Davy McGregor. Not good.

After shaking his head and looking out the car window, Stevie turned back to Patterson like a moody teenager.

'This is no' real, man. Ah'm getting pulled up cos Ah knew Susan?'

'Just answer the question,' Simpson said, annoyed because he'd got his own clothes wet while waiting to cross the road.

'OK, Ah, just met her, right? Got talking and stuff. Nothing special.'

Patterson decided to stay quiet and let Simpson ask the questions.

'Where did you meet her?'

'Cannae mind.'

'Listen, Stevie. There's no problem here. We just want to find out more about Susan, that's all. Like my colleague said, we can easily take this down the station if you want, but a young lassie was killed. We're trying to find out who did it. I'm sure you want him caught as well as us. Unless you've got something to hide, that is.'

'Ah've no' got anything to hide.'

'So just tell us what we want to know. The truth. Where did you meet Susan? It's a simple question.'

'A pub.'

'What pub?'

'Bay Horse. Bath Street.'

'So you went to the Bay Horse, and she was there? Or did you arrange to meet there?'

'Naw, Ah mean Ah went there; she was already there.'

'Was she with someone?'

'Naw, we wur both on our tod. It was like—' Stevie seemed reluctant to give details. Both Patterson and Simpson were getting more suspicious by the minute.

'What, Stevie? Come on.'

'It was like… a karaoke competition.'

'Karaoke?'

'Aye, karaoke.' Stevie rubbed a circle in the side window, which had steamed up.

'Karaoke? So you fancy yourself as a bit of a singer, do ye?' Simpson couldn't resist a little dig.

'Ah like a bit o' singing if that's what ye mean, aye, so what? It's a bit of fun, know? Well, she – Susan, Ah mean – was there 'n' all.'

'Are ye definite she wasn't with anyone else?'

'Naw, no one. Ah'd seen Susie about loads

of times, but. She was dead quiet like. Dead nice 'n' all, by the way. Ah fuckin' liked her. Ah'd never do anythin' to hurt her. Swear it, man.'

'So you and Susan met at this karaoke night. Did you both get up to sing?'

'Aye. Like Ah said, Susie was all shy 'n' that, but once she got up to sing, she was like a different person. Some voice, man. Unbelievable, seriously. She came second that night. Should've won it, but.'

'What about yersel'?'

'Naewhere.'

'So Susan was into karaoke then?'

'Oh aye, well into it. Like Ah said, Susie was brilliant. There's like a circuit, know? Different pubs that have karaoke. Ah'd always seen her about, but that was the first time Ah got talkin' to her.'

'When was this?'

'I'd say it was about two month back.'

Patterson chipped in. 'So you go to this karaoke night, Bay Horse. You get talking to Susan. What did you talk about?'

'Just stuff. Singing 'n' that. What music we was into. Ah dunno. Just stuff.'

'You took her to the Emerald one time. What was that about?'

'How the fuck dae ye know that?'

'Never mind. Just tell us.' Patterson was just as interested in what relationship Susan had with McGregor.

'It was just after that first night Ah met her at the Bay Horse. We wur talkin' away, gettin' on 'n' that. Really liked her. We arranged to meet a couple of nights later. So next time Ah met her, Ah thought I'd take her tae the Emerald.'

Patterson interrupted. 'So you end up taking her to the Emerald? Not exactly the place to take a nice young lassie like Susan, is it?'

'We wur gonnae go tae a club. But, well—'

'By that time, you were out of it?'

'Aye, well, partly that, but Ah dunno, Ah know the Emerald; Ah wisnae in the mood for a club.'

'So you took her to the Emerald and introduced her to McGregor.'

'Aye, well, see, that's the thing. To be honest… Ah kind of said to her that Ah knew this big music producer.'

'Aw, don't tell me. McGregor? You tried to pass McGregor off as Glasgow's Simon Cowell?'

'Ah wis jist talkin' shite. Like Ah said, Ah was fuckin' gone, man, that day. Just ended up saying Ah knew this big music guy, mad man.

Ah, wis half-joking, but the thing is, Susan believed me. Ah was gonnae tell her Ah was joking but ach, Ah dunno, it just went too far.'

'Did you tell McGregor about this?'

'About what?'

'About you saying he was a big shot music producer.'

'Oh aye, course. Just had a whisper in his ear like as soon as Ah got in the pub. Told him to play along. He was pissin' himself laughing. Kept telling Susan how he thought Ah was the new Robbie Williams and all that. Did ma heid in, to tell ye the truth. Thought she'd click. Point is, Ah ended up getting smashed. Meantime McGregor's giving it all this and that, about how he could introduce her to this other music guy and all the rest of it. Take her down tae London, etc. Shite like that. And then Ah go to the bog, Ah come back, and the cunt's fucked off wi' ma bird!'

'Do you know where they went?'

'Into town. A club he said. Prick. Told me the next day they went back to his place and everything, but he was just bullshittin'. Windin' me up. John, ma pal, seen him getting out a taxi on his own about midnight that same night. Anyhow, even so, next thing Ah know is Davy's seeing Susie regular. Tryin' to get in her drawers. Still kiddin' on he's a big man in the music scene. Didnae work, though. Susan wisnae like that.'

'How often did you see Susan after that first night you took her to the Emerald?'

'Dunno. Cannae mind exactly. Ah'd say about three, four times. Couple of times, at the karaoke nights, and McGregor brought her to the pub a few times. One time when he was doing his stand-up shite.'

'Did ye not talk to her again, tell her McGregor was taking the piss? That the only music industry he was involved in was selling fake CDs?' Patterson asked, taking up the questioning.

'Aye, course, but she seemed to have sussed it out herself by that time.'

'So why was she still hanging around with him?' Patterson asked as if he was also asking himself the same question.

'That's the big sixty-four million dollar fucking question, innit! Ah'm fucked if Ah know. Fucking Chuckles. To be honest, when Ah seen them together, Ah sort of got the impression Susan was stringing him along, no' the other way around.'

'How'd you mean?'

'Well, Ah dunno, Susan was all right. She was innocent like, but she wisnae as daft as all that. Ah dunno. Ah think she just liked the attention.'

Patterson made sure to catch Stevie's eye before asking his next question, 'So can you account for your whereabouts on the night Susan was killed?'

'Ah was at ma mum's. Springboig. It was my aunt's birthday. Was there till four in the morning. Got plenty of witnesses.'

'Of course.'

'Ah swear. God's honest. Besides, Ah'd never hurt Susan. Heard about the murder the next afternoon. Ah really liked her; Ah wis heartbroken when Ah heard about her. Went 'n' laid flowers outside the close.'

'Just between us, Stevie: you think Chuckles knows more about her murder than he's telling us?'

Stevie shook his head. 'Naw, seriously, you know him. Ah did think aboot it when Ah first heard she was done in, aye, straight away in fact. But naw, he seemed really upset about her murder like Ah wis.'

'What, you think he had feelings for her?' Simpson was asking the questions again.

'Naw, no chance; Chuckles only has feelings for himsel'. It was mair sumdae killing her just hurt his pride, the cunt.'

'Did Susan mention anyone else? A boyfriend, an ex-boyfriend?'

'Naw. Didnae say anything tae me at least. I mean, she said she didn't have a boyfriend.'

'Did she mention anyone she was seeing or anyone else at all? Say that she'd been threatened by or was being followed or anything unusual?'

'Like Ah said, even though we spent some time together, Ah really didnae know Susie that well. She was quiet. Gorgeous but. Really something. Great singer 'n' all. Ah told her she should go on one of these shows, know?'

'What shows?'

'Ach ye know, Natural Talent UK and all that.'

'Do you know if she did?'

'Nah, dunno, she should've but.'

Simpson looked at Patterson, seeing if his superior had any more questions. He didn't. 'OK, Stevie. That's all for now, 'said Patterson. 'You may have to come down the station sometime and make a statement, all right?'

Stevie nodded. 'Aye, OK. If it helps ye find who done it. She was all right, Susan, by the way.'

Stevie looked behind out the car window and, seeing the road was clear, opened the door and got out. Patterson and Simpson watched him run back across the road and take a cigarette off one of the guys standing smoking outside the snooker club, shielding from the rain in the doorway.

Jack Simpson looked at Patterson. 'What do you think?'

Patterson shrugged. 'Not sure. You know, Susan's mum didn't mention anything about her interest in singing, neither did Shona. OK, Jack, first, I want you to get a list of these karaoke pubs, this circuit Stevie was on about and get their CCTV. Ask a few questions. you know the score.'

Simpson nodded. 'But what do you think about Stevie? You think he's hiding something as well?'

Patterson looked out the front windscreen, thinking. 'Not exactly. Except I get the impression Stevie could have fallen for Susan big time and would have been pissed off if she started hanging around with McGregor. Could be a motive. What I don't get is how come Susan would continue to hang about with a sleazeball like McGregor if she knew he was just a badly-dressed thug?'

'Maybe she was playing him instead of the other way around. Like Stevie said, I get the impression Susan was as innocent as all that.'

'Meaning?'

'Meaning, she knew what she was doing.'

'Aye, maybe. Come on, let's get back to the

station, and you can make a start on getting a list of these karaoke pubs.'

As Patterson drove back, he thought again about how no one seemed to know Susan knew Chuckles or about her interest in karaoke or even about her knowing Stevie. Her mum and friends would need to be questioned again. Also, seeing a lowlife like Chuckles was the kind of thing a girl would usually tell her best friend at some point. A secret too juicy to keep a secret. Yet it seemed as if Patterson was right about Susan. She not only knew what she was doing, but she had secrets. Secrets she kept from everyone else, and Patterson had no doubt there were a few more waiting to be discovered.

Once back at the station, Patterson had other things on his mind. He was already thinking about and dreading going home to Stephanie after what had happened the night before. Of course, he knew he had to go home at some point, but he didn't want to do so just yet.

Patterson decided to test the water and gave Stephanie a phone call. To his disappointment and despair but not to his surprise, it was immediately evident Stephanie was drunk again. Patterson listened by holding the receiver a distance from his ear as Stephanie shouted and swore and raged at him.

After putting the phone down, Patterson

decided this was as good a time as any to catch up on all the loose ends of the case. It was also a good time to use the overnight sleeping facilities at the station.

Chapter 16

Kelvingrove Art Galleries

It was simply in Emma Booth's nature to care. That was one of the reasons she'd first applied to become a police officer and then a family liaison officer. She wanted to help people; it was as simple as that. Perhaps it was because she never forgot the help and care she'd received herself as a nine-year-old when both her parents and older sister had been killed in a car crash. From that moment on, as she was brought up by her gran, all kinds of support workers were part of her childhood.

At the same time, Booth always had a restless streak in her, a desire to do the unexpected. So, on one hand, it was a surprise to colleagues when she announced she was transferring down to Glasgow, and yet no surprise at all. She was going to live in a place she didn't know, had only visited on a few occasions and where she had no connections, family or otherwise. Still, three months after her transfer to Scotland's biggest city, Booth was pleased with her decision. Apart from one thing.

She felt incredibly lonely.

She got on with her new colleagues all right and had been on a few dates, but there was no one she'd really connected with. Booth needed that connection. Of course, it was still early days in her new home. Nevertheless, she was disappointed she hadn't come across anyone she could feel that spark with. Except, perhaps, for one person.

Detective Chief Inspector Michael Patterson.

On first impressions, tall, bespectacled and rather old-fashioned, she wouldn't have imagined this would be a man she felt attracted to. She couldn't even put her finger on why she liked him exactly. But for all his debatable taste in clothes, his bookish manner and his age, there was just no denying she felt a spark with Patterson. She suspected it was mutual too.

This morning, when Patterson called and said he wanted to meet her at the vet's surgery where Susan worked, Booth couldn't help but break into a smile. As far as she was concerned, it was almost like a date.

So it was that just before noon, as arranged, she pulled up in a taxi in front of the surgery to see Patterson waiting for her, leaning against the side of his car. She paid the taxi driver, took a deep breath and got out of the cab.

'Emma, thanks for coming,' Patterson greeted her. 'What's with the taxi?'

'Oh, my car was playing up, thought it best not to take a chance it would break down. I need to get it looked at.'

'Do that. So how are you anyway?'

'Fine, thanks, sir. Thanks for asking me here.'

'Yes, well, I would have asked Pettigrew or Simpson, but they're both up at the university again interviewing Susan's tutors and classmates, and Brian McKinnon has a court case to attend. Any developments with Susan's family?'

'No, I mentioned about Susan's interest in karaoke, and Susan's mum was a little surprised. She knew Susan liked singing but didn't know Susan was a regular at karaoke nights.'

'Yes, it seems Susan liked to compartmentalise her life to some degree. Anyway, this delightful Portakabin is the vet's where Susan worked. I've arranged to have a talk with her manager. I could do with a fresh pair of eyes to give an additional insight into him. You don't have to say anything. In fact, I would actually prefer you didn't – I'm hoping your silent presence will have more of an impact. Just listen and give me your impressions afterwards. OK?'

'Fine. Apart from being Susan's manager, is there any other reason he's of particular interest?'

'Not as such. I had an initial talk with him a few days ago and suspect he could know more about Susan than he's letting on. Anyway, the surgery closes for lunch now, so the manager – his name's Andrew Williams – said this would be a good time to see him. It shouldn't take long. As I said, I just want your impressions of him in addition to me forming my own.'

Patterson and Booth then entered the Portakabin, which was empty and even more grey and dull than Patterson remembered from the previous time he had been there. They were ushered through to see Williams by the receptionist, who then left for her lunch. Patterson and Booth entered a small room dominated by a large stainless-steel examination table in the middle of the room. As they entered, Williams was opening a white plastic shopping bag but stopped on seeing his visitors and smiled warmly in greeting. He indicated a couple of chairs against a wall as he sat on the steel table. He took a clear plastic triangular packet of pre-packed sandwiches out of the bag and placed them beside a Snickers and a can of Tizer next to him on the table. As with the last time he had visited, Patterson noticed a video game was on pause on one of the computer screens.

'Apologies, this is the only time I get to eat – we're so busy nowadays.' He indicated the sandwiches. 'You don't mind, do you?' He noisily opened the can of Tizer.

Patterson put his hand in the air. 'No, no, of course not. This is my colleague, Emma Booth. She's assisting me with the case.'

Williams nodded. 'So how can I help you? I don't think there is much I can add to what I said the other day.'

'I know,' said Patterson. 'It's just formalities. We're still trying to get an idea of who Susan was, what she was like as a person and as a worker. Anything at all you can say about her could still be of help.'

Williams took a bite of a sandwich, chewed for a moment and then replied to Patterson. 'Well, Susan was a quiet girl, as I said. Got on with her work. Pleasant. She was well liked by everyone.'

'She didn't mention any problems; she seemed happy as far as you were concerned?'

Williams nodded. 'Yes, as far as I know. All we seemed to talk about was work. She was so keen to learn. Always asking me questions. I was still surprised, though, that she hadn't mentioned about someone hassling her on the way home. As I said, I would have ordered a taxi or driven her home myself.'

'You never socialised with her at all outside of here?'

Williams shook his head again and took another gulp of fizzy drink before answering. 'No.'

'Did you never go out for a drink with your employees – altogether, I mean, as a group?'

'Well, I suppose there may have been one or two occasions, Christmas and suchlike.'

'Only, I heard that you may have known Susan more than you said.'

Williams gave a small laugh. 'Ah, has one of my minions been gossiping?'

'It may be gossip – you tell me.'

Williams looked at Patterson and then at the silent Booth.

'OK, hands up, come to think of it, Susan and me may have gone out for a drink together, once or possibly twice. It was a while back. I don't know why I didn't say… so yes, I admit I did see Susan outside of work a couple of times, but it was just a drink in a pub, nothing more.'

'That's fine. I just want to know more about Susan. You're not a suspect.'

Williams stared at Patterson. 'Who said I was a suspect?'

'I said you weren't a suspect,' Patterson repeated. 'I just want to know how well you knew Susan.'

Williams had stopped eating his sandwich. His hands were by his side, lightly pushing down his palms on the table. 'Like I said, I went out for a drink with her at the pub. Must have been an hour or two each time. Can't remember exactly. That's about it.'

'What did you talk about?'

'If I remember, it was work mostly, but we were just getting to know each other. She told me about her plans for the future, her career and such. That's right, I do remember one time I mentioned that I would love her to work here full time after she gained her qualifications.'

So, how many times did you go to the pub?'

'Like I said, just a few times.'

'A few times, not a couple?'

'A few, four or five times, maybe.'

'You never went back to her flat?'

'No, never.'

'In that case,' continued Patterson, 'you wouldn't mind giving us a copy of your fingerprints?'

'Why on earth would you want those?'

'We have fingerprints taken from Susan's flat. We'd just like to ensure none belong to you.'

'But I told you, I haven't been to Susan's flat.'

'Exactly. We'd just like to verify that. Again, it's just a formality.' Williams looked at Patterson and the ever-silent Booth who stared back at him.

'OK, listen, I'll be completely honest with you, and this is the god's honest truth, I swear,' Williams shook his head again, 'it's possible I may have visited Susan's flat a couple of times.'

'It's possible? You mean you did go back to her flat?'

'If I remember correctly, I went with her a couple of times to where she lived. It's not that far, as you know. Nothing happened, though, if that's what you're thinking. I just had a coffee, we talked about this and that and left.'

'And that's the truth?' Patterson asked.

'That's the truth, yes. I admit it wasn't my choice – leaving, I mean – but Susan said it wouldn't be right, you know...because I'm her boss or something. Maybe it was just an excuse. Probably was, or maybe she was right. Whatever. As I said. Nothing happened. Why would I lie about that?'

'But you said yourself wanted it to happen, that's what's important.'

It was Booth who spoke, and her unexpected interruption after some silence led the two men to look at her in surprise. Especially Patterson, who wasn't best pleased.

'I'm just trying to be truthful as I can with you. I said it wasn't my choice, but I left, end of. Listen, I'm not sure I'm comfortable with this questioning. I get the impression you're implying I could have had something to do with Susan's murder which is absurd. However, if that's the case, I'd rather do this formally with a lawyer present.'

Before Patterson could reply, Booth spoke up again. 'You really expect us to believe you simply left Susan's flat? Just like that! A young woman invites you up for a coffee, and you get, let's say, friendly, and then it doesn't go further, and you just leave? Are we really supposed to—'

'Yes, OK, Emma, we'll leave it there for now.' Patterson interjected. You will need to come down to the station at some point. I would advise you to get your facts straight beforehand, even with a lawyer present.' Patterson stood up, followed by Booth and then Williams.

Once Booth and Patterson were back in the car, Patterson turned to his colleague. 'Well, what do you think?'

'Clearly, he's hiding something,' said Booth. 'It took enough time to admit he had visited Susan's flat. I also found out his business is indeed struggling. He's also had a couple of issues with the Inland Revenue.'

'Yes?'

'Yes, and by the way, Emma, when I tell you to do something, I expect you to do as your superior officer tells you. Is that understood? I told you to keep quiet, not start making accusations to put him on his guard.'

'Yes, sir.'

'We'll talk more about it later this afternoon at the station.'

'Sorry, sir.' Patterson started the car, and they drove up towards Dumbarton Road. 'Do you know if Susan ever talked to her mother about Andrew Williams?' 'No, at least he's never came up in conversations so far. Except that Mrs McLaughlin said Susan enjoyed her work. I can ask specifically about Williams if you like.'

'Do that. I'll also want you to type up a full report of what you've learned about the family so far. One other thing about Williams is the alibi he gave for the night Susan was murdered. It doesn't check out. He says he was at a restaurant with a friend. He did make a reservation but didn't turn up. I think there's a lot more we need to find out about Mr Williams. Anyway, I'm going to get a bite to eat. Can I drop you off at the station or somewhere else?'

'Actually, I need to get a bite to eat myself. If you just drop me off somewhere, I'll make my — Hope I'm not being out of order, sir, but would it be possible for us to grab a bite to eat together? We could go over the case. I have one or two thoughts about Mr Williams I'd like to run past you.'

'Sure,'

As the car pulled up the narrow road onto Dumbarton Road, Patterson looked across the road.

'Have you been to the Art Galleries yet?'

'No,' Booth replied.

'Would a coffee and a sandwich be enough for you?'

'Sounds good to me.'

'Then let's go to Kelvingrove, they have a cafe that's quite decent.'

After parking the car, Patterson and Booth walked up the wide stone steps to the front entrance. Inside, they were faced with the open space of the main hall and surrounded by the echo of voices and footsteps.

Booth looked up, clearly impressed by her surroundings. 'Wow, I didn't realise it was so big.

It's quite a building, isn't it?'

'It is,' Patterson agreed as he led her towards the ground-floor cafeteria.

The café was relatively busy, but they found a free table, sat down and ordered food. 'So, what are these thoughts you have about William's then?' Patterson asked.

'For one thing, I think he had a motive for murdering Susan,' replied Booth.

'You do, do you?' asked Patterson as he tore open a sugar sachet to put in his coffee.

'Yes. Let's say Williams goes back to Susan's flat with her. They get intimate, but Susan resists. Williams loses his temper, loses it altogether and kills her.'

'What about the person seen climbing the drainpipe?'

Booth thought momentarily. 'He could have done that to cover his tracks.'

'Cover his tracks?' said Patterson with undisguised scepticism.

'Yes, maybe Willams was banking on being seen. He's a fit young man from what I can make out. Climbing that drainpipe wouldn't be that much of a challenge. Scary, yes, but he would have known what was at stake. He makes it out to be an intruder, and his plan works; he was spotted by the neighbour.'

'It's a possibility, but I'm not convinced.'

'Then why was he so reluctant to admit he was in the flat? It was only after you mentioned taking fingerprints he told the truth.'

'I can see your point of view, Emma, but Andrew Williams didn't come across as a murderer.'

'Who does?'

'When you've been in the game as long as I have, you get a feel for these things. I take your point. As I say, we'll be checking him out further. As for motive, I'm more interested in the business side of things.'

'How do you mean?'

'You seen the state of the so-called surgery. I think the animals are more likely to catch something there instead of being cured. I can't give an opinion of Williams as a vet, but as a businessman, he leaves a lot to be desired. If the business went bust, which I think it will, he knows he'll have his dad to bail him out. I sometimes wonder if Susan knew something else about him.'

'Such as?'

'It's possible she discovered something about Williams and his business she shouldn't have done.'

'You think?'

'It's a possibility, an outside one admittedly, but still. I'll get one of the team to check out Williams's business dealings even more.'

Patterson and Booth talked a little more about Williams before Booth asked, 'So how long have you been married?'

The sudden change of subject took Patterson slightly by surprise. 'A good few years now,' Patterson answered without expanding further.

He was going to change the subject back to work when Booth asked another question. 'Happily married?'

'Yes, I guess so; there are one or two problems as with everyone, but—'

'Problems?'

Patterson felt as if he was being interrogated. He didn't like it. He liked Booth but was seeing that unpredictable side to her again. The unruly side that saw her ask Williams questions when Patterson had specifically told her to keep quiet. However, Booth's question brought Patterson's thoughts back to his marriage and the 'one or two problems'. Should he tell Booth about those? She probably knew already – everyone else did. 'Stephanie, my wife, has been battling a drink problem for a few years now. It's partly my own fault, really—'

'What do you mean it's your own fault?'

'You know how the job is. It can overtake everything else. I got too wrapped up in my work. I neglected her. Once the kids left home – we've two kids, both at uni down south – once the kids left, Stephanie was stuck in the house on her own. Nothing to do. Usual story. She started drinking; it became a habit and then a need.'

'I don't see how that's your fault. You work hard – there's nothing wrong in that. Long hours are part of the job. I don't think you can blame yourself for that or your wife drinking.'

Patterson felt uncomfortable talking about Stephanie to Booth. He'd already said too much. Yet he couldn't deny the desire to talk about it more. Besides, maybe Booth had a point. Maybe he did blame himself too much at times. He stayed silent, thinking about Stephanie as he watched a line of primary-school kids being led across the main museum gallery by a couple of teachers.

Booth continued. 'Have you never thought about leaving her?'

Patterson looked at Booth, still wondering if his younger colleague was being a bit too forward but gave her the benefit of the doubt. 'No, I'd never leave Stephanie. It's hard sometimes, but I can't leave her. I—'

Booth interrupted again. 'So you're

prepared to go down with the sinking ship?'

Patterson glared at her. Now she was overstepping the mark, and Booth knew it too. 'Sorry, I shouldn't have said that.'

'No, you shouldn't have. Listen, Emma, I don't think you understand. You're not married yourself, are you?'

'No,' Booth replied. 'Or in a relationship?'

'No, but I don't see—' It was Patterson's turn to interrupt. 'Then get back to me when you're in a long-term relationship. There's such a thing as loyalty. And love. Apart from anything else, I still love my wife, always loved her despite everything. It's not a case of going down with the sinking ship, as you put it. It's staying with someone through thick and thin.' Patterson smiled. 'Listen, let's just—'

'No need to explain,' Booth said as she finished her sandwiches. Another silence occurred between them, allowing Patterson to change the subject. 'You know, I used to come here as a kid. Grew up not far from here, in fact. There's a beehive behind a window, a glass panel just along that corridor if I remember. You can watch bees in a kind of honeycomb hive.'

'Really,' Booth said like an excited kid. 'Where is it? I'd love to see it.'

'You should come on one of your days off.

I think you'll love the whole museum. It's a great place, but I'm afraid, for now, we need to get back to the station.'

'Can't we just have a look around for five minutes?'

Again, there was something childlike about Booth's request.

'I'd like to, but we've really got to get back. Check up on Williams's background for a start. See if Pettigrew and Simpson have found out anything from the university.'

'Oh, come on. You said yourself you can't let work take over everything. The station won't miss you for an hour, and I'd love to see the bees you mentioned. I really would. Go on, be a devil. Do something daring for a change. Break the rules.'

There was something odd about a younger colleague talking to him like this, but Patterson let it pass once again and laughed. Besides, maybe this young woman had a point, and, truth be told, he would like to see for himself if the bees were still there. 'OK, I'll give you a quick tour so you can get your bearings for when you come back another time.'

Booth stood up, as excited as one of the numerous children who passed them by. They did see the bees, and it gave Patterson as much pleasure as it did Booth. He wasn't to know Booth had already seen them and had been to the Art Galleries a couple of times since she'd arrived in the city.

It didn't matter. One hour turned into two, and for those couple of hours, Patterson really enjoyed himself walking around the museum with his excited younger companion. He liked Booth. Really liked her. He couldn't deny it. Wandering around the galleries amongst the exhibits, paintings and the ages, Patterson found himself, for the first time in a long time, switching off and content at doing nothing at all. In fact, for both Patterson and Booth, it was a wonderful afternoon they spent together.

Chapter 17

Stephanie

Patterson and Booth eventually arrived back at the station late in the afternoon. Walking into the office together, they drew curious glances from their colleagues. Although Patterson was trying to keep a more sombre, professional demeanour, Booth wore a broad smile and seemed very happy. Pettigrew, who was showing McKinnon some information at his desk, nodded in the direction of Booth and said quietly, 'She's trouble that one.' McKinnon didn't reply.

As Booth later left the office to visit Susan's mum once more, Patterson caught up with some of the paperwork that constantly arrived on his desk. He still made time to hear the latest developments, or lack of developments as was more often the case, relayed by his team. Jack Simpson told him he didn't think there was anything worth following up on at the University. Claire Pettigrew agreed. Susan was a quiet, studious girl who was well-liked and didn't seem to have any problems. Her friends and tutors all basically parroted what the team already knew. Other enquiries gave a similar response. Yet, although there was no major breakthrough in any one area of the investigation, Patterson felt some progress was being made overall. His team were still busy, and that in itself was a good sign.

Back in his office, Patterson continued to get on with his paperwork, but he found his thoughts pulled towards Stephanie. He hadn't called her all day and had a curious feeling something might have happened to her. He picked up the phone and called home.

There was no answer. He waited ten minutes and phoned again. Still no answer. He realised he was probably being paranoid, but images of Stephanie lying at the bottom of the stairs or collapsed on the bedroom floor played over in his mind. Picking up his jacket, he informed his colleagues he had to leave and almost ran down the stairs to his car.

The drive home seemed to take an eternity. All the while, Patterson just knew something wasn't right. His stomach was churning, and he felt a dread that pushed his anxiety levels to breaking point. For some reason, he also felt a guilt about the time he had spent with Booth.

Finally pulling into his driveway,

Patterson quickly exited the car and strode to the front door. He stopped mid-motion as he put the key in the lock. Something was indeed wrong; he could sense it as he slowly pushed the door open. Most nights, silence greeted him, the air heavy with foreboding, a sign of storms to come. Now though, he could hear music playing, and there was a smell – an aroma of cooking.

Still unnerved, Patterson stepped inside and closed the door. He now heard the sound of frying. Sizzling and clinking were coming from the kitchen. The porcelain clap of a couple of plates hitting together. He could make out the music clearer. Piano music. Classical. These were sounds from the past when he was a young copper coming home after a hard shift. It only unnerved him even more.

Patterson took the key out the door and quietly closed it. He walked cautiously up to the closed kitchen door and prepared himself. It had to be Stephanie, even more drunk than usual. Patterson sighed. He was already shattered. Would this be yet another night he spent in a bed and breakfast? Patterson pushed open the kitchen door. Stephanie hadn't heard him enter over the noise of the radio. She stood at the cooker with a look of concentration on her face, biting her bottom lip. With a spatula, she was prodding some beef sizzling in a pan. Suddenly realising Patterson was there, she turned around and gave a start. 'Oh'.

Patterson couldn't help but ask the most obvious question. 'What are you doing?'

Stephanie reacted as if the question was silly. She shrugged, then smiled, a little embarrassed. 'What does it look like I'm doing? I'm cooking. Stir-fry as it happens.'

This obviously wasn't enough of an answer for both of them, so she continued. 'I just thought I'd make you some dinner, that's all. I didn't know when you would be back, but I thought I'd make a start.'

'I called, but there was no answer.'

'Did you? Sorry, I've had the radio on; I mustn't have heard it.

Patterson continued to look at her, still trying to identify signs of drunkenness such as a slurred word, an occasional stumble or slow-motion blinking eyes. Yet, Patterson could only detect sobriety in his wife. Nevertheless, when she spoke, Patterson could also discern some emotion in her voice. Stephanie gave a slight cough, and he could see her swallow as if trying not to cry.

Patterson instinctively walked up and put his arms around her. Stephanie turned and dropped the spatula on the top of the cooker, she held him so tight he found it difficult to breathe.

He rubbed her back, put his hand through her hair, and she continued to hold him as her shoulders slowly heaved up and down as if she was taking in huge gulps of air. Then she started to cry, releasing long-trapped emotion from deep inside her. It was a couple of minutes before she could begin speaking again. When she did, it was muffled as she kept her head buried in his shoulder. Yet the words spilled out of her mouth at breakneck speed as if she had been wanting to say them for such a long time.

'I'm so sorry, Mike; really I am. I hate the way I've been, hate it. I've decided to make a real effort this time. Honest. I promise. I'll get help. Honest. I mean, I really promise. I swear. I made an appointment with the doctor. And I looked up where the next Alcoholics Anonymous meeting is. There's one just around the corner as it happens.

Patterson knew enough to know there was always an AA meeting just around the corner. This was Glasgow. He tried to calm his wife down. 'Enough Steph, enough. It's OK, just take it easy.'

Stephanie still talked rapidly, though out of breath. It was as if she had to say the words quickly, or else she may not say them at all. 'I mean, I'm not quite ready just yet, but I'll go some time, I promise. I know I have been a right bitch recently. I know it. I hate myself. I never want to hurt you. Never. It's the last thing in the world I want, but it's been so hard recently the drink...' Stephanie added as she wiped away the tears.

Patterson kissed her on the cheek. He didn't know what to say in reply. Yes, there were times when Stephanie would be sober. Yet, at that precise moment, it seemed different for some reason. It was as if his wife had just returned from somewhere far away. Maybe it was his imagination. Perhaps he was kidding himself on. However, he thought he could already sense Stephanie's real determination to get better.

'You don't have to apologise,' Patterson said. 'I know it's the drink – I see its effects every day. I'm the polis remember?'

Stephanie took another deep breath, and now, not knowing what else to say, she tried to gather herself together. She gently pushed her husband away and turned back to her cooking.

'This stir-fry is going to be absolute rubbish.'

'No, it's not; it's going to be wonderful.'

And it was. Stephanie had always been a good cook. It was just one of many things Patterson had missed about her.

Later, during the meal, they talked more about her addiction, that subject which was completely taboo when she was drunk. It was such a release for both of them. They knew that Stephanie's battle with alcoholism could very well end in defeat. It probably would. Yet, at least Stephanie was trying one more time, and as long as Stephanie kept her determination and with Patterson supporting her, she still had a fighting chance.

After dinner, they sat down on the settee to watch television, though they didn't pay much attention to what was on the screen. They just sat holding each other's hands, most of the time in silence, both lost in their own thoughts. When they did speak, they caught up on what the other had been thinking or doing in the past few weeks. During the time Stephanie had been away. They talked about Calum and Aisling. Both children avoided coming home, even phoning, only doing so on rare occasions. Yet, if things went well, Patterson said he would invite them up sometime. See what they said. Then Stephanie asked her husband about his anxiety, about how he was coping. Patterson admitted he had been struggling big time in recent weeks. What with the case he was working on and everything else. He admitted it scared him. He was scared that one day he would crack.

Patterson also apologised for his own behaviour. In his view, he knew he had neglected his wife – that he'd become too immersed in his work while Stephanie had nothing to do all day at home.

'I'm due at least four weeks' leave,' Patterson said. 'Dunard is always telling me I should take my holidays. As soon as this enquiry is over, we can go on a long trip somewhere. Maybe go see the kids or go on a cruise if you like.'

'Not a cruise,' Stephanie said, 'I don't want to be stuck on a boat. We'll go somewhere, though. That would be nice. What's the enquiry you're on, by the way?'

He ignored the fact Stephanie didn't even know that Patterson was working on such an important case.

Instead, Patterson started to talk about the murder of Susan McLaughlin. It was an opportunity to go over the details, wondering again if there was something he'd missed. He spoke of this innocent girl who had been murdered whilst lying in her bed at night at home. This immoral murder. He told how it turned out Susan knew Davy McGregor, and, talking to Stephanie, he realised the presence of McGregor could be far more significant than he had let himself believe. It was indeed possible his threats about catching Susan's killer were a bluff. Perhaps, he was simply covering his own tracks. He needed to question him again. Then Patterson's mobile rang, and he glanced at

Stephanie as a way of apology.

It was Pettigrew. 'Sir, I just thought I'd let you know that one of the patrols was passing Markus Sepp's home tonight, you know the man from the gym? Well, the light's on, and there's movement inside. Want me to go down and see him?'

'No,' Patterson said. 'It can wait. We'll pay him a visit together tomorrow morning. What are you doing working this late anyway, Claire?'

'Just catching up with a few things. I've been going over the CCTV trying to locate the vet guy. Still haven't identified him yet.'

'Well, get yourself home. You've a busy day tomorrow with me; I need you sharp and alert.'

'Aye, sir.'

Patterson put the phone down and switched it off. He noticed Stephanie's hands shaking a lot of the time. A sign that even these last few hours, not having a drink was difficult for her. Patterson said he would attend the AA meetings with her if she liked. She declined the offer. She would do this herself, she said. Talking to her husband, she also realised how important this case was to him. She knew more than anyone her husband could keep an emotional distance with the enquiries he worked on. Yet, it was clear something about this murder had got to him. He seemed as determined to find this murderer as Stephanie was to beat her alcoholism. It remained to be seen just how successful either of them would be.

For now, they spent this one night together as they had in the past. Only pleased to be in each other's company, and even if it was for a relatively brief few hours, distant loving times became present loving times, and with that, nothing else mattered.

Chapter 18

The Greenock Gazette

It was rare that Stone came into the office on Saturday morning, but he knew it helped now and then for the passing public to see Stone Investments was open on a weekend. Besides, if his TV show took off, his career would be going in a new direction, and there would no longer be a need for Saturday morning visits to the office.

Yet he couldn't help but sense that the BBC seemed more hesitant than before. He couldn't quite put his finger on it. Maybe it was the lack of an actual start date for his show, final confirmation that his show would definitely be going ahead. He'd contacted Greg to explain that his meeting with Geneva at the Turque à la Ronde hadn't gone quite as well as planned. He wondered if it was the trouble in finding a suitable sidekick holding things up.

Naturally, Greg wasn't happy about what had happened with Geneva. When Greg contacted Peter Webb at the BBC, Peter wasn't pleased either. They still believed Geneva was perfect for the show and as a foil for Stone. They suggested that Stone try to smooth out any difficulties with her whilst the BBC would also contact her directly. However, Stone still held off making contact with her, but in any case, the call from the BBC didn't do any good. Geneva said she was flattered by the offer, but she just couldn't work with Stone.

Even Stone, in spite of his earlier impressions, had to admit that Geneva would be good for the show. However, he wasn't going begging to another here-today-gone-tomorrow reality TV star. Besides, was it really that big a deal that he'd slagged off her friend? What was his name again? Crack? What sort of shit name was that anyway? Crack, for fuck's sake. And that haircut he had. Blonde with purple sides. He'd just looked plain weird. In fact, he was weird. Had Stone really been in the wrong to think Crack was just another pleb wanting an autograph? Or should he just give Geneva a call? On the plus side, phoning Geneva again would put him in Peter Webb's good books. An extra tick for Stone could be what was needed to get the show's start date confirmed.

So it was that his mobile rang while Stone was pondering whether or not to give Geneva a call. Talk of the devil. It was Greg. Stone's heart quickened – perhaps his agent had a confirmed start date for the show. Curiously though, his agent didn't start the conversation with a hello or a 'hey, bud' but with a question, and the randomness of this question immediately struck Stone as strange.

'Stone. Have you seen the Greenock Gazette this morning?'

As far as Stone was concerned, the question deserved nothing more than a very sarcastic, 'Er, no,' which Stone duly delivered in reply.

'Then go to the Greenock Gazette site online now, then give us a call back.'

Greg rang off, and Stone soon found the local newspaper site, only to be faced with bold letters next to a rather unflattering photograph of himself.

'TV FINANCE EXPERT IS A FRAUD' said the headline. Reading on, the first impressions didn't get any better.

Stone Johnson, the Greenock-born TV financial expert on the popular cable TV channel Caledonia Television was today accused of being a fraud by his ex-wife. Sue Johnson. Sue, who was married to the TV personality for over eight years, stated that he has not paid any child support since he abruptly walked out on her three years ago. His ex-wife now looks after their three children on her own in a small two-bedroom flat in Forsyth Street. She also alleges that in addition to not paying child maintenance, her ex-husband has cheated clients out of money and left her with a string of debts when he suddenly 'disappeared' after saying he was going to the local shop. Now, with rumours circulating that Mr Johnson has just landed his own show with BBC Scotland, she has decided to speak out exclusively to the Gazette.

Stone read on with a mixture of anger and disbelief. How could Sue do this to him – and at such a critical time? He stopped reading, picked up the phone and rang Greg back.

Before Stone could say anything, Greg asked a question. 'Is it true?'

'Of course not,' Stone replied emphatically.

He could hear Greg cursing to himself.

'It is true, isn't it? I knew it.'

Stone decided the best line of defence was attack. 'Let me ask you a question, Greg. Do you think you can call and start shouting at me? You work for me, in case you've forgotten, so if you're going to get all... pernickety' – it was the best word he could think of – 'then think again. As for your question, she's nuts. I could tell you a thing or two about her. I—'

'I'm not interested in her. I just want you to tell me if there's any truth about what she says.

Have you been paying child maintenance or not?'

'OK, I may have missed one or two payments, but—' Once again, Stone could hear Greg swearing on the other end of the phone.

'You know this could affect the BBC show going ahead – you do know that, don't you?'

Stone was having none of it. 'What do you mean this could affect the BBC show? It's just a few missed child-maintenance payments—'

'What about the other stuff she alleges: the womanising, leaving her with debts, the fact she says you've cheated clients out of money—'

'You're right, those are serious allegations. Sue's on dodgy ground there; I've a good mind to sue Sue—'

'Listen, we need to nip this in the bud ASAP. You do realise there's a clause with your show which stipulates if you bring the BBC into disrepute for any reason, they can cancel your contract with immediate effect.'

'Greg, it's the Greenock Gazette we're talking about here, not the Financial Times. Besides, I'm sure the BBC won't do anything rash.'

'Well, I certainly hope so, Stone, for your sake. You deserve this break. Listen, if any journalists try and get in touch with you, don't say anything for now. I'll get in touch with James, and he'll tell you what to do later on.' James was the lawyer Greg used when need be. 'For now, Stone, keep your head down, and with a bit of luck, this will blow over, and no real damage will be done. I'll give James a call now, so expect him to be in touch this afternoon. Bye, Stone.'

Stone clicked off the phone and put his head in his hands. Yeah, it wouldn't become anything serious with a bit of luck. Surely he was too good an asset for the BBC to drop. Yet even Stone was beginning to doubt his worth. He couldn't help worrying.

He buzzed through to his secretary. 'Cancel any appointments, Jenny. We're closing early.' Stone needed time to think.

Chapter 19

On the Corner of Allison Street

It was Saturday morning. Eight minutes to eleven. The early clouds of dawn had been blown eastwards by a fresh breeze, and now the sky was painted the lightest of blue. Daniel stood on the corner of Allison Street and Victoria Road, waiting for the pubs to open. It was hell. Even at the weekends now, Daniel just went to the pub. He was beginning to feel sometimes he needed to go to the pub. Not a good sign.

Could things get worse? A flash of remembrance from the night before came into Daniel's mind. The night before! Getting thrown out of that pub for calling that fucking arsehole of a barman a fucking arsehole. Nightmare.

Six minutes to eleven. Daniel walked further up Victoria Road and found himself stopping outside a jeweller's shop. He stood looking aimlessly at the different clocks and watches with their non-moving hands. This scene, however, quickly faded as the brightening of the sun materialised his reflection in their place.

Boy, he looked rough. No doubt about it. Crumpled shirt. Crumpled jeans. Crumpled face. Great blue bags hung below his eyes, and his whole face looked bloated. His hair, cemented by dirt and grease, pointed up in various directions. He tried to convince himself that this pointy hair could be seen as trendy. As could his unshaven look. In truth, though, being unemployed for what seemed an eternity now, Daniel didn't see the point in shaving – and unshaven, the stubble grew on his chin like green mould on a stale piece of bread.

His attention wandered down from head to body. There was a noticeable potbelly pushing out his crumpled brown shirt. He pulled his stomach in for a couple of seconds before the stomach stubbornly inflated itself back to its natural state.

Was that really himself who stood there looking back? Was he really that short? He'd never been tall, but short? In the reflection of the jeweller's window, he found himself to be a small and withered old man.

Daniel really needed a drink now. No, seriously. Now.

He looked at his watch. Four minutes till opening time. Thank God. Time to head to the pub, but as he turned, he thought he saw Deborah, his ex-girlfriend, standing across the road.

It couldn't be her, though. Daniel imagined seeing Deborah all the time. Any girl walking up the road with long black hair he always imagined to be Deborah. This was just another time. Or was it. This girl actually looked like her, and as she turned and looked down the road, Daniel's heart missed a beat. It was her – Deborah; it was really Deborah, standing outside the butcher's shop across the road.

Such was fate. He forgot all the heartache that had gone before. The fact that she'd left him when he was at his lowest ebb. If ever there was one person he needed at that moment, it was Deborah. At a moment when he felt so low, when he couldn't feel any lower, Deborah was truly a godsend.

His first instinct was to call across to her, but something stopped him. No. He wouldn't do that. Caution. He would walk across to her instead. Casual like, across the road. Via the traffic lights.

So he walked down to the traffic lights, his heart beating strong and fast, keeping his eye on the woman he'd shared three years of his life with. She continued to look into the butcher's shop window, still not noticing Daniel. She turned her head sideways, giving him a better view of her. She looked as beautiful as ever. Her hair was a little shorter than he remembered, but he liked it. Yeah. And she looked in good health. Radiant.

As he waited for the lights to change, he remembered the times they'd spent before, the nights of old when they would snuggle up in bed and read a book and then each other, or even just the little things like shopping on a Saturday morning. Like she was doing now... with someone else.

A man walked out of the butcher's shop. A man he recognised from somewhere, and he couldn't quite place... Steve Pritchard. Bastard Steve. His ex-boss. The man who'd made him redundant.

The lights changed, the green man beeped and flashed, and Daniel didn't cross the road. He stood motionless, lost at this sight of his ex-boss and his ex-girlfriend apparently shopping together. On a Saturday morning, they were shopping together. If Daniel had caught them screwing against the butcher's shop window, it wouldn't have hurt so much. He was in shock. He continued to stand at the traffic lights and watch.

Steve had walked out of the butcher's shop with a big grin on his face. He was parading a small white plastic bag up in the air. This proceeded to crease Deborah up in hysterics. Daniel wondered what Steve could possibly have bought that would cause such hysterics in Deborah. Mince? Pork chops?

Then a cold, shivering shockwave went through Daniel's body. Steve, still holding the bag in the air, placed his other arm around Deborah and kissed her passionately on the lips. She responded in kind.

It was all too much. Daniel had never seen Deborah act in such a way. Especially on a Saturday morning. Then Deborah, still laughing herself silly, took the little plastic bag (Black pudding? Chopped liver?) and put her arm in Steve's so they could walk arm-in-arm up the road.

A sudden rage overcame Daniel. Steve! Of course. What an idiot he'd been not to realise sooner. The whole office had probably known! All those nights she'd said she'd spent at Susanna's. Bitch! Whore! Slag!

Daniel had to do something to quell the rage inside him. He would kill Steve. That was it. He would kill Steve. Now. Take his funny plastic bag (Bacon? Steak?) and shove it down his throat.

He straightened himself up, tucked in his shirt and waited for the lights to change once more.

As he waited, though, he remembered his reflection. He looked down at his clothes. Although he'd tucked his shirt in, he was still a mess. Perhaps it would be better to confront Deborah and Steve when he was a little bit smarter.

The traffic stopped, and the green man beeped and flashed, but once again, Daniel didn't move. He just stood there and let the emotions run free through his being. Rage. Loneliness. Shame... He probably smelled. He turned away from the road and walked in the opposite direction from Steve and Deborah.

Half an hour later, Daniel sat in the corner of a small pub, drinking his second pint. There had been times in his life when he'd felt low, but surely, honest to goodness, never this low like a piece of dog shit not good enough for other people to stand on. He decided to take up smoking just for the hell of it. He had nothing to lose. Now and then, he would go outside to experience the pleasure of inhaling smoke while being gawped at by passing traffic and pedestrians.

At least, looking on the bright side, he couldn't feel any worse. Things could only get better. That was a good thing.

He finished his second pint and ordered a third. As he drank, though, like a needle stuck in a groove of his brain, the image of Deborah and Steve walking hand in hand up the road played over and over in his brain. He still couldn't get over the way they'd kissed. The way Deborah had pissed herself laughing at that little plastic bag (Haggis?) – that pissing-yourself-laughing laugh, which was a clear sign of being in love.

He needed to get drunk. Get so fucking drunk he'd pickle his brain. Which he did. One drink, one pub led to another. He drank as fast as the alcohol would go down his throat. Beer, whisky, vodka, cocktails of alcohol... He drank until he couldn't talk in a straight line, let alone walk one.

Later on, to get served, he went to even darker, dodgier pubs where they would serve a camel if it had a quid. The anger which seethed and boiled inside grew with every drink. The drunker he got, the angrier he got. The angrier he got, the drunker he got. He wanted violence, needed violence. To kick the shit out of someone, anyone. The next cunt that says something to me, as much as looks in my direction, he thought, I swear, I'll rip his fucking head off.

At twenty minutes to nine, he sat swaying on a bar stool of a back-street pub in Govanhill. He was working his way through the bottles of spirits from left to right.

An old man next to Daniel tapped him on

the shoulder. 'Calm down, son. You'll be putting yersel' into an early grave drinking like that.'

Daniel looked at him. Both of him. 'Don't worry about me, mate,' he slurred. 'I'm immortal.'

'Aye,' the old man answered, 'but for how long?'

Daniel shrugged as he took a cigarette out his pocket and was about to light it when the barman tapped him on the shoulder.

'Yeah?' replied Daniel, surprised.

'You the only guy who's no' heard o' the smoking ban or sumfin'? Outside.'

Trying to overcome the staggering rage which rose inside him, Daniel slowly took the cigarette out of his mouth, looked at it and then looked back at the barman. No use. Looking at the barman was the last thing Daniel would remember about that night.

Chapter 20

Markus Sepp

Patterson had left his home on Saturday morning happier than he'd been for some time. Waking up, Stephanie seemed more fragile than the night before. However, she was still talking about making an effort to beat her addiction. She sat at the kitchen table with Patterson as he had breakfast. He couldn't remember the last time Stephanie had been up at the same time as him. Patterson didn't know how long it would last, but it was nice to have a wife again. He promised Stephanie he would come home as early as he could.

This morning, he reminded her he was going to see someone called Markus Sepp, who seemed to know Susan at the gym. It was probably nothing, but Patterson thought he was still worth checking out.

So it was that half an hour later, Patterson got out of his own car and walked towards Pettigrew's car, which was parked just down from Sepp's flat in Gilbert Street.

Gilbert Street was a quiet, fairly run-down street which stood on a hill and was set amidst garages, small industrial workshops and undeveloped wasteland in Yorkhill. A large red-brick school stood on the corner, which was now used as council offices. Further down the hill were more modern buildings built to accommodate students from Glasgow University.

Patterson got in Pettigrew's car and sat next to his fellow officer in the front passenger seat.

'Morning, sir,' Pettigrew greeted him. 'It's the ground-floor flat, red curtains. I've seen him walking around since I've been here.'

Patterson looked at the unassuming building in dirty brown cladding and the window Pettigrew indicated.

'OK, let's go and pay Sepp a visit.'

'Before that, sir, I've got something for you.' She handed him some photos.

'What are these?' Patterson asked.

'They're stills from CCTV. We believe this is the vet guy.'

Patterson found himself looking at the black and white, slightly blurred stills of a slim young man walking along a main road. His very slight frame was accentuated by skinny legs themselves accentuated by very tight jeans. 'Excellent. Any idea who he is yet?' Patterson asked.

'Not at the moment, but with the CCTV, we're trying to trace his movements before and after he was seen hassling Susan.'

'When was he found on CCTV?'

'Last night.' Patterson looked at her. 'You mean you found these last night after I told you to go home?' Pettigrew didn't answer.

'Claire, I appreciate the work, but you need your rest as much as anyone else.'

'I know. The thing is, we have the footage now, and although I haven't checked it all, we can clearly see this vet guy talking to Susan and following her home on at least one occasion.'

'I'll look forward to seeing that footage later on. Has anyone else seen these apart from yourself?'

'I showed the stills to Simpson and McKinnon when they came in this morning. No one has yet seen the actual CCTV apart from myself.'

'OK, it's probably a good idea to get these images out to the press soon as possible. It could scare this vet guy off, but there's got to be someone in the area who recognises him.'

Patterson handed the photos back to Pettigrew. 'In the meantime, let's see if Markus Sepp has anything interesting to say.'

Patterson and Pettigrew got out of the car, walked across the street and went up the small flight of dirty, cracked concrete stairs which led to the front door. On either side of the stairs was a small sloping patch of unkempt grass enclosed behind chipped black-painted railings.

Pettigrew chapped on the door, and almost immediately, the door opened to reveal Markus Sepp standing before them. He was a tall, well-built man who filled the doorway space. He wore a light-blue baggy V-neck jumper, his bare chest showing underneath. His long, straggly dark hair was damp, and in his left hand, he held a red towel. A smell of unsubtle cologne wafted out the door. Sepp looked at Patterson and Pettigrew with undisguised suspicion.

'Mr Sepp?'

Sepp nodded.

'Partick CID.' Patterson showed his warrant card. 'Sorry to trouble you at this hour, but we're conducting some local enquiries. May we come in?'

'What about?' Sepp's Eastern European accent was pronounced, his voice deep.

'It's about Susan McLaughlin. You may

have heard about her murder last week. She was a member of the same gym as yourself at the Kelvin Hall. We're contacting all the members, just routine enquiries,' Patterson repeated. 'It won't take a minute, I promise you.' Not for the first time, Patterson felt like a door-to-door salesman.

Sepp still stood defiantly at the door, looking back at Patterson and Pettigrew. His muscled arms were tense, his stance obstructive and his hostility towards the two police officers very clear. So much so that Patterson thought if Sepp had the opportunity, there was a possibility he would make a run for it. Surprisingly though, Sepp's manner suddenly changed – he smiled and stood to one side to let them both in. He then ushered them through the small hallway and into the living room. The place was immaculately tidy, yet with little furniture. A couple of large, open holdalls sat next to the TV.

Patterson sat down next to Pettigrew on a worn-looking tan settee while Sepp sat on a sofa chair. A solid-looking table was between Sepp and the two officers. Sepp still smiled at his unexpected visitors, though the smile seemed more forced than natural. Nevertheless, Patterson appreciated the effort.

'Sorry I not let you in straight away; I just not used to police.' Sepp rubbed his hair a little with the towel, then let it rest on his lap.

'Of course – everyone's the same,' Patterson said, wanting to put him at ease. 'As I was saying, it's about Susan McLaughlin – you may have heard about her murder in the news.'

Sepp didn't reply as Patterson brought out the photo of Susan he carried everywhere nowadays as part of his enquiries. He handed it to Sepp. 'We're just wondering if you ever spoke to each other at the gym?'

Sepp picked up the photo and looked at it before glancing at the two police officers. 'Yes, I see her, pretty girl, but I not talk to her, sorry.' He handed the photo back to Patterson.

Both Pettigrew and Patterson took in the clear lie before Pettigrew spoke for the first time. She thought if she indulged in a little small talk, maybe he would be less defensive.

'You like to look after yourself then – going to the gym, I mean,' Pettigrew said.

'Yes, I go now and then, not all time, but it good for stress,' Sepp replied modestly.

'Are you working?' Pettigrew continued.

Sepp nodded. 'I am barista,' he said with a certain amount of pride.

'Where's that?'

'Greenbean. In town.'

'Oh yeah, I know it,' Pettigrew said. 'Big

place. Just on the corner of Buchanan Street and West Nile Street, isn't it?'

Sepp nodded; now he was relaxing more, smiling at Pettigrew. 'You should come down sometime. Both of you. I make best coffee in Glasgow,' he said, laughing.

'We will,' Patterson said. 'For now, we just want to check you didn't know Susan at all. I mean, you're absolutely sure you didn't talk to her at any time?'

Again, Sepp said he didn't, although his manner was a little more unsure than before.

'Only,' Patterson continued, 'one of the staff members there said he was sure Susan and yourself were often in conversation with each other.'

Sepp acted surprised. 'Yes? Wait.' He asked to see the photo again and this time, looked at it a lot longer. 'Sorry, I really not remember first time. Of course, I talk to her, not much but yes. I talk to a lot of women at gym; they talk to me.'

'So you definitely did talk to her then?'

Pettigrew asked. 'Yes, I do. I remember now. Not much; a little.'

'What did you talk about?'

Sepp shrugged. 'If I remember, it was little things. I don't know. Yes, but I remember now, I think she said she liked my tattoo.' He pulled down the right arm of his jumper over his shoulder to reveal a small tattoo of a mermaid. 'My hometown. We have story of mermaid; many in town have this tattoo, even ladies.'

'Did Susan talk about herself, what she was doing? Anyone who was bothering her. Anything like that?'

Sepp looked blank again, thinking about the question he was asked or perhaps the answer he should give. 'No, she was quiet girl, shy. She not say much.'

'Do you remember anything she may have said, anything at all, apart from the tattoo?' Pettigrew asked.

'I just did not remember. She not talk much, nothing really.'

Patterson leaned forward 'You haven't been back to the gym since last Saturday – why is that?'

'Yes? Oh, I see friend in Manchester. I am away all week.' Sepp pointed to the two holdalls. My friend from Estonia also. I go to see him there and sometime he comes here. I leave last Monday and am back yesterday afternoon.'

'Just a routine question,' Patterson added in as light a manner as he could find, 'but where were you on the 19th of July, the night Susan was killed?'

Sepp thought for a moment, his eyes nervously darting back towards the holdalls. 'I think I was here, yes, I was... you know, with woman.'

'Your girlfriend?' Pettigrew asked.

'No, I have no girlfriend,' he replied, clearly thinking Pettigrew had additional reasons for asking, 'She just someone I meet, you know.' He smiled, implying a casual conquest.

'Would you have her name, contact details?'

Sepp shrugged. 'No, sorry. I don't have her number. She, er, come here, you know, but she don't tell me her number. I know her first name is Megan if that help. That all I know, sorry.'

Patterson nodded, still in two minds about what to make of Sepp. Wouldn't the woman have given her phone number? Or was Sepp a disappointment?

'OK, if you can get her details, know how to contact her, it would be a big help. And that goes for your friend down in Manchester. Don't think anything of it. We just ask these questions of everyone.'

Patterson stood up, followed by Pettigrew. 'And if you do remember anything else, get in touch with me. Ask for DCI Michael Patterson, Partick police station, Dumbarton Road. Here's my card.'

Sepp stood up, putting the damp towel on the chair before taking the card. 'Of course,' he said. 'I do that, and hey' – he directed his comment mostly towards Pettigrew – 'don't forget, you want best coffee, you come to Greenbean and ask for me.'

'We'll be sure to do that. Bye now,' Pettigrew said as both Patterson and herself shuffled out the narrow hallway and out the front door. Sepp shut the door behind them as they went back down the small steps to the cracked pavement below.

'Well?' Pettigrew asked as they stood by the side of Pettigrew's car. 'What do you think, sir?'

Patterson looked into the distance and thought for a moment.

'He seems innocent enough. If he was in Manchester, maybe I was reading too much into his disappearance after the murder. Maybe we were, or I was, barking up the wrong tree. I dunno; I just had a feeling. Anyway, we'll still keep a check on him. Now we've got these CCTV images, I'm more interested in this vet guy, to be honest. Hopefully, we can find out his identity quickly, someone must know who this guy is.'

'Like you said, though, you don't think putting out an appeal could scare him away?'

Pettigrew asked.

'Possibly. But it's a chance we have to take, I think.'

'So what now?' asked Pettigrew.

'Well, I'm off to meet Simpson at Susan's flat. I've asked Susan's landlord to meet Simpson and myself there. See if he can add any more information to what we know. Simpson should be there already, in fact. So I want you to head back to the station and check up on Sepp in the meantime. See if he really did go down to Manchester. Then I want you to find out when he made the booking. Whether it was made before or after Susan was murdered.'

'Sir, if you don't mind me asking, why are you so interested in Markus Sepp? I mean, all he did was talk to Susan at the gym. You just said yourself, he seems innocent enough – what's the big deal with him?'

Patterson nodded. 'I know Claire, I know. No reason, really. Just a feeling - especially with him going away just after the murder. Even if it was pre-arranged, the trip away just seems, whatever.' Patterson seemed lost in thought. 'It's probably just coincidental in Sepp's case, but I don't like coincidences. That's why I'll be happier once we know if he made that booking to go away before Susan's murder or after.' Patterson and Pettigrew parted as Patterson walked back to his car.

Patterson then drove through the narrow, tangled streets of Yorkhill and turned left at the Kelvin Hall onto Dumbarton Road. It wasn't long before he arrived at Gardner Street and Susan's flat.

Patterson stood for a moment outside the stairwell of Susan's address and wondered himself why he was so interested in Sepp. He knew he was clutching at straws, and that was because there was a big danger this enquiry could end up going nowhere fast. He needed a breakthrough of some kind soon, and that thought made him feel that little bit more anxious once again. He was aware his pulse was beating a little faster, and he tried to calm himself down by taking deeper breaths.

As he waited for a moment downstairs, he decided to give Stephanie a call to see how she was, but there was no answer. She was probably still asleep, he thought. Patterson put the phone back in his pocket, pressed the buzzer for Susan's flat, and Jack Simpson buzzed the door open for him in return.

Chapter 21

Pressure

Patterson was out of breath by the time he had climbed the stairs to Susan's top-floor flat. He wondered how much of that was down to his lack of fitness and how much was down to the tangible anxiety rising within him. There seemed no reason why he should feel more stressed than usual, yet the hints of unease he did feel, self-perpetuated like storm clouds gathering on the horizon. He knew one of the best ways to combat these simmering feelings of anxiety was by concentrating on the job in hand. With that in mind, Patterson took another deep breath and lightly tapped on the half-open front door of Susan's flat.

Entering the flat reminded him that Susan was a real person, not just a photo he carried around in his pocket or a name written in felt-tip pen on an incident board. He was also reminded that the two-bedroomed flat was well cared for and spacious enough to accommodate three people, let alone one. Why didn't Susan at least have one flatmate to share the rent?

In fact, one of the reasons Patterson wanted to meet the landlord that morning was to understand how Susan could afford this lovely, spacious flat on her own. She had to make her student loan last and was just getting a nominal wage plus expenses from the Riverview surgery. Patterson suspected that Davy McGregor might have been paying the full rent or at least part of the rent for her. That this would explain why Susan tolerated his company for so long after learning he wasn't a music mogul. He wondered if the landlord, in turn, would know anything, or suspect something, about this.

As Patterson stood in the hallway and looked around, the property was still notable for its cleanliness, yet now the air felt dead as if the flat had been drained of life.

Jack Simpson appeared out of the main bedroom and greeted his superior. 'Morning, sir.'

'Morning, Jack. Is the landlord no here yet?' Patterson asked.

'Nope. I said around ten, though; it's still only ten to.

'Ah, well. I guess it gives us time to look around.'

Patterson walked through to the living

room. Everything in the flat was a reminder this was a young woman who had all of her life before her. The furniture., personal items, decor...he could see, feel, and imagine Susan everywhere he looked. She was like a million other young people in many ways – looking to the future, building her life, and living it as best she could.

It led to Patterson asking the question he kept coming back to. What was the motive for Susan's murder? What led this murderer to take so many risks? To climb so high up the outside of a tenement, to risk his own life, to stop someone else's life? Patterson hated it sometimes, trying to figure out the logic behind someone's personal evil. He often wondered if he would be better off doing a job where he didn't have to deal with the worst of human nature on a daily basis - whilst all the time trying to deal with his own demons every single day.

For the umpteenth time, he reminded himself it is as it is. He just had to get on with it. Glasgow had a layer of dirt he had to clean. Sometimes the dirt was clearly visible; sometimes, you only noticed it by looking a little closer. Then, sometimes, you had to dig deep under the surface to find it. But the dirt, the badness was always there in this city– it was always there.

Patterson walked over to the bay windows and looked down onto Gardner Street below. To the left was the high hill that led to Hyndland Road. To his right, the street led down to Dumbarton Road. He walked back through the rooms, lost in his own thoughts. He again imagined Susan doing the same, even on the day she would die - completely unaware her life would end so suddenly that warm summer's night.

Patterson knew he had to find this murderer come what may. It angered him that someone could have carried out this most immoral of murders. The killer of Susan McLaughlin needed to be brought to justice, and it was down to Patterson to do just that. That was what her friends and family depended on him doing, not to mention his colleagues and superiors. So, what if Patterson failed? Granted, he had had numerous successes in the past, but what if, this time, he completely failed? What if, because of his own weaknesses, his own failings, the murderer of Susan McLaughlin would not pay for this horrific crime? And what if Stephanie was right? Even if it was said as part of a drunken rant, maybe Patterson was pathetic. Maybe he was the lowest of the low.

Plus, there was always the possibility this murderer would kill again. Another innocent life would be lost, and all because Patterson wasn't up to the job in finding him. So far, there didn't seem to be any reason Susan was murdered.

No motive at all. So maybe Susan was indeed murdered just for the sake of it or perhaps for the thrill of it, which meant the murderer would be looking for that thrill again. Maybe –

'You all right, sir?' Simpson could see, not for the first time, that Patterson wasn't quite right. His superior was hunched over, breathing heavily and sweating. 'You want me to get you a glass of water?'

'No, I'm fine. It's just these damn stairs.'

Patterson straightened up in defiance of his thoughts and fears, brought out a hankie and wiped his brow while coughing. He had to pull himself together. Get a grip. He hated how his insecurity could be so random. By trying not to think too much, he had fallen into the trap of thinking too much. He just had to get on with what he had to do. He just had to get on with it.

'What's the name of the guy that owns this property again?'

'Mr Zach Papadakis. Greek – or at least his family is.'

'Right—' Patterson was about to say something else when he heard the echo of the main door downstairs clicking shut and footsteps coming up the close. 'Hopefully, this is him now.'

In quick time, there was a tap on the half-open front door, and opening fully, there stood a young man in his twenties. With dark hair and tanned skin, he was strikingly good-looking. He smiled to reveal over-whitened teeth. He wore a bright yellow open-necked shirt with smart, dark trousers.

Walking in and seeing Simpson, he went over to him as if he was greeting a long-lost friend. 'Good to see you again, Jack. I hope you've been keeping well?'

His charm was as loud as his shirt.

Simpson gave a muted but polite response before adding. 'Zach, this is my colleague, DCI Patterson. As I said before, we just want to get some more information on Susan and see if you could tell us anything to help with our enquiry.'

'Of course,' Zach replied, his tone suddenly more solemn with what appeared like a genuine look of concern on his face. 'I think I've said everything I could, but anything I can do to help the police, I'm happy to do so.'

As Patterson was going to ask the first question of Zach, he looked over the youthful landlord again. There was something familiar about him. Patterson definitely recognised the landlord from somewhere, although he couldn't put his finger on where exactly. Then it dawned on him.

'Aren't you the son of Vardis Demetriou?'

Zach didn't answer immediately but looked at Patterson as if he had now recognised the DCI in turn. Still, though, Zach didn't answer; he just continued to look at Patterson as if deciding what to say in return. Eventually, he broke into a smile and shrugged.

'Yes, I am. Do I know you from somewhere, Inspector?'

'Sorry, but I was under the impression your last name was Papadakis, not Demetriou?'

'It is. Zach Papadakis is my business name.'

'Your business name? Really? I didn't know that existed. What's that then, like your stage name?'

Zach continued to smile. 'Not quite. It's just that I prefer to keep my business dealings separate from my personal life.'

'Bit dramatic to change your surname, is it not? I thought family names were a matter of pride in Greece.'

'First of all, I'm a Glaswegian, Detective, er...'

'Patterson.'

'Patterson. A Glaswegian of Greek descent, but I'm as much a Scot as you are. Second, it's not that big a deal. I find it comes in handy when, as I said, I can keep my family life away from my work life.'

'So, it wouldn't be anything to do with the fact your father has been done for being a slum landlord in the past? Nothing to do with that?'

Zach stopped smiling and glared at Patterson. 'Nothing at all,' he replied, keeping his composure, yet the annoyance and anger with Patterson were still apparent.

'How is he, by the way, your father?'

Zach continued to stare at Patterson, now with undisguised dislike in his eyes. 'He died two years ago. Heart attack.'

'Oh, sorry to hear that,' Patterson said in a neutral voice, looking over at Simpson. 'Zach's father, Vardis Demetriou, was a well-known landlord around these parts one time. Unfortunately, some of his properties weren't up to the standard you would expect, at least going by the rents he charged. In fact, as I recall, wasn't there a case of a tenant being killed because he couldn't escape a basement flat. A fire. Something to do with bars on the windows?'

'As you no doubt know as well, Inspector Patterson, that was not proven. Besides, any problems my father had with properties in the past are gone now. I took over the property business after my father died, and as you can see' – Zach indicated the clean, spacious flat they were standing in – 'we've all moved on from then. I'm a respectable landlord. I make a point of looking after my tenants.'

'Yes, I believe you looked after Susan?'

'Looked after her? I liked her if that's what you mean. She was never any trouble, a dream tenant.'

'Always paid her rent on time?'

'Always.'

'How did she pay her rent?'

'What do you mean?'

'I mean, was it cash? Weekly? Monthly?'

'It was monthly, direct debit.'

'And the money came from her bank account?'

'Yes, as far as I'm aware. Why wouldn't it have been from her bank account? You would have no doubt checked this already, I would have thought. Why are you asking this?'

'Nothing. I just want to double-check. So she never had any trouble paying the rent?'

'None whatsoever, as I said, she paid it monthly via the bank. Always on time, never a problem. In fact, I actually charged her a lower rent than other places.'

'Ah,' Patterson said, 'You gave her a lower rent because she was such a good tenant, is that it?'

'Exactly. A good tenant is worth their weight in gold. I didn't want Susan to leave, so I kept the rent low.'

'Wouldn't it have been better, or easier for you, if someone else moved in with her? There's more than enough space for two here.'

'True, but Susan didn't want that.'

'Didn't she? And do you usually allow your tenants, even the ones you say you like, to dictate the terms of a tenancy?'

'Of course not,' Zach replied in a more agitated tone of voice. Listen, I've done nothing wrong. I kept Susan's rent down, so what? Isn't that a good thing?'

'You kept her rent down in exchange for what?' Patterson's question drew a glance from Simpson, who was wondering if his boss was deliberately trying to provoke Zach. If so, then he had succeeded in his goal.

'Sorry?' Zach said in a raised voice and was visibly angry now; he clearly had a temper. 'What do you mean by that?'

'I mean...' Patterson hesitated, trying to find the right words. 'Let's be frank. Susan was an attractive girl. You're telling me you didn't keep her rent down for any other reason other than goodwill? You're a businessman. You have overheads and expenses, and yet you let this young woman dictate the terms of the rent to you?'

'What are you implying?' Zach asked loudly.

'I'm just wondering if you didn't have some kind of arrangement with her, that's all?' Patterson added quickly, 'Listen, maybe it's best if you come down to the station sometime and make a formal statement about your involvement with Susan. I do think there are one or two things to clear up here. It may also be wise to bring your lawyer too.'

'Forget the lawyer, I can come now if you want. I've got nothing to hide.'

'No, it won't be necessary right now, but we'll let you know when to come down.'

Zach looked at Patterson, then Simpson before looking back at Patterson again. 'You're completely out of order, Inspector. I do not take advantage of my tenants - and I am not a slum landlord either.'

Patterson smiled. 'You can go now, Mr Demetriou.'

Zach was going to say something more before thinking better of it. He turned without a word and went out the door.

Once they heard the main front door downstairs click shut, Simpson turned to

Patterson. 'Sir, with respect, what the hell was all that about?'

'Well, for one thing, I wanted to find out if our landlord had a temper or not. He was too charming by half on arrival, and I'm always very suspicious of charm. As it turns out, he clearly is indeed a hot-headed young man. Plus, once I recognized him, I knew he wasn't to be trusted. I know a number of his family; they can be charming too and right corrupt individuals at the same time. The fact he uses two names is a sign he has something to hide, and it's not just the corrupt past of his father. I initially suspected that McGregor was paying the rent here, which was why Susan still hung around him. Yet, on recognising Demetriou, I realised it was also quite possible Susan had an arrangement with her landlord that was of a sexual nature.'

'Don't you think you're getting ahead of yourself with that assumption? Besides, you really think Susan would be part of an arrangement like that?'

'Whether by choice or necessity, it's at least a possibility and could very well be a precursor to a disagreement between them.'

'You mean Susan wanting out of the agreement?'

'Something like that. Of course, I noticed

on the bank statements the rent payments were lower than the average for this area, but it still would have been a struggle for Susan to pay the rent here without fail.'

'But, as for McGregor, if he was paying the rent somehow, that would surely have shown up in Susan's bank statements. As far as I know, nothing showed up.'

There's always simple cash in hand. However, with someone like Zach Demetriou and his dodgy dealings and dodgy family, I think we have ourselves a new suspect...' Patterson's voice tailed off and the main reason he didn't take Demetriou down the station there and then became apparent. Patterson's anxiety, which had been patiently building up in the last hour or so, and was always lurking as he was talking to Zach, now saw its chance to make a dramatic entrance. It was as if it had suddenly grabbed Patterson from behind and was holding him tight around the chest. Patterson felt he couldn't breathe properly, and the sights and sounds in the flat became blurred reflections and echoes he couldn't quite make out. He knew he was having a panic attack, and there was nothing he could do to stop it. He felt as if his head was literally going to explode with the pressure from inside pushing out.

Patterson tried to resist the extreme tension that was squeezing the life out of him, but his thoughts, doubts and fears were far too powerful to fight against. Most of all, there was fear. A bone-clenching, organ-stopping fear that enveloped everything.

Simpson noticed Patterson's sudden turn for the worse and held him upright. His superior's breathing became increasingly laboured as the seconds passed. Having seen it many times before, Simpson immediately knew what was happening.

'Come on, sir,' he said, 'let's get you some air.' He took Patterson by the arm, and both men left the flat like someone leading his drunk friend out of a pub.

Simpson carefully guided Patterson down the close stairs and outside into Gardner Street. Patterson leaned with his back against the light orange sandstone tenement wall beside the stairwell entrance. He breathed in the welcome fresher air and started to regather his thoughts into some kind of order. After a few minutes of deep breathing and focusing his thoughts on recovering, he felt better. He was glad, as always, that Simpson had been there to help him.

Patterson straightened up and looked around the narrow street as he continued to regain his composure. All the time, Simpson patiently waited by his side.

'Feeling better, sir?' Simpson asked

eventually, and Patterson nodded, still bent over with his hands resting on his knees. He then stood up straight, took another deep breath and looked at the people walking left and right along Dumbarton Road at the end of the street.

Someone caught his attention.

It was a glimpse of a person standing but turning away. Patterson vaguely recognised the man from somewhere. In fact, hadn't he just seen that skinny youth recently? Very recently? The figure turned around again and looked directly at Patterson before casually looking away again.

Patterson turned to Simpson. 'Claire said she showed you some CCTV stills of the vet guy this morning.'

'Oh, that's right, forgot to say, I — '

Patterson interrupted him by nodding in the direction of Dumbarton Road. 'Check him out over there with the blue top on. Is it my imagination, or does that look like the same guy?' Simpson looked in the direction Patterson indicated but couldn't see who Patterson meant. Then he noticed the blue top and the tight blue jeans covering spindly legs. It certainly resembled the guy in the photographs, but it was still hard to say for definite. Whoever it was still stood at the corner, trying to act nonchalantly, but the more he did so, the more suspicious he looked.

The young man then turned and looked directly back towards the two officers once more. Patterson and Simpson now knew for certain it was indeed the vet guy who, realising he'd been sussed, suddenly turned and made to run along Dumbarton Road.

'Get him,' Patterson said, and Simpson immediately set off in pursuit.

Chapter 22

The Vet Guy

The vet guy had got a good start on Simpson, so by the time Simpson had turned left into Dumbarton Road, the vet guy was already bombing it halfway up the road. The vet guy also had a fair pace on him. With Simpson wearing his smart and shiny but non-athletic brogues, running along the pavement was already killing his feet. Yet what Simpson lacked in sportswear, he made up with fitness and was already starting to catch his prey by the time the vet guy reached the corner of Dowanhill Street.

Soon Simpson was almost within reach, but just as he was about to lay an arm on the vet guy, he tripped and went flying across the pavement, landing in front of a surprised and not too impressed young woman pushing a stroller with an even less impressed toddler inside it.

'Bastard. Me fucking keks!'

Ignoring the pain he felt and trying to immediately forget about another ruined pair of trousers, Simpson picked himself up and headed after the suspect once again. He saw the vet guy take a sudden left turn and run into the entrance of Kelvinhall subway station, where people were beginning to stream out – a sign of a train having just arrived. As Simpson reached the entrance himself, he heard the hollow toot of a train leaving the station, along with the cold rush of sour air from the tunnels down below.

Knowing the back entrance to the station had recently been closed off, Simpson had no hesitation in jumping over the barrier. He bounded down the steps and onto the sole central platform, where he saw the vet guy standing all alone at the far end of an otherwise empty station. Having just missed a train, the vet guy was still trying to act as nonchalant as before and still failing just as miserably.

The rumble of the recently departed train faded and was soon replaced by the sound of dripping water echoing from the tunnels.

The vet guy's shoulders were visibly heaving, and there was sweat pouring down his forehead, which showed that running wasn't a regular occurrence for him.

As Simpson sauntered up to him, some sweat covering his own forehead, the vet guy continued to look straight ahead at an advert on the curved wall facing him which encouraged him to visit the Highlands.

With the vet guy still determinedly trying to ignore his sole companion on the platform, Simpson placed his hand on the man's shoulder. 'Thinking about going somewhere? You know, that may not be a bad idea.' Simpson said as he led the vet guy back along the platform and towards the exit of the station.

*

Back at Partick police station, the vet guy was soon identified as Blair Travers. Travers sat in the interview room next to the duty solicitor, with Simpson sitting opposite. Travers was a tall, skinny 21-year-old, although he looked anywhere between the ages of thirteen and thirteen and a half.

He had prominent cheekbones and noticeably small eyes as if he was permanently squinting. At regular intervals, Blair would slowly run his fingers through his long thick brown hair as if he enjoyed the sensation of touching himself at any opportunity.

When Patterson first heard about a teenager hanging around the vet's surgery and hassling Susan, like Becci, he'd expected the vet guy to be a typical Glasgow ned, ned being Glaswegian shorthand for 'non-educated delinquent'. Yet Susan was right: Blair Travers was anything but. Travers had gone to Glasgow Academy, a private school where one of the most common qualifications was money. It turned out his father was a well-respected businessman who owned several companies throughout the city.

It was also evident in his manner of speaking that Travers had a high opinion of himself. He proudly wore his sense of entitlement in full view of everyone else, and his utter contempt for Simpson was in no doubt whatsoever. All this didn't really matter, of course. What did matter was to find out if he'd had any involvement in the murder of Susan McLaughlin.

As Patterson looked on at the interview via a monitor, Simpson placed a photo of Susan on the table and asked the question he already knew the answer to. 'Have you seen this woman before?'

Travers looked back at Simpson without answering.

Simpson tried again. 'Listen, the sooner you help us and answer the question, the sooner we can get this over with. Have you seen this woman before?'

'No.' Travers had barely glanced at the photo.

'This is Susan McLaughlin; she was murdered on the 19th of July. You must have read about it or seen it on the news. The thing is, shortly before she died, Susan said she'd been hassled by someone on more than one occasion outside her work by a man fitting your description. In fact, you were seen on CCTV, following Susan home, talking to her.' Simpson brought out a photographic still taken from the CCTV. 'Now, this is murder we're talking about, and you're a suspect in that murder, so I would advise you to tell us everything you know now. Did you in any way know this woman?'

'No,' Travers replied. His permanent sneer gave the impression that even to speak to Simpson was beneath him.

'Fine, have it your way. If you don't cooperate, we'll have to detain you overnight. I'm sure your parents would be very pleased about that.' It was with satisfaction that Simpson noticed Travers flinch at the mention of his parents.

'I told you, this is a murder investigation. If you're hiding something, the consequences could be very severe. Just tell us the truth.'

Travers' solicitor leaned over to him and whispered something in his ear. Travers put his hand through his hair again as if he was trying to show he was really, really worth it. He then shrugged, sighed, and for the first time, looked directly at Simpson. He then proceeds to speak in a faux American accent.

'OK, man, I have no idea why this chick would say that.'

Simpson let the 'chick' comment go by, thinking that maybe that's what young people were saying these days. Then again, perhaps it was just Travers. Simpson tried another tactic.

'OK. So why did you run away when you saw my colleague and myself earlier today?'

'Hey, man, let's just say I knew you were after me, capiche? I mean, you want the truth? Huh? Yeah, well, fine, I'll give you the truth, bro. I was good friends with Susan, yeah sure, you got me on that one, happy? But I didn't hassle her, no way, Jose.' Travers' Californian Glaswegian came across as pretty strange and deeply annoying to Simpson. Still, he tried not to let it show.

'What were you doing in Dumbarton Road when we saw you earlier?'

'What do you mean what was I doing there? What kind of dumbass question is that?'

'Just as I said. You're linked to Susan McLaughlin, who was murdered, and you just happened to be hanging around near her address?'

'Go figure. I told you, man, I live in the

neighbourhood. I was passing by. I mean, yeah, I told you I knew her, so I know a lot of chicks, big deal.'

'So how well did you know Susan?'

'Well. Not well. Who knows. It was complicated. Think she liked me.'

'Then why would she say to a friend you were harassing her?'

'Don't know, man. Who can understand the female species at the best of times – know what I'm saying?'

'Where were you on the night of the 19th of July, Saturday, the night Susan was murdered?'

'I dunno. In my bed or at home playing on the computer, I guess. Don't remember exact.'

'Late Saturday night?'

'That's what I said, didn't I?'

'Would you mind if we checked your computer to verify that?'

Travers gave a nervous glance to Simpson before shrugging and saying, 'Cool by me, cop. Do what you want.'

Simpson asked more questions, but it seemed as if Blair Travers had an answer for all of them. The most important thing they now knew was who the vet guy actually was, and they could now check up on his whereabouts and his links to Susan. First, they would make arrangements for his computer hard drive to be examined.

The interview ended, and after consulting with Patterson, it was decided to conditionally release Travers pending further enquiries.

Travers got up, noisily pushing his chair away. He wanted to show he wasn't happy.

As Simpson led him out the door and sarcastically thanked him for his time, Travers turned back round to him and stopped. 'Hey, bro, word of advice. I heard you guys on the news saying that Susan was an angel. Well, I got news for you. She ain't the angel you think she was – take it from me.'

'What do you mean by that?'

'Just sayin', my man, just saying.' Travers laughed and sauntered out the door with a swagger Huggy Bear would have been proud of.

Once Travers had left the room, Simpson turned in the direction of the camera Patterson was watching through and said, 'What an absolute dick.'

Further checks were made immediately on Travers by the whole team. They couldn't find any immediate link he had to Susan, but additional checks were still being followed up by McKinnon. For now, Patterson decided to call it a day and told the team to come back in the morning.

As Patterson tidied up some final paperwork, he decided to give Stephanie a phone call to see if she wanted anything from the shops on his way home.

'Hi, Steph, I just wondered—'

What the fuck do you want?' Stephanie's shouted question was both slurred and angry.

A feeling of complete despair instantly overcame Patterson. He took a deep breath and tried to ask another question, but it was no use. Stephanie didn't seem to understand, and her speech soon became incoherent mumblings, crying and screaming. Patterson put the phone down. He'd known that Stephanie's sobriety could end at any moment, but he hadn't expected it to be so soon. At the same time, he knew he'd kidded himself on, once again, that Stephanie's pledge of sobriety was somehow different this time.

He felt a complete fool.

As he pulled on his jacket, picked his papers up and switched off his office light, he also knew he was in for another night of misery.

Chapter 23

Further Investigations

As expected, when he got home, Stephanie was completely drunk and impatiently waiting to wage war on her returning husband. On the plus side, she was so drunk that after shouting the usual obscenities and telling him how pathetic he was, she soon slumped down on the settee and fell into a heavy sleep. Patterson tucked a blanket around her and headed into the kitchen. He laid papers relating to the investigation on the kitchen table and went over once again aspects of the case, wondering if there had been anything he'd missed. He made himself a sandwich and had a cup of coffee as he studied everything in front of him. Then he, too, fell asleep at the table before he woke in the early hours, checked Stephanie was all right and took himself up to bed.

It was with a heavy heart that he left for work the next morning. Stephanie was still fast asleep on the couch, but checking on her once again, he knew she would probably be all right.

She seemed so peaceful when she was asleep, so different to when she was awake. When he looked down at her still sleeping on the settee, it saddened him that the woman who would wake up would be so destructive, not just to those around her but to herself most of all.

Patterson gathered his papers once more, then his jacket and headed out the door. With issues at home preying on his mind and his anxiety also waiting to make another reappearance, Patterson again found it hard to concentrate on his work. What some others at the station took for absent-mindedness was actually worry. However, at least regarding the case, there had been some promising developments. For one thing, now that the vet guy was identified, extensive investigations into his background could begin. If he was the murderer of Susan, then sooner or later, they would find proof.

As for this day, Patterson started it with another briefing to his colleagues. He stood in front of the incident board while Simpson, Pettigrew, McKinnon and a few other select officers sat in front of him.

'OK, here's where we're at today,' Patterson began. 'We've already established, according to one of McGregor's sidekicks, Steven Armstrong – otherwise known as Stevie – that Susan liked going to karaoke nights; in fact, she didn't just like karaoke, she loved it apparently. Now —'

'Excuse me, Sir,' Pettigrew asked, 'but how come we didn't know this before? Shona, her best friend, didn't mention it. Her mum didn't. How come we're only finding out about it now?'

'Because Claire, it seems that Susan liked to keep secrets. One of those secrets was her going to karaoke. Why did she like to keep secrets? Heaven knows, but that's the way Susan was. Now it's just possible Susan could have met her murderer at one of these karaoke nights. That's why, in addition to some good work done by Jack already, I've already got a few more uniforms going around and getting CCTV from all known karaoke bars in the city, as well as asking questions about Susan being seen and if she was with anyone else on a regular basis. If Susan was into karaoke as much as has been said, hopefully, she should turn up on CCTV somewhere.' Patterson turned back towards the board. 'Apart from that, we finally know who our mysterious vet guy is.' Patterson tapped Blair Travers' name, which was written underneath his photo. 'Brian, you were looking more into him. What have you found out? Anything of interest so far?'

Brian McKinnon shook his head. 'No joy, I'm afraid. It turns out he does have an alibi for the night Susan was murdered. He was at home, which his family have confirmed. They say he went to bed around eleven that night and was there the next morning. However, he does have had a habit of hassling several women in the area. We've a report from another woman who made a complaint to Maryhill about him and one in Woodside. He was cautioned and let go on both occasions. Yet, apart from following women home, there's no evidence he has done anything more than that. We're still checking his computer. He has made searches for Susan. Yet, he didn't get far because Susan had a very limited presence online. That's to say almost none, which is quite unusual for a young woman like Susan. There's also no evidence so far that Travers had any contact with her apart from the times we know he hassled her in the street.'

Patterson nodded. 'OK, at this stage, until we find out something more, I get the impression Travers may be nothing more than an annoyance. Of course, we'll keep an eye on him, and we can at least charge him with harassment. Perhaps more women will come forward when we release his photo to the press.'

Patterson then turned to a photo of Markus Sepp. 'Now, Claire, any developments on our friend from the gym.'

'Afraid not,' Claire Pettigrew replied. 'Another dead end. We managed to locate the woman he was with the night Susan was killed. She confirms she was with Sepp up till past eleven. It's possible Sepp could still have went to Susan's flat later on, but for now, his alibi checks out. Plus, we've confirmed he did go down to Manchester for a few days, as he says. The trip had also been booked three weeks in advance of Susan's murder. We've also nothing whatsoever linking him to Susan apart from the fact he was talking to her at the gym.'

Patterson was disappointed once again. His hunches were being proven wrong on a regular basis. 'OK. Brian, I want you to coordinate the officers finding out more about these karaoke pubs. Jack can help you out as well. Posters with Susan's photo are arriving this afternoon. We'll get them put up in the relevant bars.'

'What about Stevie and Chuckles?' Simpson asked.

'Again,' Patterson replied, 'both have got an alibi for the night of the murder, but we'll be keeping an eye on them too, of course. If either are involved with the murder of Susan, we'll get them. Granted, it would help if forensics had given us something, but so far, zero. Still, something may turn up.' Patterson tried to keep an optimistic tone. 'OK, I know it doesn't seem like we've much to go on at the moment, but we have to keep trying. We—' Just then, an officer came in the room and shouted over to Patterson. 'Sir, a body's been found in a flat in Peel Street. A young woman. According to one of the officers, apparently, there are similarities to the murder of Susan McLaughlin.'

Chapter 24

Close

'The victim's name is Kimberley O'Hara. Aged twenty-seven. Lived alone, been here two years, local girl. Worked in the bookies across the street.'

As McKinnon read from his notepad, there was definitely a case of déjà vu for Patterson this Sunday morning. Only a couple of weeks ago, he'd walked up a tenement close to be faced with the corpse of Susan McLaughlin. Now, he was attending another killing in Peel Street, only two blocks distance from where Susan McLaughlin had been murdered.

The feeling of déjà vu was even more apparent as Patterson took in the scene before him. He found himself looking down at the body of a woman who'd died well before her time. He noted her arms placed across her chest, just as Susan McLaughlin's arms had been. It appeared as if there had been some care taken with her position overall. As if she'd been laid out on the bed. Just like Susan McLaughlin.

Yet there was one immediate difference to the murder of Susan McLaughlin.

Placed across the stomach of Kimberley O'Hara was a bright red rose.

'Brian, bag that rose and don't inform anyone about it unless I say so.'

McKinnon did as he was told as Patterson looked around the room. As with every crime scene, he immediately looked for signs, first impressions could often be the best impressions. Messages that came from anything unusual, something out of place, something that just didn't seem right, or that just didn't add up.

Patterson then moved out of the way to let the forensic pathologist, Tasmina Rana, come by and do her stuff.

Once McKinnon had carefully placed the rose in an evidence bag, he reappeared at Patterson's side.

'How do you know she worked in the bookies across the street?' Patterson asked.

'A neighbour from downstairs,' McKinnon replied. 'Simpson is with her now—'

As he was about to continue, Simpson himself appeared at the door, and McKinnon decided to let his colleague fill in the details.

'We might have a bit of luck, sir,' Simpson said.

My God, thought Patterson, will this déjà vu ever stop?

'Don't tell me, we have a witness?'

Simpson smiled. 'No, not quite, but Mrs Addington, a neighbour, saw a man running away from the scene.'

Patterson waited for the catch, the but, yet it didn't come. He looked at Simpson with rising expectation. 'Did she get a good look at him?'

Simpson nodded. 'She did indeed. The man was running down the stairs full pelt, she said, nearly knocked her right over. He had, quote, "a wild look in his eyes" Claire's with her now.'

Patterson nodded. 'So it was this neighbour who found the body?'

'Yes. Mrs Addington thought he might have been a burglar. So she came up here to check if everything was all right. Unfortunately, it wasn't. She saw the door open, went inside and found the victim's body as it is now. She's still pretty shaken, as you can imagine.'

'Tell Claire I'll be down shortly and make sure she's asking the right questions.'

Simpson turned to leave the flat, and Patterson called McKinnon back over. 'So, Brian, what else do we know so far?'

McKinnon looked at his notes as he guided Patterson round the flat. 'Well, there's no sign of forced entry. There may have been someone else here recently, though. If you'll follow me through.' McKinnon squeezed past his tall, slim senior officer and took him through to the living room.

He pointed to a small coffee table. 'Two coffee cups, possibly from last night.' McKinnon seemed quite proud of this piece of detective work.

'Anything else?'

McKinnon didn't have anything else to offer, as he'd been hoping Patterson would be satisfied with the coffee-cup deduction.

At McKinnon's shrug, Patterson shook his head and made his way around the flat, going from room to room, occasionally giving instructions to his colleagues. He walked through to the kitchen and looked around the window. It was shut, nothing to indicate an intruder, but with it being a warm night previously, the window could well have been open earlier. However, a few thoughts had occurred to Patterson. Yes, there were clear and obvious similarities to the murder of Susan McLaughlin, and yet something felt different. Not just the rose but something.

He turned back to McKinnon. 'What time

did you say the neighbour saw the man running down the stairs?'

'I didn't. But it was this morning. Just after eight.'

'This morning? Is that a definite time?'

'Yes. The local shop opens at eight round the corner; Mrs Addington had just returned after it opened.'

Patterson went over to where the coroner was still examining Kimberley's body and then turned back towards McKinnon again. 'Hey, do we know who the landlord is here?'

McKinnon looked down at his notes. 'Man by the name of Livingstone. John Livingstone. Ex-policeman, apparently.'

Patterson couldn't help but be a little disappointed. 'Tasmina, what can you tell me?'

Tasmina stood up. 'Well, if you want probables, on first impressions, it looks fairly straightforward. It's almost certainly asphyxiation, and going by the bruising, she was manually strangled by her attacker. You can see the bruising around her midriff —'

'I see,' Patterson interrupted. This wasn't just a similar murder to Susan's; it some ways it seemed almost identical. 'So you're saying her attacker was on top of her when he strangled her?'

Tasmina nodded and spoke aloud the thoughts they were both thinking. 'Yes, it does seem we've been here before. There is one thing, though.'

Tasmina pointed to the back of Kimberley's head. 'There's a large bruise and cut here. Very recent. Most probably happened around the time she was attacked. Some fresh blood loss.'

'You think she was hit with something?'

'Could be. Can't say for sure. By the way, the cut is with the bruise, I would guess it's also possible she hit her head on something, something blunt, falling backwards.'

Patterson noted the bruising on the right of Kimberley's face. 'It also looks like she could have been hit or punched.'

'Yes, I'd say so,' Tasmina agreed.

Patterson looked around the bedroom. If she fell back, there wasn't much space in this room. She could have hit her head on the side of a cabinet, but there was no sign of that. He looked at the floor. There were thick light-coloured carpets in the bedroom as well as in the sitting room. They seemed spotless in both rooms – there was no sign a struggle had taken place in this room at all.

He walked back through to the hallway

and looked at the carpet. In the middle of the floor, there was a small dark patch, like the floor itself had been bruised.

Patterson called the photographer through. 'Donna, over here, please. Get me a couple of shots of that.'

Once the photographer had done so, Patterson kneeled down. Almost definitely a smear of blood and recent too. About six feet from the front door. Kimberley would be around five foot eight or nine, he thought. 'So let's just say she opens the door to someone, who hits her, she falls down and hits the back of her head here. The killer gets on top of her and kills her in the hallway before positioning her on the bed.' Patterson said this in a quiet voice, almost to himself.

McKinnon was at once impressed with Patterson's immediate deduction yet convinced it was completely wrong. 'One thing's for sure, sir. It surely can't be a coincidence – the similarities between the murders, I mean. It seems whoever killed Kimberley here most likely killed Susan McLaughlin as well.'

Patterson thought it was still too early to say that for definite but could only agree the similarities were striking. It was very possible he was now looking for a double murderer. His heart was beating a little faster, and he felt a little out of breath. This second murder was what he'd been afraid of ever since the body of Susan McLaughlin had been found.

Patterson was troubled by something else. The similarities between the murders and yet the differences. He turned to McKinnon as a sounding board. 'Some things still don't add up here. If it is the same murderer, Susan's killer climbed up a drainpipe and entered via the kitchen window. Why did they just come up to the front door this time?'

'Maybe he's a quick learner. Realised there are easier ways to enter a flat than climb a drainpipe. Apart from that, I checked. No drainpipe goes near enough to the windows here for someone to climb in,' McKinnon said. Was that the reason for the change?

Patterson went back to the front door. There were no marks or signs of forced entry. Then he noticed something else outside on the landing.

On one of the white tiles on the opposite wall was possibly another tiny smear of blood. Looked very recent too. Could that be Kimberley's blood? Or the blood of her murderer? Patterson tried to fit this further piece of information into his original scenario. Perhaps there had been a struggle on the landing before the murderer killed her.

He was thinking this over as he returned to the bedroom to talk to Rana.

'So what estimate do you have for the time of death, Tasmina?'

'I'd say the early hours of this morning, possibly late last night. Should be able to be more precise later, as per.'

Early hours of the morning or late last night? Yet a man was seen by the neighbour running away from the scene just after eight, Patterson thought. Why would he be running away this morning if the murder had taken place in the early hours? Had he stayed in the flat? Waited for some reason? Then why run down the stairs when he did eventually leave?

Patterson gestured to McKinnon. 'Brian, look around the flat again. Get some addresses. More – details of family, work, etc. – if you can. I'm going downstairs to talk to this neighbour, Mrs Addington.'

Chapter 25

Mrs Addington

Patterson went downstairs and entered a large living room to see Mrs Addington sitting in a straight-backed, primrose-yellow flower-patterned armchair. The elderly lady was crying, dabbing her eyes with an embroidered handkerchief. To the right of her, large bay windows looked out onto tenements opposite and the street below. The room itself was old-fashioned in style and atmosphere. The slightly tanned wallpaper could have dated from the fifties. A black Singer sewing machine stood on a green baize table in the corner while ornaments and family photos sat on surfaces all around the room. On the mantlepiece above an unlit gas fire, pride of place went to an old black-and-white photograph of a young, moustached man in an RAF uniform. Only the extra-large black and shiny flat-screen TV seemed out of character with the surroundings.

Pettigrew was sitting in another chair, leaning forward towards the elderly lady, gently asking her questions while Simpson stood beside her taking notes.

As Patterson entered, Pettigrew stood up. 'Margaret, this is Detective Chief Inspector Michael Patterson. Sir, this is Mrs Addington – Margaret – who found Kimberley.'

Patterson smiled towards the lady, who he guessed was in her seventies. He took a small brown, wicker-backed chair from against the wall, placed it next to Pettigrew and sat down. 'Mrs Addington, I know this whole business is upsetting, but the sooner we can get information, the sooner we can catch whoever did this to Kimberley.'

Margaret nodded, still dabbing at her eyes with the tissue.

'I was just saying to Claire,' Margaret replied in a quiet voice, 'I'll tell you what I can, but it's so terrible. Kimberley was such a nice young woman. I can't imagine anyone wanting to hurt her.'

It struck Patterson that almost the exact same thing had been said about Susan. He started his own questions, unconcerned if they'd already been asked by Pettigrew. 'So, how long had Kimberley lived in the flat?'

'About two years... roughly, yes, two years, I'd say.'

'Did she live alone?'

'Yes. She used to live with someone before, though. Her boyfriend, a flash young man. Didn't like him to be truthful, full of himself, you know? In fact, he ended up running off with my neighbour across the landing. Poor Kimberley. Poor lassie. First that and now this.'

'Do you know the name of the boyfriend?'

Margaret thought for a moment. 'Craig, I think. His name was Craig. Don't know his second name.'

'And what about the neighbour he left with?'

'Oh, I know her name, all right. Fiona Wallace. Think they moved down south somewhere, London or thereabouts. Strange woman. Why he would ever want to leave a lovely young girl like Kimberley for a trollop like Fiona Wallace, heaven knows.'

'So, you knew Kimberley quite well?' Margaret nodded. 'Quite well, yes. She would pop in for coffee occasionally, or I would pop upstairs. Take parcels in for each other. That kind of thing. Now and then, we'd have a good natter with one another.' 'Last night. Did you hear anything unusual?' 'I'm not sure. I was saying to Claire, I was fast asleep, but I woke up suddenly, you know when you think you hear something? It was like a door slamming or a thump – some kind of commotion. I thought it could have been my imagination. Just went back to sleep.'

'And would you know when that was roughly?'

'It was in the early hours; that's all I know. I didn't really think anything of it at the time, to be honest. As I said, I went back to sleep eventually. Though it is quite unusual to hear any noise here, I have to say. We're all quite respectable in this close. Kimberley was never one for bringing people back. Not that I spied or anything. Just sometimes, you can't help but know about each other's business. No, more often than not, I'd hear Kimberley come home from work around six, and that would be that.'

'And she worked in the bookmaker's, is that right?'

'Yes, just across the road. Fred Burnett's. I sometimes went in myself for the odd flutter and to say hello.'

Patterson glanced over and made sure Simpson was still noting everything down. Pettigrew continued with her own questions. 'Margaret, you were also saying about this man you saw running down the stairs this morning.'

'Yes?'

'What else can you remember about him?'

Margaret sat up in her chair, trying to compose herself, remembering. 'He was in a right state. Practically ran into me! Quite a shock, I can tell you.'

'Did he say anything to you? Or you to him?'

'No, nothing. We just looked at each other. He stopped in front of me, stared at me for a moment and then continued running down the stairs.'

'What did he look like?'

'He looked like a student, actually. Thick black hair. Brown eyes, Not thin, bulkier. I think. He looked suspicious.'

'Suspicious in what way?'

'I don't know, just shifty, flustered – like he was up to no good. That's why I went upstairs.'

Patterson cut her off; he was more interested in facts than impressions. 'What height would you say he was?'

'Not tall; quite small actually,' Margaret said, nodding towards Patterson.

'Small? How do you mean small?'

'Well, not small, that's not the right word. Short, say about five-seven or five-eight then. Not tall.'

'What else?'

'Could have done with a shave. His eyes were red. Like he'd been up all night.'

'What was he wearing?'

'A grey jacket if I remember, dark trousers perhaps; I don't know, it happened so quickly. Oh, but he also had a blue shirt on, a dark blue shirt if I remember correctly.'

'And you said he seemed in a right state, flustered?'

'Oh, aye, that's right. Like I said, I knew there was something wrong immediately.'

'But you'd never seen this man before?'

'Funnily enough, his face looked slightly familiar, but I can't picture where I may have seen him.'

Simpson chipped in. 'Maybe he lives in the neighbourhood.'

'Maybe, that could be it, but I don't know. It changes so much around here. No one seems to want to stay in one place nowadays. Margaret brought her hankie up to her eyes again. 'You see it on the news, all these murders, but Kimberley... She had her whole life ahead of her...'

As much as Patterson was interested in what Margaret had to say, he knew Pettigrew would be better at getting answers while he went back upstairs.

'OK, Mrs Addington, Claire will stay with you a little longer, but I'll need you to come down to the station later if you can. It's obviously important we find this man as soon as possible. We'll need you to look at a few photos and give a statement.

Margaret nodded. Patterson stood up and indicated to Simpson to follow, then left the flat with Simpson by his side.

Patterson looked at his watch. 'If the bookies is open on Sunday, it should be open soon.'

Simpson looked at his own watch. 'Yep. It's ten to eleven now. By the time we walk down and see, it might be open.'

Patterson agreed. The walk would at least give him time to mull over what he'd learned so far. It seemed that they not only had a definite lead in this murder but, as such, a possible breakthrough in the killing of Susan McLaughlin. Even if it was at the expense of another young woman's life, he had to admit it was good news.

Chapter 26

Bookies

Patterson and Simpson walked out the close into Peel Street. A silver undertaker's van stood waiting across the street. Its driver was tapping the steering wheel and bopping his head along to some music while his assistant read the paper. Noticing Patterson come out the close and give him the thumbs up, the driver nudged his work colleague on the shoulder, and they both made to get out of the van.

Patterson and Simpson walked the short distance down Peel Street onto Dumbarton Road. They ducked under the white-and-blue police tape, where a small crowd of onlookers, mostly kids, had already gathered. From the end of the street, they could see across to the yellow-and-blue facade of the independent bookmakers on the main road where Kimberley had worked. At first, it seemed the shop was closed. Nevertheless, Patterson looked through the glass front doors and could see a middle-aged blonde woman inside, standing behind the main counter. A cleaner was busy wiping the blue plastic seats.

Patterson tapped on the glass door. The blonde woman looked up before pointing at her watch and mouthing the word twelve. Patterson tapped on the door again and held his warrant card against the glass.

The woman was naturally suspicious of anyone arriving early at the bookmaker's wanting to be let in. Particularly as there had been a spate of robberies at bookmakers across the West End in recent weeks. However, she came out from behind the counter through a door, locking it behind her, walked up to the main glass doors and meticulously studied Patterson's ID before giving both officers the once-over again.

She spoke to them, via a muffled conversation, through the door. 'What is it you want?'

'I want to speak to you in relation to one of your colleagues.'

'What about?'

'Listen, can we talk inside?'

The petite woman in her forties rechecked the ID, then finally opened the door and let them in. She locked the door behind them. 'Sorry, can't be too careful these days.'

'Of course. And quite right too,' Patterson said. 'Are you the manager here?'

'I'm the acting manager. How can I help?'

'Is there somewhere we could talk. Sit down?'

'Certainly, there's an office in the back. Come through.'

Patterson and Simpson followed the neat, smartly dressed woman into the small back office under the curious gaze of the cleaner. The acting manager straightened her dark blue skirt as she sat down. 'So is this about the robberies that have been taking place then?'

'No, this is... it's about... can I just take your name?'

The woman said her name was Mrs Julie MacMillan. Patterson continued, 'This is about one of your work colleagues – Kimberley O'Hara.'

'Kimberley?' Julie's face suddenly turned very pale. She knew straight away something bad had happened. Only now did she remember the commotion up the road as she'd been coming to work. Near where Kimberley lived. The police sirens and the road being closed off. 'What about her?' she asked, hoping against hope her instincts were wrong.

Patterson spoke softly. 'I'm afraid we

found Kimberley's body this morning. She died sometime last night. At this moment, we're treating her death as suspicious.'

'Oh, my God. No. Not Kimberley.' Julie's eyes filled with tears. Her hands started shaking.

'Mrs MacMillan, I know it's going to be difficult, but we have to ask you some questions now.'

Julie shook her head, tears slowly rolling down her cheeks. 'Kimberley? But—'

'How long did Kimberley work here?'

'About six months. She's a lovely girl. Good fun, hard-working. We were just out last night as well. Oh my God, this is terrible. Are you sure it's Kimberley?' All the time the manageress answered the questions, she looked intently at Patterson.

'There'll be a formal identification later,' Patterson said, 'but for the moment, we're quite sure it's Kimberley. You said you were out with Kimberley last night?'

'Yes. Kimberley, me and a couple of the other girls. I can't believe it.'

'Did anything happen last night? Anything unusual?'

'No.' Then Julie looked surprised. She remembered something. 'What am I saying? Aye, as a matter of fact, you could say something unusual happened. Kimberley went to talk to a couple of men who came into the pub. It wasn't like her. Kimberley, I mean. We thought she kind of knew these two men. I mean, she did, but... I mean... she didn't... well, we all did, in fact. In a way at least.'

'I don't know what you mean, Mrs MacMillan. You're not making sense. Did you – do you – know who these two men were or not?'

'Well, Kimberley went up to talk to them. One of them was off the TV. That's what I mean by we kind of knew him. The other used to visit the betting shop.'

'TV? I don't suppose you know his name by any chance?'

'I can do better than that. The guy off the TV— Hang on. You won't believe this...' She picked up one of the Sunday papers and turned to a double-page spread where the chiselled features of a well-bronzed man grinned back at them. 'That's him there. What's his name? Stone Johnson! That's it. I couldn't believe it when I saw him in the newspaper this morning. That's a coincidence, I thought. He was in the pub last night. And now this! But... No! Do you think he may have had something to do with Kimberley's death?'

Patterson and Simpson looked at each other in surprise.

'Can I see that?' Simpson took the paper and started to read the article.

As Simpson read, Patterson continued with his questions. 'So you're absolutely sure that this man here, Stone Johnson, was one of the men with Kimberley last night?'

'Oh aye, one hundred per cent. The other girls could identify him as well. I think Kimberley took a fancy to him, to be honest with you. He took a fancy to her as well, I think. You could tell if you know what I mean.'

'So what happened in the pub?' Patterson continued, trying to get back to facts. 'Did you all leave together?'

'No, Kimberley stayed with the two men. I went home to my husband. The two other girls went into town. A club, probably.'

'We'll also need to talk to these other two girls.'

'Yes, yes, of course. Actually, they should both be in any minute,' the manageress said, looking at her watch.

As Simpson continued to read the exposé on Stone Johnson, Patterson pursued his questioning. 'So Kimberley stayed in the pub with the two men, one of which was Stone Johnson?'

'Aye. I know what it sounds like, but

honestly, Kimberley wasn't like that. You know the funny thing is, she seemed to know Harry Potter quite well, but she never said to us she knew him outside work so—'

Patterson interrupted. 'I'm sorry, Harry Potter?'

The woman nodded. 'Oh aye, that's what we called the other man. Not the TV man. The other one. The one who used to come to the betting shop. We used to call him Harry Potter. You know Harry Potter?'

'Yes, I know Harry Potter. That's his real name?' Patterson asked.

'Och no. It was just a nickname. It was just because he looked liked him, a wee bit, at least without the glasses. See, we sometimes gave nicknames to customers. To pass the time, you know? Just a little fun me and the girls have. Here, you know, Inspector, one thing we noticed, in the betting shop, that is, was that Harry Potter was always staring at Kimberley. Kind of creepy like.'

'I don't suppose you would know his real name, would you – this, er, Harry Potter, I mean?'

The manageress shook her head. 'No idea. Sorry.'

Patterson turned to Simpson, who was still reading over the newspaper article. Simpson raised his eyebrows before informing Patterson as to why Stone Johnson was in the Sunday paper.

'It's an exposé. This Stone Johnson is a financial consultant of some kind. Seems a bit of a character, to say the least. And not a nice one at that. Says he runs an investment company, and he's fleeced customers out of thousands of pounds. Whenever someone went to see him, he would always promise to transfer money into their bank account, but never did. He also appears on a cable TV channel as a financial expert. That's why there's the heightened interest in the paper. He's been up to all sorts of wrongdoings, apparently. For instance, according to the paper, at least he's not paid any child maintenance to his wife and kids for two years. And there's no shortage of other people queuing up to have a go at him. Clients mostly, but even his TV colleagues are slagging him off. It seems he's certainly made a few enemies in his time.'

Patterson turned his attention back to the other man seen with Kimberley. 'Could you give me a description of this Harry Potter? I take it he looked a bit like the actor – Daniel Radcliffe, is it?'

Julie nodded, trying to concentrate. 'A wee bit. Actually, for some reason, he looks more like Harry Potter than Daniel Radcliffe. Without the glasses, as I said. I'd say he's slightly chubby, first of all. Dark hair. Smallish. Always came across as a bit of a loner.'

'What about his clothes? Do you remember what he was wearing last night?'

'I do because he was wearing a suit. Well, grey jacket and trousers at least. He still looked creased, mind you. We always were laughing at him because no matter when you saw him, he always looked creased.'

When you say smallish, what do you mean? Five-eight? Five-seven?'

'Five-eight I'd say.' Patterson glanced across at Simpson. The description matched the man seen running away from Kimberley's flat this morning.

'You say you and your two colleagues left Kimberley with these two men, Stone Johnson and this Harry Potter, in the pub. What was the name of the pub again?'

'The Fox and Hounds, Castlebank Street.'

Patterson looked surprised. 'The Fox and Hounds? A bit rough there, is it not?'

'Oh, I know, but Tracy's – Tracy's one of the girls who works here – Tracy's uncle is the manager there, so we get cheap drinks. And the lounge isn't that rough... you know... they have karaoke and things.'

'Karaoke?' Patterson looked up at Simpson.

Julie shook her head again. 'My God. I still cannae get ma head round it. Poor Kimberley…' She started to cry.

Patterson looked at Simpson once more. They had enough to be getting on with at the moment. 'OK, Mrs MacMillan. Thanks for your time. One of my colleagues will be along later to ask a few more questions.'

'Is it all right if I take this paper?' Simpson asked.

The woman nodded, still trying to comprehend that her young work colleague was dead. She walked the two detectives to the main door, where a couple of other girls stood outside, waiting to be let in.

Realising Patterson and Simpson were police officers as she slipped inside the shop, one of the girls asked their manageress anxiously, 'What's the matter? Don't tell me there's been another robbery?'

Julie ushered them inside, crying. 'Officer, the other two girls who were out with us last night, Tracy and Jade. Do you not want to talk to them now?'

'Not yet. We will do. I presume you won't be opening the shop today.'

Julie shook her head. The girls looked at their acting manageress, confused.

'If you'd all like to stay here for the morning, though, it'd be much appreciated. I'll send down a colleague later to ask you all a few more questions.'

Julie nodded before closing the door and turning to her colleagues. Looking back through the glass door, Patterson noticed one of the girls put her hand to her mouth as Julie started speaking.

Simpson turned to Patterson. 'Don't you think we should question the other two girls now?'

Patterson shook his head. 'I'd rather Claire do it. She has a knack for getting information. Besides, we've got other things to do right now. I want you to get this Stone Johnson's address. Head back to Kimberley's flat and see what else you can gather. Tell Claire to get down here and interview the work colleagues after she's finished with Mrs Addington. I'm going along to the Fox and Hounds. See if they can tell me any more. I'll pick you up in around half an hour, and then we can pay this Stone Johnson a visit.'

With that, Patterson made for his car as Simpson headed back to the crime scene.

Chapter 27

Macaroni Pie

Patterson drove the short distance to the pub on Castlebank Street in Yoker. As Patterson arrived, a man came out of the pub's front door to put out a sandwich board. 'Today's Menu' was scrawled in chalk, informing customers that the 'Plat du Jour' was macaroni pie. As Patterson exited his car, he called across to the bearded, heavily built man.

'Hello there. Are you the manager?'

The manager didn't admit to this immediately, glancing over Patterson's garb before replying, 'What if I am?' He realised Patterson probably wasn't from *The Good Food Guide*.

Patterson walked over and showed the man his I.D. 'My name's DCI Patterson, Partick CID. Can I have a word inside, please?'

'What is it you want?'

'If we could talk inside.'

The manager reluctantly led Patterson into the cool, dark interior behind the front entrance. The door closed behind them with a long, tired creak, and the two men sat in one of the booths. Patterson could smell the lingering aroma of stale beer, which the constantly whirring air conditioner could never completely shift. The lounge wasn't as bad as Patterson remembered it from his previous visit a couple of years back. Still a dive, but now a dive with carpets.

He turned his attention back to the manager. 'Were you working last night?'

'Aye.'

'Just yourself?'

'Naw. Christine, one of the barmaids, was on.'

Patterson brought the paper out and showed him the photo of Stone. 'Do you remember seeing this man at all?'

The manager squinted before nodding. 'Aye, I think I do, think he was here in the lounge, in fact, but Christine would know better. I mostly serve the public bar.'

The manager turned and called across the bar counter without getting out of his seat. 'Hey, Christine, come out here a minute!'

A few moments later, an attractive but

harassed-looking woman in her thirties with short dark hair came into the lounge holding a dishtowel.

'This gentleman is a police officer. He wants to know about someone in the pub last night.'

She came across, and Patterson showed her the newspaper.

'Do you remember him?' Patterson asked.

'Ah, sure do,' Christine answered. 'Good-looking bugger. Bit of a rarity around these parts. What's he doing in the paper?'

Patterson didn't answer but asked another question. 'Was he here by himself?'

'Naw. He came in with this other guy, pissed out his head he was – this other guy, I mean.'

'What did this other guy look like?'

'Dark hair, small, chubby.'

'And did anything happen?'

'They started chatting to a woman.' Christine looked at her manager to explain further. 'They were chatting to Kimberley – you know, Tracy's workmate?' The manager nodded, and Christine continued. 'This guy left with her around eleven, I'd say.'

'So, this person in the paper, Stone

Johnson, left the pub with Kimberley around eleven? Are you sure about that?'

'Oh aye, they phoned a minicab.' Christine walked over to the public phone and returned to give him one of the taxi's business cards. 'Yoker Cabs. Check with them.'

Patterson took the card. 'What about the other guy?'

'Blootered he was, but I'd stopped serving him by then. In any case, he fell asleep at the table, so I let him sleep it off for a while. Had to wake him up eventually, course. Put him outside about midnight.'

'Did you call him a taxi?'

'Naw. I offered like. He mumbled something about just living around the corner. Tottered off into the night.'

'Could you describe him a little more?'

'Dunno. Five-foot nine. If that. Roundish face. Not much to add. Dark thick hair. Kind of scruffy. Looked in his mid-twenties, I'd say.'

'What was he wearing? Do you remember?'

'Light jacket, possibly grey or cream – didn't fit right, too short. Can't think what else. Not too sure, to be honest. Hang on, a blue shirt. He had a dark blue shirt on. I remember cos I thought it might have been a Rangers top at first.

Wouldn't have served him if it was.'

'He wouldn't have been allowed in the pub,' the manager added, wanting it known that apart from having a plat du jour, his pub was a respectable joint that didn't allow football tops.

'Did anything else happen last night with them? Any arguments or anything?'

'No, not that I can remember, like I say,' the barmaid continued, 'this Stone person in the paper there and the other guy were sat at the table with Kimberley.' The barmaid tried to remember more. 'As I said, she came in with Tracy and her mates from the bookies.'

The manager interrupted. 'Tracy's my niece.'

'Aye, Tracy is Frank's niece, so they usually come here for a drink on a Saturday before they head off into town. Ah, hudnae seen they two guys before, though. Hud you, Frank?'

'Naw,' Frank agreed. 'Me neither. Strangers.' Frank was beginning to get worried about his niece or Kimberley. Something had happened.

Patterson nodded. He had to call Yoker Cabs to confirm where Stone and Kimberley went. He hoped they kept records, but they were one of the dodgier private cab firms in the city. And that was saying something.

'OK, well, thanks for your time. One of my colleagues will be down later to ask a few questions. Are you here all day?'

''Fraid so.' The manager rose at the same time as Patterson. 'Till four at least. There's nothing bad happened, I hope?'

'I'm afraid Kimberley O'Hara was found dead this morning. We're treating her death as suspicious.'

Christine gasped. The manager swore. 'Fuck. Ye're kidding me. Kimberley? She can't be! My God. What a waste of a beautiful wee lassie! What about Tracy?'

'She's fine. I just seen her turning up for work at the bookies. As you can understand, we're trying to get as much information as we can at the moment, piece together Kimberley's last movements. As I said, though, a colleague will be down later to ask some more questions. So if you make sure you stay here for the next couple of hours at least... thanks.'

The manager and the barmaid looked at each other without saying anything. As Patterson was walking out the door, however, the barmaid called out to him. 'Here! Wait a minute, I just remembered.'

Patterson turned and looked at her.

'The name of the other man. I know his

name! I asked the guy what his name was, meaning just what his first name was, but he told me his full name. He said Daniel McLeod. I remember cos it was the same name of a guy I went to school with, but it wisnae him. That was his name though, Daniel McLeod. At least, that's what he said.'

'You sure about that?'

'I'd stake a Bacardi Breezer on it. Aye, I'm sure that's his name.'

Patterson nodded. This was another break he gladly welcomed.

'OK. Thanks to both of you. You've been a great help.'

Patterson watched the barmaid and manager put their arms around each other, then walked back outside into the bright mid-morning sunshine. It had been a very productive morning. Now Patterson didn't just have one suspect for the murder of Kimberley O'Hara but two. One who'd left the pub with Kimberley last night and another who was seen running away from her flat this morning – Stone Johnson and Daniel McLeod. However, a lot of questions had still to be answered. First things first – it was time to pay a visit to the home of Stone Johnson.

Patterson pulled his seat belt on, put the car into gear and headed back towards Peel Street. Once there, Patterson sent a uniformed officer up to fetch Simpson, who quickly came down and informed Patterson that Stone Johnson lived in Burnside, an affluent suburb on the southern outskirts of the city. With it being Sunday morning and with a couple of uniforms as backup in a car behind, they made good progress to the address.

Patterson felt as if he was finally close to finding Susan's killer, and he had butterflies in his stomach. It was a feeling of trepidation along with excitement. A case possibly coming to an end and a killer being caught and brought to justice. A thousand thoughts were going through Patterson's mind while Simpson kept quiet beside him, his own thoughts keeping him occupied.

*

After half an hour, they pulled up outside a semi-detached Victorian villa. Patterson and Simpson walked up to the front door with two officers behind them. Patterson didn't expect any trouble, but you could never tell. There was no noise coming from inside the house, but just as Patterson went to ring the doorbell, the door opened, and there stood not only Stone Johnson but someone else too – a man who matched the description of Daniel McLeod.

Chapter 28

Interview Room A

In interview room A, Simpson sat opposite Stone Johnson, who had his rather dapper lawyer beside him. Like others, Simpson had taken an instant dislike to Stone Johnson. There was something false about Johnson, Simpson thought. Perhaps it was just his name or his overconfident manner, but for whatever reason, Simpson just didn't like him. Nevertheless, Simpson asked Stone to go over his version of events once again. So, starting with a sigh, Stone repeated what he'd already said a couple of times before.

Stone said he didn't know and had never met Daniel McLeod before Daniel had turned up at Stone Investments last Thursday. At the appointment, Daniel had explained to Stone that he wanted to invest some of his redundancy money as he'd recently been let go by an insurance firm in town. Daniel said he didn't want to squander the money – it was only around £4,000, Stone said – and thought investing it would be a way to avoid that. Stone had listened to everything Daniel had to say and thought he could indeed help him by investing his money wisely on his behalf. At the end of their half-hour meeting, Daniel had said he'd think about it more but had seemed very keen on making some kind of investment.

Although slightly unusual, Stone, as part of wanting to finalise the investment deal, had invited Daniel for a drink on Saturday. Yes, Stone repeated, it wasn't his standard practice to do this, but the fact was he kind of liked the guy and had felt sorry for Daniel since he was clearly down on his luck.

Once they were out in a city-centre pub, it was Daniel who'd mentioned going to this other pub in the West End. At first, Daniel hadn't mentioned Kimberley, but it was clear later on that she was the reason he'd wanted to go to that particular place. So Daniel had taken Stone to the Fox and Hounds to meet Kimberley O'Hara. Stone repeated that he'd had no idea who this Kimberley was and had actually been wanting to go home, but Daniel had insisted he go with him. So they'd ended up getting a taxi to this really dodgy pub, which Stone immediately regretted agreeing to.

Nevertheless, this Kimberley had been there with her mates, and as it turned out, Stone had immediately hit it off with her. Once

Kimberley's mates left, Kimberley decided to stay on with Daniel and Stone. However, Daniel, having had far too much to drink by this time, had fallen asleep at the table. Kimberley had then invited Stone back to her flat for a coffee, and he'd accepted.

Stone admitted that, perhaps, it hadn't been kind to leave Daniel sleeping at the table like that, but Daniel only had himself to blame. He couldn't handle his drink. So yes, Stone freely admitted he'd gone to Kimberley's flat, though nothing had happened between them because not long after they'd arrived, whilst drinking coffee, they'd ended up arguing. The reason for the argument, Stone said, was that he'd tried to warn Kimberley about Daniel since Stone could sense, having spent the day with Daniel, that there was something creepy about him – and he obviously had a thing for Kimberley.

However, Kimberley hadn't wanted to listen to Stone's warnings, they'd had words, and it was then that Kimberley had literally thrown him out the flat. Stone said he'd fallen and hit his head against the wall on the stairwell landing, then he'd left, hailing a taxi in Dumbarton Road to take him back to his home in the Southside.

Stone had then quickly fallen asleep, and it was only the next morning, this morning, when he'd woken up and turned on the news that he'd heard a woman had been murdered in Partick.

At first, Stone hadn't thought much about it, but the more he'd listened, the more he'd realised – to his horror – that the murder had happened in Peel Street, and he was sure that was where Kimberley lived. When Kimberley O'Hara was named locally, it must have been mid-morning, Stone said, he'd been shocked, but he knew he had to get in touch with the police straight away.

While Stone was still trying to get his head around it all, the doorbell had rung. He'd opened the front door and, much to his surprise and horror, found none other than Daniel standing there. Before Stone had been able to say anything, Daniel charged headfirst into him, knocking Stone backwards onto the hallway floor. They'd struggled, fighting, and Stone said he was petrified. He realised straight away that it must have been Daniel who'd murdered Kimberley and was now going to kill him because Stone was like a witness or something. They'd then fallen into the kitchen, still fighting, where Daniel had grabbed a knife and forced Stone upstairs. Stone had been sure he was going to be murdered too, and upstairs, while in the bedroom, Daniel admitted he'd killed Kimberley.

However, miraculously, before Daniel could kill him, Stone had managed to overpower Daniel, and somehow they'd got talking. Daniel was obviously crazy, completely nuts. Still, incredibly, Stone said he'd persuaded Daniel that the best thing he could do was go to the police with Stone and confess all, which, miracle upon miracle, Daniel had agreed to do. Stone and Daniel had just been heading outside to the police station, which was just up the road, when on opening the front door, who should be standing there but DS Simpson and DCI Patterson.

That was it, Stone said – that was exactly how it all happened.

Chapter 29

Interview Room B

Daniel McLeod was finding it hard keeping it all together as he tried to explain precisely what had happened over the previous twenty-four hours. Every now and then, he would have to take a deep breath, clenching his fists tight together to keep talking and not break down crying.

Nevertheless, Claire Pettigrew listened patiently as, in interview room B, Daniel sat beside the duty solicitor and relayed his explanation in a voice shaking with emotion. Pettigrew then asked Daniel to repeat his story one more time.

Daniel began by saying things had been rough recently. Not only had he just lost his job, but his girlfriend, Deborah, had left him around the same time. It then turned out that Deborah had been having an affair with his boss, the very guy who'd let him go. Daniel also wanted to say that he'd been drinking a little too much recently and started gambling; it was a bad couple of weeks he'd gone through.

So Daniel had been spending quite a bit of money and was now scared he would end up squandering his redundancy payment. It was a few thousand quid he had, quite a lot of money, and he thought he needed to put it into a bank or building society account where he couldn't touch it for a year or two. It was then Daniel had seen an advert for Stone Investments in the local paper. He'd thought it could be ideal, just what he was looking for, so he's made an appointment to go to the office of Stone Investments on Dumbarton Road.

It was there that Daniel had met Stone Johnson for the first time. However, at the meeting, Daniel hadn't liked Stone Johnson; Daniel thought he was smarmy as hell and well suspect. Nevertheless, he listened to Stone's spiel before managing to get away without agreeing or signing anything. And that was that, or so he thought. Then to his complete surprise, on Saturday morning, Daniel had received a call from Stone asking him to go for a drink. Yes, Daniel thought it was a bit weird, and yes, Daniel didn't like him, but still, he was going for a drink anyway. So partly out of curiosity, he'd met Stone at a pub in town, the Second Movement on Sauchiehall Street.

Once there, Daniel regretted it

immediately. Stone hadn't said so explicitly, but it was clear he was after Daniel signing some kind of contract. To be honest, Daniel said, he felt a right mug agreeing to meet Stone, and the whole time he'd been dying to get away from him. Then he remembered something. He knew Kimberley O'Hara, and she'd told him she drank at this pub, the Fox and Hounds, every Saturday after work. So Daniel thought he would go there and decided to invite Stone along, thinking Stone would say no – but, in fact, Stone said yes.

Once they'd arrived at the Fox and Hounds, Kimberley had indeed been there. She'd seemed really pleased to see Daniel, and Daniel had realised that Stone was even more of a problem for Kimberley and himself. Daniel just couldn't get rid of him, so Kimberley and himself could be alone. Then, unfortunately, because he'd had too much to drink, he fell asleep at the table. When he woke up, Stone and Kimberley had disappeared.

He didn't remember much after that, apart from somehow staggering home and then waking up the next morning with a hangover. He'd decided to head down to the local shop early; the only one open at that time in the morning was on Dumbarton Road.

When he was outside the shop, he'd realised Kimberley literally just lived around the corner. So, because she'd simply disappeared the night before, he'd thought he could pop up to see if she was all right.

The door to her close was broken, so he'd gone straight up to her flat. No, he hadn't been there before, but he'd seen her name on the doorbell for 3/1.

Daniel had gone up the stairs and, to his surprise, found her front door was slightly open. He'd had a horrible feeling about it all. It must have been intuition, he said now. He'd knocked on the door and went inside. It was then he'd seen Kimberley lying on the bed. At first, he'd thought she was asleep but quickly realised she was dead. With the marks on her body, it was also clear she'd probably been murdered. Well, Daniel said, his voice trembling, he was in absolute shock.

Of course, he was going to call the police, but then something had come over him, and he'd just sort of panicked and ran out of the flat and down the stairs. In the process, he'd nearly knocked over this elderly woman, and then he'd just walked in a daze along Dumbarton Road, then all the way to the Southside. Then he'd thought about the night before.

Stone. He'd thought about Stone – Stone must have murdered Kimberley. He'd been trembling with rage, out his mind. At the very least, he would go and confront the bastard. So he'd got his address (there was only one Stone Johnson in the directory) and then headed down to Stone's home in a taxi.

He'd had no idea what he was going to do once he got to Stone's place – but as soon as Stone opened the door, Daniel had charged at him, half through fear and half through rage. He was scared as hell because he was certain Stone had murdered Kimberley. They'd fought each other, struggled with one another, but eventually, Stone had persuaded him it was best to go to the police. Daniel had been surprised as hell that Stone had suggested this but readily agreed to it. The police station was five minutes up the road, Stone said. So they went to leave, but as they opened the front door, who should be standing there but DS Simpson and DCI Patterson.

That was it, Daniel said – that's what exactly what happened.

Chapter 30

Superintendent Dunard

'They're both talking bollocks.'

Superintendent Dunard was clearly unimpressed with both Daniel McLeod and Stone Johnson's versions of events. Certainly, it wasn't clear which of the two suspects, if either, had murdered Kimberley O'Hara. Still, given their respective stories, Dunard thought it was likely one of them had.

In front of Dunard, on the opposite side of his desk, sat Patterson, and on either side of Patterson were Simpson and Pettigrew.

Apart from Dunard, all three officers had already formed their own suspicions about who was telling the truth and who wasn't. Simpson was leaning towards Stone being innocent, while Pettigrew favoured Daniel. Patterson, meanwhile, was keeping an open mind. He knew that evidence would ultimately prove or disprove each man's version of what really happened, and it was still early days in that regard.

Likewise, Dunard wanted to review each man's statements and started with Daniel's version of events.

'So let's assume that Daniel did make the appointment with Stone, which Stone doesn't dispute. They meet and then go to this pub where Kimberley is. How well did Daniel say he knew Kimberley?'

Daniel's appointed spokesman Pettigrew answered. 'He said he knew her from the bookies where she worked, and then they met by accident one day in the supermarket. Apparently, it was then that Kimberley told him she usually went to the Fox and Hounds on a Saturday after work.'

'So that's it?' said Dunard. 'That's his full acquaintance with her? He was making out they were good friends. It seems he didn't really know her at all.'

'But he did know her to some degree,' Pettigrew felt the need to add.

'The point is,' countered Simpson, 'if that was Daniel's only acquaintance of her, apart from the bookies and the accidental meeting, how come he knew where she lived?'

Whether by accident or design, Pettigrew

felt she was turning into Daniel's defence lawyer. 'Well, there he admits that when he bumped into her in the supermarket, he saw her afterwards go across the road and into her close. He said he then knew her flat number by her name being on the doorbell downstairs.'

'So he followed her home?' Dunard asked.

'Not quite; she practically lives opposite the supermarket,' answered Pettigrew.

'What I also don't get is,' continued Simpson, 'if he didn't really know her well, how he felt he could go up to her flat on Sunday morning. Who does that?'

Pettigrew didn't have an answer for that, but Patterson filled in for her. 'Well, I would say the shop Daniel went to is as good as right next to her flat. It's possible curiosity did get the better of him. Though it's still one hell of a coincidence, he should decide to go up to see her on the very morning she's murdered.'

'And then when he finds her body, he doesn't call the police? He just makes a run for it?' Dunard said. 'No. I'm not having it. He's either a very unlucky innocent man, or he's more likely guilty of her murder.'

'It has been known to happen,' Pettigrew said whilst everyone else looked at her. 'I mean, it certainly wouldn't be the first time someone finds a dead body, panics and doesn't call the police. We know that logic sometimes goes out the window in a situation like that.'

Dunard shook his head. 'Well, there's something not right about it all. And what about this Stone Johnson? From what I can tell, he's clearly lying as well.'

'Not necessarily,' said Simpson, who was now his appointed defence lawyer. 'I've checked up on much of his story, and it adds up.'

'Such as?' Dunard asked.

'Well, he admits he went to the flat with Kimberley. It's a small point, but we did find two coffee cups in the living room. We have a record of him getting a taxi from Dumbarton Road to his home in Burnside just after midnight. Would a guilty man get a taxi home? He's not that stupid, and according to the taxi driver, Stone seemed annoyed but not in any major, agitated state that you'd expect from someone who'd just committed murder. There's no doubt Stone is a dodgy character, but there's nothing in his past to suggest he's violent.'

'Yet, said Dunard, 'you found both men together this morning in Stone's house. It actually gives a suspicion both men could be complicit in her murder. And now, with both caught together, they're trying to blame each other. Could both of them not have gone back to Kimberley's, and one or both of them murdered her? Or could Johnson have gone to her flat first, and then McLeod joined him? Maybe after a call from Johnson? What gets me is why they would meet up this morning, two men who apparently didn't know each other well. So maybe they did know each other. First, Daniel goes up to Kimberley's, and then he goes to Stone Johnson's? Even when he suspects Johnson is a murderer?' Dunard shook his head again at all the questions he found himself asking. He was also wondering why Patterson was keeping so quiet. 'OK, so let's get your views on where we are, Mike. Who do you think, if either, may be responsible for Kimberley's death?'

'Well, putting all else aside,' Patterson started, 'we have witnesses who say Daniel was paralytic when he left that pub in the early hours, so was he even capable of carrying out the murder? Plus, going by the timings, the murder had probably already taken place by the time he left the pub anyway. We also have CCTV of him in the shop this morning. Why would he go there and then back to Kimberley's flat in the morning if he'd killed her hours before?'

'Because it's the perfect way to cover his steps,' answered Simpson, 'or to see if there was anything he'd left behind?'

Pettigrew still wasn't convinced. 'So why was Daniel clearly distressed when he ran from the flat in the morning? The downstairs neighbour he ran into, Mrs Addington, said he looked in a state of shock. The murder had taken place hours before, and the CCTV of him in the shop this morning shows him to be relatively relaxed. No, sir.' She addressed her comments to Dunard. 'I believe if either of the men is guilty, then it has to be Stone Johnson. Yes, he hasn't a history of violence, but we know Kimberley was killed just after midnight, and the fact remains that Stone was there in the flat at that time or thereabouts. He even admits they had a fight. It's too much of a coincidence. As for Daniel, it is plausible he just wanted to go up and check she was all right. He'd been in her company the night before, he knew where she lived and was practically outside her close by going to the shop. We know it was indeed the only one in the area open at that time in the morning and very popular with the Sunday-morning hangover crowd. The fact he went to Stone's house could also be a sign of his own innocence. I think he did believe Stone Johnson had something to do with her murder and, still not in his right frame of mind, went to see him.'

Simpson couldn't contain himself any longer. 'It's just as possible that Daniel McLeod was angry about Johnson and Kimberley being together. Woke up in the pub, sobered up on the way home, went to her flat just after Stone left and murdered her. Otherwise, we have the timings wrong for her murder, he woke up in the morning, remembered the night before, was angry about Stone and Kimberley leaving him in the pub, went to her flat in a rage and then murdered her.'

All through this, Patterson was still keeping relatively quiet, which Dunard noticed once more. 'So, again, Mike, I want your views on this. What do you think overall ?'

'Well, for one thing, we're missing an important point. We know that whoever murdered Kimberley almost certainly murdered Susan McLaughlin as well, and so far, we've found nothing to link either man to Susan. That's what we have to do now. I think if we find out which one of them has a link to Susan, then we'll find out who murdered both women. We also have forensics to come through, and, for all the circumstantial evidence, there's no direct evidence, at the moment, either man murdered Kimberley. Yes, Daniel was seen running away from the flat, and yes, Stone was in the flat the night before, but I think our best way forward is to see if either or both even have a link to Susan McLaughlin. As of now, we've actually got nothing to hold them on.'

'And both of them haven't any previous?'

'Actually,' Patterson answered, 'There's nothing on Stone Johnson, but it turns out

Daniel McLeod has been arrested on common assault charges.'

'How long ago was this?'

'Last Saturday.'

'Last Saturday! Daniel was arrested for common assault last Saturday?'

'That's what I said, sir, yes.'

'And when you say common assault, did he threaten or actually assault someone?'

'He assaulted someone. He punched a barman in a pub.'

'Any reason why he would do that?'

'The barman told him to put out a cigarette.'

'He was smoking in a pub? Had he not heard of the smoking ban?'

'That's what the barman said.'

'So, was he charged?'

'No, since he had no previous and there was an Old Firm game on last Sunday, meaning they needed as many cells as possible, they let him off with a caution.'

'And before this assault, he has no previous before that?'

'None whatsoever, no.'

'Doesn't that strike you as strange?'

'In what way?'

'Here we have someone who has no previous dealings with the police at all in his life, and yet last Saturday he assaults a barman in a pub. Around a week later, he is brought in for questioning on suspicion of murder? You think that is simply coincidence?'

'Hitting a barman is hardly the same as murder.'

'Of course, it isn't, but it's an indication that someone is beginning to lose control. OK, I want Stone Johnson released under caution and Daniel McLeod kept in.'

Patterson looked at his superior 'Really? Both men could have easily murdered Susan, just because Daniel assaulted someone last week, it doesn't mean he could murder someone the week after.'

'It's not just because of that. Although I do think it's highly significant Daniel was in trouble last week. It's the sign of a disturbed mind or a mind becoming more disturbed. However, the thing is, I think for now, we should also increase the distance between both men. I can't help suspecting that either Daniel is guilty or both men are guilty. That's to say, they were working together in some way. So what I suggest is we release one man and hold the other by creating a distance it could make one of them talk. I get the impression Daniel McLeod is the more likely to crack if we hold him overnight.'

'Sir?' replied Patterson, wondering about the logic of Dunard's logic. Dunard ignored Patterson's clear doubts, lost in running after his own thoughts. 'Personally, I have to say do feel Daniel is more likely to have been involved in the murder of Kimberley O'Hara rather than Stone. I'm not convinced Daniel just happened to go up to her flat this morning. He hardly knew her. Then once he finds her body, he runs away? No, I don't like it. Keep Daniel in and let Stone go.'

'Really, sir?' pursued Patterson. 'Surely, if, as you say, we want to increase the distance or tension between the two men, we should keep both in for as long as we can. Let each one think the other will confess. Plus, there are still a lot of enquiries to be made which will prove or disprove either man's story.'

'No, I've made my decision,' Dunard said. Patterson stood up in disbelief.

'Fine, we'll let Stone go then, but I want it put on record I strongly disagree with this decision.'

'Noted,' Dunard said, bringing the meeting to a close.

So it was that a short time later, Stone Johnson was released under caution while Daniel McLeod was kept in overnight.

Looking down from his office window, Patterson watched Stone standing outside the police station, talking into his mobile and then climbing into a taxi he'd flagged down. He strongly disagreed with his Superintendent's decision to let Johnson go. Yet, he had to be as open-minded as possible. So Patterson did indeed keep Daniel in overnight and asked him more questions. However, Daniel was sticking to his story, and nothing would budge him from it. So the next morning, Patterson decided to release Daniel under caution without informing Dunard.

Chapter 31

Headlines

After being unexpectedly released by DCI Patterson, Daniel stood on the steps of Partick Police station, wondering just what had happened in the last few days. It didn't seem that long ago he was leaving his steady job to go home and have a meal with his steady girlfriend in his nice comfortable, steady life.

Daniel glanced at his watch. It was 6:32 am. At least he knew things couldn't get any worse. Yet, deep down, he knew even that was a lie. Daniel now knew that things could always get worse. Especially when you thought things couldn't get worse, that was when they usually did.

A car pulled up in front of the police station, and the nearside window rolled down to reveal a waving hand and then a sideways head. It was Jamie. The car door swung open.

'Daniel, jump in; I'll take you home.'

A surprised Daniel walked down the steps and got into the car.

'What are you doing here?' said Daniel as he put on his seatbelt, 'and how did you know I was being released this morning?' asked Daniel.

'I didn't. I was passing earlier and, on the off-chance, thought I'd pop in and ask if you would be released any time soon. I explained I was a friend, the desk sergeant made a call, then said you should be released in the next hour, so I waited.'

'How did you even know I was being held here in the first place?'

'Well, that's why I waited for you. I wanted to warn you.'

'Warn me about what?'

Jamie Campbell reached down between the seats and pulled out a folded-up newspaper, which he handed to Daniel. Daniel unfolded the newspaper and was presented with a headshot photo of himself looking guilty on the front page. He immediately recognised the photo as being from his security ID at Campbell and Hill.

Above the photo, it read, *Drainpipe Killer Suspect Revealed.* Daniel's heart pounded as he saw the photo and read the words above.

After the headline, the paper told its readers to turn to pages four and five for the full story. Daniel duly turned to pages four and five and began to read.

Our paper can exclusively reveal that the man arrested in connection with the Drainpipe Killer murders is Daniel McLeod, a 28-year-old from the Partick area of Glasgow. An irresistible curiosity made Daniel read other snippets, although it felt like a foolish act of self-harm.

McLeod, currently unemployed...Neighbours and work colleagues described him as a 'loner'...His office manager Steve Pritchard revealed he recently let him go as he had concerns about the welfare of his office staff...

Daniel read the words as other people, some nameless, some not, popped up to confirm that Daniel had all the hallmarks of your typical serial killer. As far as the paper was concerned, Daniel was already presumed guilty and deserved a whole life sentence. On the right-hand side of page five, there was a separate column with a photograph of a serious-looking Steve Pritchard next to the sub-headline *'I just had to get rid of him.'* It continued, *'I felt I had to protect the other office staff... As office manager, the safety of my crew is always my number one concern...'*

Daniel's vision became slightly blurred as the blood thumped against his temples. He still managed to read on a little further. Steve Pritchard catalogued a series of reasons that made it impossible to keep Daniel on at the insurance firm. Daniel stopped reading, folded the newspaper and let it rest on his lap. He was in a semi-state of shock before another thought struck him. How come there was no mention of Stone Johnson? It wasn't just Daniel who had been arrested on suspicion of murdering Kimberley O'Hara and Susan McLaughlin. Yet, Stone wasn't mentioned at all.

Jamie looked across at his friend. 'I know, mate. It's unbelievable. Luckily, I was out last night and got a late edition. I couldn't believe it when I saw the front page. That's why I came down to the station this morning.'

Daniel still didn't say anything. He was utterly shattered, both physically and mentally. His whole body ached, and he had a splitting, thumping headache.

'Listen,' continued Jamie, 'don't take any notice of it. It'll soon be forgotten about. They don't know what they're talking about. Arseholes.'

Daniel nodded absentmindedly, but his face and name being headline news was his worst nightmare. Besides, did people really think of him like that. A loner? Strange? He always thought most of his workmates at Campbell and Hill liked him.

'I think I just want to get home and sleep,' Daniel said quietly.

'Yeah, course you do.' Jamie said sympathetically.

In no time, they arrived outside Daniel's flat.

Daniel was half expecting a crowd of reporters to be standing outside his close.

When the car stopped, Daniel turned to his friend. 'Do you want to come up for a coffee?'

'Nah, I'll let you get to your bed. Like I said, I just wanted to try and catch you on the off chance and give you a head's up.'

'Thanks.' Daniel opened the car door. 'Hey, what's with the car anyway?'

'Didn't you know I could drive?'

'Yeah, I knew you could drive; I just didn't know you had a car.'

'Actually, it's part of my new job. I left the call centre.'

'Really? Well, I guess some things are back to normal.'

'Yeah,' Jamie said, smiling. 'I'll explain it all another time, you get some kip, and I'll see you later. You can keep the paper.'

'Thanks,' Daniel said sarcastically.

Daniel exited the car and headed to the stairs leading up to his close. Suddenly everything seemed different. He wondered if people were watching him, saying there is that man from the paper. That loner. That man who is unemployed. That serial killer. Part of him felt frightened. Part of him felt like crying. Part of him just wanted to go to bed and sleep forever. He had fallen for it one more time.

Just when you thought things couldn't get any worse, they usually did.

Chapter 32

Suspects

The next day Patterson walked down the back-corridor stairs of the police station, having just come from Dunard and a dressing down. One more stunt like letting Daniel McLeod go without permission, Dunard had told him, and Patterson would face a disciplinary hearing. Patterson hadn't responded for fear of saying something he might regret. Yet he was still bemused as to why Dunard had wanted to let Stone go in the first place and keep Daniel in. Either keep both in or let both go, he thought. Especially if there was a possibility both were acting together. Still, he let Dunard have his moment of indignation with the dressing down while inwardly thinking, as always, that the sooner his superior retired, the better.

Patterson came to these fire-exit stairs when he needed a moment to calm his nerves and to escape his colleagues. No one ever used them unless there was a fire drill which was quite rare. Patterson stopped on the landing between the second and third floors and looked out the large plate-glass window. His view was of Glasgow's Southside, towards the dockside warehouses of Govan and further south towards Cardonald and Pollok. Patterson felt agitated again, but it wasn't simply anxiety. Kimberley O'Hara's murder had been a development Patterson had dreaded. He now had two crime scenes to investigate, even if, with this second murder happening, two clear suspects had come into view. Since the murder of Kimberley, he'd also been given an additional number of officers to work on the case, and this was a big help, albeit an additional responsibility as well.

With the murder investigation of Kimberley O'Hara still gathering momentum, Patterson thought back to the murder of Susan McLaughlin. He thought about some of the people she'd known. Had Patterson already met Susan's murderer and, therefore Kimberley's murderer too? And if so, who was it? In addition to Stone Johnson and Daniel McLeod being prime suspects in Kimberley's murder, other people still had his interest. People like Susan's landlord Zach Papadakis or Demetriou, or whatever he was calling himself that day. Patterson strongly suspected that Zach wasn't giving Susan a lower rent simply out of the goodness of his heart. Had he been getting sexual favours from Susan in return? He'd already gathered from multiple sources that Susan wasn't as innocent as he'd first believed her to be. There was a darker side to this angel. And Patterson suspected Zach was just as shady as his father had been. Could something have then happened between Zach and Susan that meant he had killed her?

Patterson had Simpson checking other tenants of his, namely young women who Zach could have a similar arrangement with. If Patterson could prove that the relationship between Zach and Susan was more complicated, then a possible motive for her murder could emerge. Granted, Zach had an alibi for the night Kimberley was murdered, but on the night Susan was killed, he said he was asleep at home with his family away for the weekend. Very convenient. Zach kept himself in good shape too. If anyone could have climbed that high up a drainpipe, he was sure the athletic Zach could.

Then there was Blair Travers, the so-called vet guy. He still seemed like an annoyance more than anything, but perhaps Patterson was underestimating him. Travers had an alibi for the night Susan was killed. He'd been at his parents' house, which his parents had verified. Yet, the large and luxurious detached villa, which was the family home, was big enough for Travers to sneak away undetected late at night. Plus, Travers clearly seemed fixated on Susan. From his computer hard drive, he'd been searching for her on social media. As McKinnon said, though, luckily, Susan's online presence was limited. Had Travers climbed up that drainpipe with the intention of raping Susan but ended up killing her? Yet, if Travers did kill Susan, then what motive had he for murdering Kimberley? Had he even known Kimberley? Efforts had been made to find out if Travers had been hassling Kimberley as well. However, so far, those efforts had drawn a blank. Still, it was possible both women rejected him in some way. Then again, did both women reject Zach?

Patterson then thought of another suspect, Marcus Sepp. Like Zach, this was an athletic man who could have not only climbed a drainpipe but easily overpowered Susan. If he got on top of her, there was nothing Susan could have done to save her life. Patterson also knew that Sepp was hiding something, and a little more probing would hopefully turn up what that secret was.

He then thought of Stevie, Davy McGregor's flunkey. It was clear that Stevie liked Susan, at the very least, and with Susan going off with McGregor, could that be why Susan was murdered? Or was it actually McGregor himself who Patterson should be concentrating his efforts on? After all, McGregor was a known criminal, the only one out of all the suspects. He had a violent past as well as a violent present.

He had an alibi, but as with all the suspects, those alibis could easily be faked. Had Susan done something which meant McGregor had lost his temper, lost control? Had McGregor sussed that Susan was using him rather than the other way around? Had that hurt his pride? Was that a strong enough motive for murder?

Another suspect who intrigued Patterson was the manager of the vet's surgery where Susan worked. Andrew Williams. The relationship between Susan and Williams was more than he was letting on, and there was a reason for that. Patterson suspected Susan and Williams knew each other intimately, and something had happened between them. As of yet, he just didn't know what. Patterson had delayed bringing Williams in for questioning, but he knew he needed to do so soon. Maybe in the pressured atmosphere of an interview room, Williams would reveal more than he had already.

Patterson thought of all these suspects as he looked over the southern Glasgow skyline. His thoughts were interrupted when he heard a door below open. Someone started to walk up the stairs. This was such an unusual event – usually, no one used these stairs. Patterson made to casually walk downstairs when he saw that the person walking up was none other than Emma Booth.

'Emma, what are you doing coming up this

way?'

Booth smiled. 'I remember you mentioned you came here when you needed a bit of peace and quiet. I couldn't find you anywhere else. So I thought I would try here.'

'Why, what's happened?'

'Oh, nothing's happened. I was just concerned about you.'

'Concerned? Why would you be concerned?'

'I just...'

Patterson and Booth were close to each other now. Very close. Booth put her arm around Patterson's waist and gently kissed him on the lips. Patterson's initial surprise made him hesitate for a moment, but then, surprising himself, he found he didn't resist. Instead, he put his arm around her in turn, pulling her closer. They were suddenly kissing more passionately with her hands searching, reaching down, and she was pleased to feel that Patterson was already excited and responding. Patterson's lips brushed against her neck, his hand on her breasts, and then they were both tugging at each other's clothes before Patterson suddenly stopped and pushed her away.

'Emma, I can't.' Booth initially ignored this and reached for Patterson again. 'I know you want to, I've seen the way you look at me.'

Patterson relented again, momentarily giving in to his desire before pushing Emma back. 'Seriously, Emma, we can't do this.' Part of Patterson wanted nothing more than to continue, yet a deeper, stronger part of him resisted. It was a voice in his head saying no over and over again. You mustn't, and it was this voice that had quickly gained dominance and led to him regaining self-control. Patterson began to tuck his shirt in, praying no-one would choose that moment to unexpectedly enter the stairwell. He avoided Booth's gaze lest he should be tempted again.

Booth's desire had grown over the previous weeks. She felt so attracted to Patterson and felt he was just as attracted to her. However, it wasn't just desire, part of her wanted to prove a point. Booth liked to do the unexpected but also wanted to show Patterson her control over him. Yet perhaps this wasn't the right time. But she knew there would be another time, that she just had to be patient. She tried to gather her thoughts and feelings, her own self-control and resist the desire she felt. She leaned against the wall and reluctantly began to tuck her blouse in and straighten her skirt and her hair.

'This isn't me, Emma. It would be - he searched for the right word - immoral. It wouldn't be right.'

'Wouldn't it?'

'No, it wouldn't.'

'Don't deny you are attracted to me?'

'Enough. I have to go. I—' With that, Patterson brushed past her and almost ran down the stairs, leaving her in the corridor. Booth watched him go down the stairs. Why did he have to be so righteous about everything? Immoral? Really? Yet part of her knew that despite his denials, Patterson liked her, wanted her, as much as she liked and wanted him. Part of her was determined that, no matter what, one day, she and Patterson would be more than just colleagues.

Chapter 33

Stonelaw Road

Despite everything that had happened to him these past few days, Stone still felt optimistic about the future. He could always turn a negative into a positive. Even though that skill had been tested to the limit in the last few days, he felt all that had occurred was an opportunity he could exploit in some way. After all, with him diverting the newspapers' attention onto Daniel whilst managing to keep his own involvement in the murder enquiry quiet, the media hadn't been chasing him up just yet. Granted, he was still getting hassle regarding his financial affairs and because of the exposé in the Sunday paper, but he'd thrown these enquiries onto Greg. It was about time his agent did something to earn his money.

What was more worrying for Stone was that he still hadn't heard anything from the BBC. Details about the new show should have been finalised in the last week or so. Not only that, as far as he was aware, he still didn't have a co-host. Yet even this BBC silence could be taken as a good sign rather than a bad one. No news was good news, he tried to convince himself. Maybe they were just comprehensively working things out before getting back to him.

So, taking everything into account, Stone still felt he was in control of his own destiny. When the time was right, he would reveal to the press his own police questioning drama and his grief at knowing Kimberley O'Hara, a woman he'd met briefly but who made a great impression on him. It would be a case of taking the initiative and clearly stating he was a completely innocent victim, accidentally caught up in the wickedness of the real murderer Daniel McLeod.

As part of his quest to make his life appear as normal as possible, Stone decided to take an early evening stroll down to the shops from his home in Burnside. Why shouldn't he? Should he change his life just because of the paparazzi? So what if he got the odd stare or comment shouted? Fucking peasants. Besides, fresh air was something he appreciated even more after his hellish Midnight Express experience at Partick police station.

So Stone left his home and walked down Stonelaw Road. Traffic was quiet, the sky a pleasant light blue, and the most noise Stone could hear was birds chattering away to each other hidden in roadside trees.

As he reached the top of a hill, a white transit van pulled up alongside him, and the driver – a man in his twenties, wearing a blue baseball cap with NY imprinted on the front – leaned over towards the nearside window and gestured towards him. 'Excuse me, mate, ye don't know how I get to Rutherglen High Street from here, do ye?'

Stone stepped towards the van driver to tell him it was straight ahead and just on the left. However, as Stone moved towards the van, he felt a hand twist his arm behind his back and another black-gloved hand go over his mouth. At the same time, the side door of the van quickly slid open with a whoosh, and Stone was thrown inside head first.

Chapter 34

The Search

With Stone Johnson and Daniel McLeod now both released pending further enquiries, it was once again time for Patterson and the team to re-evaluate where they were with the murder investigation overall. So far, there was still nothing whatsoever that connected either man to Susan McLaughlin, and that was a major problem. With no forensic evidence tying either man to either murder, the team needed to regroup and find another line of attack. So now they concentrated on the murder of Susan McLaughlin and the one previous line of enquiry that might still bear fruit – that Susan was a regular and enthusiastic visitor to karaoke bars across town. It was almost certain Susan knew her killer, and it was just possible that Susan might have met her murderer through the Glasgow karaoke circuit.

So it was that previous efforts in this line of enquiry were stepped up. Every bar known for holding karaoke nights in Glasgow that hadn't already been visited, particularly in the

West End and the city centre, was contacted. CCTV was obtained and studied, especially on or around the date that Susan was murdered. Every establishment was visited by officers asking if any staff recognised or remembered Susan.

Following on from what Stevie had said about Susan thinking about entering one of the national talent contests that regularly pulled into town, one new, possibly important piece of information was collected – Susan had indeed entered a national TV talent contest that had been held at the Clyde Auditorium, otherwise known as the Armadillo. More than that, the audition date was the 19th of July. The day that Susan was murdered. Coincidence? Patterson knew all about coincidences. At the very least, he now knew why Susan seemed excited when her mum spoke to her on the Friday. Throughout the investigation, it was apparent that Susan liked to keep secrets. Yet, the fact she had managed to keep this audition a secret was quite something. Susan hadn't told anyone about it and had managed to keep it a secret, even from her mother. At the same time, Patterson was disappointed no attendees had come forward to say they had recognised Susan from the audition.

'Right,' said Patterson to McKinnon, 'We need a list of everyone else who attended the audition at the Armadillo on that day checked and double-checked. Everyone who has a criminal record first of all, with priority on those living in Partick and the West End.'

Patterson knew he could rely on McKinnon to do a good job, and later on, in the afternoon, he checked up on how McKinnon was doing.

'Found anything of interest yet, Brian?'

'Oh aye,' McKinnon said. 'Among our budding stars attending that day, I've already identified two child abusers, countless convicted for GBH, burglary, you name it. It seems our criminal fraternity is dying to show the other hidden talents they have. Having said that, I haven't found anyone so far with an address in Partick or the West End who's known to us, but I should have this list complete by sometime this evening.'

'Good,' said Patterson. 'Once you have some names, I want you to get them to me ASAP. Then once you've finished that, both Pettigrew and yourself can go through the audition tapes to see if anything else of interest crops up.'

Patterson went back to his office, shut the door, sat behind his desk and let out a sigh. He wasn't only thinking about the case but also about Stephanie, as always. He took a deep breath as he once again tried to calm his nerves. Stephanie had been even worse than usual these last few days. He wondered how much longer he could carry on.

Patterson also thought about Booth. He hadn't seen her since the 'incident' on the stairs and assumed she was avoiding him. Apart from anything else, the situation between them wasn't doing the investigation any good. He needed to talk to her and get everything straightened out. Just in case she was in any doubt. If worse came to the worst, he could always have her transferred. Although would that be right? He was as much to blame as her. In the meantime, he sat at his desk and tried to calm himself down. His anxiety, that inner pressure, was building again. He went to drink the cup of water on his desk before realising his hand was shaking so much he wouldn't be able to hold the cup. Everything seemed to be coming to a head, and although some excellent progress was being made in the investigation, with more than one definite line of enquiry, now he just wanted this case to be over with and the double murderer caught. At that moment, though, he felt the world was on his shoulders, and there was nothing he could do but continue to take deep breaths, focus on the job and try to calm his anxiety down. He also hoped the double murderer didn't become a triple murderer anytime soon.

Chapter 35

Three Pairs of Legs

When Stone regained consciousness, he found himself sitting on a freezing, dust-covered floor in a large, bare room. Spiderwebs were hanging in the corners of the ceiling, and he could see a couple of boarded-up windows. Stone quickly sensed his hands were tied behind his back, and his legs were bound together. Yet it was only as he tried to cough that he also realised there was tape over his mouth. He breathed audibly and with difficulty through his nose and shivered in the cold as he tried to figure out what the hell had just happened.

There was a flash of memory of him getting thrown into a van – yet nothing else after that. Just the single scene of his head hitting the dark grey metallic floor playing over and over.

Coming back to the present, he was now aware of the wind howling outside, and one of the boarded-up windows let in a chink of light where he could make out a slice of darkened grey sky outside. Turning his head as best he could, he saw a light-green wooden door, the paint faded and curling in strips. As he continued getting his bearings, he knew he had to get out of there fast.

However, as he tried to move, he involuntarily fell over onto his left side, so he was now lying sideways with his left cheek pressed against the freezing cold floor. He breathed dust in through his nostrils and, for a moment, panicked he would suffocate. Trying to regain his focus, he slivered like an overweight snake very slowly towards the door. He didn't get far before the same door opened.

'He's awake,' a voice – grainy, hard and somehow stupid – called through to the other room. Stone tried to look up to see who it was but could only make out a pair of dirty jeans and even dirtier old-school trainers. A more distant shuffling could then be heard, and Stone could now make out three pairs of legs, two in jeans and trainers, one in a pair of green trousers which seemed to be flares matched with bright red shoes.

As Stone contemplated the gaudy shoes, he felt a hand grab him by the shoulder, pull him upright and drag him back to where he came so that his back was leaning against a wall.

Having a better view now, Stone didn't like what he saw. The man in bright red shoes had a power drill in his hand. The man to his left was carrying a baseball bat, while the other to the right had a knife in one hand and a dirty white towel in the other. It was the man in the red shoes who worried Stone most, though, and not just because he was the one with the power drill. Apart from the dodgy foot attire, he just looked more dangerous for some reason. It was as if his natural skin tone was violent.

'We're gonnae untie ye and take the tape aff yer mouth. So don't fucking move and don't open yer fucking gob!'

Although it was Baseball-Bat Man who gave this command, it was obvious Power-Drill Man was the guy in charge. The grey masking tape was then ripped off Stone's mouth by the Knife-and-Towel Guy like Stone was having his face waxed at a very down-market health club.

Yet Stone knew full well this definitely wasn't a health club. In fact, if Stone had looked more closely at the floor, he would have seen dried bloodstains. Even more closely, he could have spotted some teeth and tiny bits of flesh, cured over time. That was because the isolated cottage Stone was now visiting was where Red-Shoes Man conducted his interviews. Interviews which were more Guantanamo Bay than Partick police station.

Red-Shoes Man spoke for the first time.

'How's it going, Stone – ye all right?' His voice was surprisingly cheerful and friendly. Stone wasn't to know the man talking was Davy McGregor, aka Chuckles.

McGregor had received an anonymous phone call earlier that day tipping him off that Stone was the main suspect in Susan McLaughlin's murder and had immediately arranged the van napping.

'What is it you want?' Stone asked with some difficulty since his mouth was so dry his tongue stuck to the top of his mouth.

'Good question,' McGregor answered. 'A little birdie tells me you had something to do with the murder of a lovely wee lassie Ah had the pleasure of knowing. Word has it, you're the lowlife that killed Susan McLaughlin.'

'Susan McLaughlin?' As DCI Patterson had earlier asked Stone if he knew the same person, Stone had a feeling of déjà vu. He shook his head and gave the same answer he'd given the police. 'No, I don't know her.'

McGregor sighed, conveying just how disappointed he was by the answer. He pointed the drill at Stone like it was a 50's sci-fi gun. 'Aye, anyway, before Ah do some DIY on ye, Ah want you to tell me how you murdered my Susan.'

'Listen, I honestly don't know what you're talking about. I told you, I don't even know this

Susan McLaughlin.'

McGregor looked at Baseball-Bat Man. Baseball-Bat Man walked up to Stone and whacked him across the knees, making Stone scream out in pain. Since there was no one for miles around, the noise wasn't a problem.

'See,' McGregor continued as if he was just explaining the rules of baseball, 'what happens here is you answer questions correctly, and we don't do things to ye. Think of it as Mastermind with attitude.' He chuckled to himself, and his two heavies laughed as well, even though, as per usual, they didn't really understand the joke.

'So just tell us. Ah know you killed that Kimberley bird, and whoever killed her killed Susan. Ah just want you to admit it first. I want to hear you say that you murdered Susan.'

'I swear, I really don't know what you're talking about.'

'Ah'll take that as a pass.' McGregor looked at Baseball-Bat Man again and nodded, and Baseball-Bat Man brought the full force of the bat down on Stone's right shoulder.

Stone had never felt such searing pain. He thought he would pass out and half wanted to. Things hadn't gone well for him in recent days. Only hours earlier, he'd been optimistic he could turn everything around. Now that optimism was being literally battered out of him. Was this how his life ended?

He was resigned to the fact that it was.

Chapter 36

Breakthrough

Constable Sarah Mulligan was very excited – it could be the breakthrough the team had been waiting for. The last couple of days, along with others, she'd been reviewing CCTV, and her eyes and mind were feeling the strain. Yet now she'd finally found something.

She moved to enter Patterson's office to tell him the news, but with the phone to his ear and one finger pointed in the air, Patterson indicated she stay out. Only once he'd finished his phone call did he then lower the finger and motion with a flick of his hand for Mulligan to enter. Mulligan did so, finding it difficult to hide her excitement. 'Sir, I've got something. On the CCTV. I think you should have a look.'

Patterson got up out of his chair and followed Mulligan back to her desk.

'This is from outside Woodlands Bar.'

Patterson watched as he saw what looked

like Susan McLaughlin entering the pub.

'I believe this is Susan entering the pub at 7:42 p.m. They were having a karaoke competition that night. As you can see, it's quite busy. We don't have CCTV from inside the pub yet, but I'll check up on that.'

She clicked on another time. 'This is Susan leaving later, at approximately 10:17 p.m., in the company of another man.'

On seeing who it was, Patterson said the name quietly.

'Marcus Sepp.'

The sudden realisation that Sepp had been lying about how well he knew Susan made Patterson surprised, angry and yet excited. He turned to Mulligan.

'What date is this?'

'Saturday the 12th of July.'

'One week before Susan was murdered,' Patterson said. 'Have you shown this to anyone else yet?'

When Mulligan replied in the negative, Patterson called Simpson and Pettigrew over to look at the footage.

Both officers came and stood on either side of Patterson while Mulligan played the clip again.

'Let's get down to Sepp's flat now,'

Patterson said, and there was a flurry of activity as he and his team made to leave the office.

Mulligan made to go as well, but Patterson stopped her. 'I need you to stay here, Sarah. I want you to get the statements Sepp has already given us, plus get in touch with the Home Office again and the Estonian authorities. Check his previous records and make sure there hasn't been a mistake made somewhere.'

Mulligan, unable to hide her disappointment, nodded and sat back down. The bustle of the office suddenly became silence.

She looked up to see Patterson arrive back.

'Forgot to say, that's great work, Sarah. Well done.' He nodded awkwardly before turning to head back down the stairs.

Mulligan smiled at herself and cracked on with what she had to do.

It would turn out later that Patterson had been right to suggest double-checking the information they'd received about Marcus Sepp. There had been a mistake. For some reason, the Estonian police hadn't informed the British authorities that Sepp had been suspected of a violent sexual assault three years ago. Although found not guilty, it was information that could have been helpful. Even after this information was eventually passed on, it had still not come to the attention of the Glasgow investigation until now. Mulligan just hoped the information hadn't come too late.

Chapter 37

Interview Room C

Patterson was relieved to find Sepp at home and pleased that he returned to the police station without too much protestation. A short time later, Sepp sat beside the duty solicitor opposite Patterson in interview room C, with Simpson and Pettigrew observing via a monitor. Sepp had refused the offer of a translator and now sat next to the duty solicitor. So far, the interview had gone much as Patterson had expected it to – Sepp having an explanation for everything and making out he was more a victim than a murderer. Nevertheless, Patterson tried once again.

'Why did you lie about knowing Susan as well as you do?'

Sepp shrugged. 'Why you think? I'm a foreigner. I know you think I kill Susan, but I did not do that. Yes, I see her at Woodlands Bar, but I meet her only one time. One time!'

'Then why did you lie?'

'I just tell you. I know you think I guilty. Yes, I have crime past in Estonia. Little crime past. I meet Susan by chance in pub. We see each other before in gym, so I say hello. That is everything.'

'It's not everything, though, is it? You left the pub with her on the 12th of July. We have it on CCTV.' 'Yes, yes, of course, I leave pub with her, so?' 'Where did you go?' 'I walk her home then go home myself. Nothing happen.'

'But you knew Susan well – at least more than you've admitted.'

'I know her little. We get on. We like each other. That is one time I see her outside gym.'

'That night you left the Woodlands Bar, you walked her all the way home to Gardner Street?'

'Yes.'

'So you walk her to the close entrance and then go back to your own flat, or did you go upstairs with her?'

'I leave her at entrance to stairs.'

'Really?'

'Really. After, I walk alone back to my flat.'

'See, the thing is, Marcus,' Patterson said calmly, 'yes, we have CCTV of you walking with Susan to her flat. Yet, we don't have any CCTV of you walking back towards your own flat afterwards. If you say you left her at the entrance to her close, her stairwell, how can you explain that?'

Sepp thought for a moment before answering. 'Sorry, yes, I forget. It is because that night, I walk back through path at side of big road, expressway. Not main road. Not Dumbarton Road.'

'The Clydeside Expressway? You're saying you walked back via the path that runs alongside the Clydeside Expressway?'

'Yes, Clydeside Expressway. There is path at side through park which leads back to my house.'

'Why not just walk back along Dumbarton Road?'

'I can't remember. I just do. I want change. It just as quick.'

'Listen, Marcus, let's save time here. Why not admit you knew Susan far more than you told us before?'

'Because I don't. Why would I deny this?'

'Exactly. Why would you deny it? Because you've got something to hide. Did something happen between you? Is that it? An argument? All you've done so far is lie about how well you knew Susan. It makes me wonder what else it is you've got to hide.'

'I tell you truth now.'

However, the more Sepp talked, the more Patterson suspected that he was lying about everything. It was the same as what had happened with Susan's vet boss, Andrew Williams – Sepp only ever admitted to anything once he was shown proof he couldn't deny. Patterson knew the path at the side of the Expressway, and it did lead back towards Yorkhill. It cut through some obscure parkland. No CCTV. The only possibility was if CCTV on the Expressway itself had picked Sepp up on the edge of a frame. As Sepp continued to deny everything, Patterson tried once again.

'So on the 12th of July, you didn't spend that night with Susan?'

'No, I walk home, I tell you.'

'You did like Susan?'

'Yes – I say that before.'

'So how many times did you see her?'

'I tell you. One time only. I go to this pub, and she sings. I surprised. I recognise her from gym. I have a drink with her, I say I walk with her home, that's it.'

'Honestly? Is that the absolute truth?'

'Yes. Perhaps. I mean, OK. I ask for coffee

with her, her flat, but she refuse.'

'So you asked to go up to her flat for a coffee?'

Sepp looked at his solicitor, who gave him a non-committal look in return.

'Yes, I ask her. She say no.'

'So you lied again?'

'Now I tell you the truth.'

'You've said that more than once before.' Patterson was getting nowhere. He tried to get more out of Marcus, but the Estonian continued to stick to his story and, above all, deny any involvement at all in the murder of Susan. In a moment of sheer frustration, Patterson decided to end the interview there and then and try again the next morning. They would keep Marcus in overnight and let him think things over. Patterson knew, without finding some clear evidence of Marcus's involvement in Susan's murder, they would have to let him go. As with all the suspects now, the key may lie in connecting him to both victims and not just one.

Afterwards, Patterson talked the situation over with Simpson and Pettigrew.

'Well,' Patterson said, 'what do we think?'

'We know that whoever killed Susan probably knew her,' Simpson replied. 'Marcus knew Susan. Whoever killed Susan knew she lived in that flat alone. Marcus knew she was in that flat alone.'

'The same could be said about Andrew Williams,' Pettigrew argued.

'Yes, but whoever killed Susan needed to be physically strong to climb that high up the drainpipe.'

'Again,' Pettigrew repeated, 'the same could be said for Williams – he's relatively fit.'

Simpson shook his head. 'But Sepp goes to the gym regularly and is a strong guy. We also know he was charged with sexual assault—'

'Yet,' Pettigrew interrupted. 'why would Sepp climb a drainpipe if he could have just gone up to the flat? If he was in some kind of a relationship with her? Why risk his life climbing 30ft up a drainpipe in the middle of the night when he could have just rung the buzzer or gone to her door.'

'Because you heard it from Sepp himself,' Simpson replied. 'Susan had already refused him entrance to the flat once, so no doubt she could have done so again. Maybe he walks round the back and sees the drainpipe, the open window and gets to thinking. Yes, he could have gone up to her door but wanted to make it to look like an intruder who didn't know her, so he climbs the drainpipe.'

'Then again, Sepp has previously been charged for sexual assault in Estonia,' said Patterson, 'but Susan wasn't sexually assaulted, and why would he murder her if sexual assault was the motive?'

'Maybe, he didn't mean to kill her,' Simpson replied. 'Maybe he tried to only overpower her, but then he loses it. He goes too far.'

It was beginning to make more sense for Patterson, but they needed more evidence instead of presumption. 'OK,' Patterson said, 'what we do know for now is that Sepp remains our number-one suspect. For the moment, we focus all our attention on whether he had anything to do with Kimberley or her murder. Jack, find out everything about his movements in the days leading up to Kimberley's murder. Claire, I want you to do the same regarding Susan and Sepp. Get Brian to dig up as much background information on Sepp as possible. I want everything focused on Marcus Sepp at the moment. He's been lying to us from the start. All we need now is evidence, proof of his involvement in one or both killings, and we have our murderer. OK, everyone? We're nearly there – let's get on with it.'

As they all rose from their chairs, Pettigrew spoke to Patterson. 'There is one other way you can prove Sepp is our man.'

'What's that?' Patterson asked.

'Get him to confess,' Pettigrew said.

'Aye, I know that already, Claire,' Patterson agreed. 'Don't worry, I'll be having another go tomorrow.' He was quite looking forward to the challenge.

As Patterson, Simpson and Pettigrew went to leave the room, McKinnon came into the office. 'Sir, we've just had a call from the West End Chronicle. They've received a letter from someone claiming to have murdered Kimberley and Susan.'

'So?' Patterson knew these crank letters, in addition to crank phone calls, came in all the time. 'What's so special about this one?'

'He mentioned the red rose found on Kimberley's body.'

Patterson looked at Simpson. 'Come on, Jack, let's visit the West End Chronicle.'

Chapter 38

West End Chronicle

The small office of the West End Chronicle was situated just off Dumbarton Road in Mansfield Street, overlooking the open space of a skateboard park and football field in the centre of a large square.

The editor of the local paper, Joy Bradley, stood next to a desk on which lay the letter purporting to be from the so-called Drainpipe Killer. Bradley and Simpson watched as Patterson put on a pair of polythene gloves before picking the letter up.

'Was it yourself who opened it, Joy' Simpson asked.

Bradley nodded, her inexplicably overlong fringe making her constantly push hair away from her eyes. Curiously, Bradley talked in short sentences as if she was continually editing her own speech. 'Aye, came in this morning. The letter was on the floor. Just by itself. Before the first post. No stamp. Someone must have put it through by hand. The regular post came later.'

Patterson looked at the letter. It was typed on standard white A4 photocopy paper neatly folded in three equal parts. The long envelope only had 'The Editor' typed on it. Patterson picked up the letter and read it out loud for the benefit of Simpson.

Publish this letter. Dear all, It is I who is the Red Rose Strangler, and it is I who killed Susan McLaughlin and Kimberley O'Hara. Yours faithfully, The Red Rose Strangler.

'Well, that was short and sweet,' Simpson said.

Bradley explained why she'd called. 'I know it's a crank. But I thought it best to let you know. Why the Red Rose Strangler?'

Patterson looked over to Simpson, both thinking the same thought. No one knew about the red rose apart from Patterson and his three close colleagues. He had deliberately kept back that piece of evidence for this very reason. Unless there had been a leak, it was almost certain this wasn't a crank. This letter had indeed been written by whoever murdered Kimberley O'Hara and Susan McLaughlin.

Chapter 39

Consequences

Daniel lay on the settee, looking up at the ceiling, thinking about everything and nothing. The last few days had been hard to get through – being suspected of murder, spending time in a police cell for the second time in as many weeks. The first time after he had hit that barman in the pub and the second time on suspicion of murder. He knew that no matter what happened, the consequences of the last few days would be at the heart of everything he would do in the next few weeks and months, possibly a lot longer.

If only he hadn't taken Stone to Kimberley's pub that Saturday night. If only he hadn't decided to meet Stone that Saturday afternoon. If only he hadn't seen Stone's advert in the paper earlier in the week. And even before all that. If only he hadn't started drinking so much after losing his job. If only he hadn't lost his job. If only Steve hadn't become office manager. If only he hadn't started work at Campbell & Hill all those years ago. All this may never have happened. If only. If only he hadn't been born. He realised that the realities of today, tomorrow and everything in the future lay in the consequences of even the most trivial past and present events.

What disturbed Daniel most was seeing his name and photo in the paper after being arrested. It had resulted in Daniel staying in, avoiding the glare of outside strangers who may recognise him as the Drainpipe Killer suspect. Instead, he spent his time tidying the house and trying to keep himself occupied.

Daniel's parents lived down in Lincolnshire, along with his little sister Bryony, his father being offered a job down there just about the time Daniel started at Campbell and Hills. They too had been in touch and told him he should come down south for a time until everything settled down. Daniel said he would definitely do that, but for now, he just wanted to take things as easy as possible.

Daniel was still trying to recover what the papers were saying about him. In fact, could the papers have been right about Daniel? Implying he had all the hallmarks of a serial killer even though he'd been released by the police?

Daniel got up off the settee and walked over to the window.

From three storeys high, he looked down onto the traffic that passed along Crow Road. He looked left, along towards Broomhill Cross, where cars stopped and started at the traffic lights in regulated little patterns. People getting on with their lives. Going to the shops. Mums and dads picking their children up from school. Delivery vans stopping outside shops. Taxis at the taxi rank, waiting for their next fare. Daniel looked out the window at life going on as usual. But that was the problem. In order to see life going on as usual, Daniel had to look out the window.

There was a knock at the door. Daniel waited, wondering who it could be. Jamie? Maybe it was Mrs Carnegie from across the landing who'd been so sympathetic and helpful to him these past few days. Then again, perhaps it was a journalist who had got into the close.

As he pondered whether to answer the door, there was another knock, this time louder than before. Daniel crept towards the living room doorway and peeked his head around to see down the hall. He saw fingers poke through the copper-coloured letterbox. Daniel ducked his head back. Then he heard a voice shouting through.

'Daniel, it's me. Are you in?'

Deborah. Daniel's heart missed a beat. Deborah? He hadn't heard her voice in such a long time.

He listened to the letterbox close with a hollow, metallic thunk as she took her hand back out the opening. He heard her shuffling outside on the landing, so he quietly tiptoed up to the door and looked through the peephole. A concave Deborah – big head, small body – was scribbling a note. He stood there, wondering what to do once more. He had to make a decision. He quickly opened the door.

'Oh!' Deborah looked back at him in surprise before breaking into a smile. 'I didn't think you were in.'

Daniel didn't answer; he just looked at her. It was so strange to see Deborah standing there in the flesh, all real and everything. Apart from when he'd seen her at the butcher's with Steve, she was like a faintly remembered dream. As if she had somehow died and this was her ghost.

Deborah sighed. 'Still talkative as ever, I see... I was just going to leave you a note.'

Daniel nodded, and much to Deborah's relief, he finally said something. 'You'd better come in.'

He pulled the door open, and Deborah

walked through with her head bowed. She stood in the hallway, looking at the open closet door.

She noticed a vacuum cleaner in the hall. 'Been doing some housework? That's good to see.'

Her jokey demeanour seemed forced and awkward. Daniel knew her too well to be taken in by her outwardly chatty attitude.

He led her through to the kitchen, where she stood next to the window with one arm holding on to her large leather handbag, which had an image of an owl stitched on it. It looked back at him with big staring eyes that made Daniel uncomfortable. He was going to ask if she wanted a cup of tea, but this only served to remind him of the day Deborah had left. If only. He wouldn't be more cordial than he had to be.

'So what is it you want?'

Deborah shrugged. 'I just thought I'd pop round. I won't stay long. I just wanted to see you.'

'Right.' Daniel wasn't in the mood to start arguing. However, there was one thing he couldn't resist asking straight away. 'How's Steve?'

'Steve?' Deborah thought about pretending for a moment but didn't. She shrugged again as if to say guilty as charged. 'You know about Steve then?'

'I saw you both coming out the butcher's

one morning in Pollokshaws Road.' Daniel was tempted to ask what had been in the little white bag. Black pudding? 'It was obvious you were more than just friends.'

'I wouldn't know how Steve is now, as it happens. And I couldn't give a damn, in fact.'

Daniel didn't react.

'Turns out he's an arsehole.'

What a surprise, thought Daniel. 'I'd like to say I'm sorry, but you know...' Daniel felt some satisfaction they had at least broken up.

'I know. I don't blame you. You're right to be angry with me.' Deborah sat down at the kitchen table. 'You couldn't make us a tea, could you? I'm gasping.'

Daniel picked up the round, fifties-style pink kettle that Deborah had bought and put its little spout under the running cold-water tap.

'You got enough in? Do you want me to go out and get some groceries for you?' Deborah asked as Daniel plugged in the kettle.

'No,' he replied, trying to keep his voice monotone. He didn't know what to think about Deborah being there. Yet he couldn't help but talk more to her. It was good to talk to someone. 'Mrs Carnegie, you know, from next door, has been really good to me. She's been getting messages for me.'

'That's good of her.' Deborah smiled and looked around the kitchen, pleased to see it was relatively nice and clean. He really had been doing the housework. 'How's your family? Your mum, dad, Bryony?'

'Fine, they've been in touch. Mum is worried sick, but I told them not to worry. I may go down to visit them for a time in a couple of weeks or so.'

Daniel then took two cups and placed them on the table. 'Isn't this what they call the elephant in the room?'

Deborah had a quizzical look on her face. 'What elephant?'

'Oh, you know, the fact I'm suspected of being the so-called Drainpipe Killer, a double killer. The fact my whole life has been in the papers this past week?'

Deborah seemed uneasy again. 'There's no need to explain.'

'No need to explain? Seriously? I've been accused of murdering two people. Aren't you even the least bit curious?'

'Of course, I am but Daniel, I just... I just don't see what there is to talk about at the minute, that's all. The whole thing's silly if you ask me. Believe it or not, I know you're not a murderer.' She laughed. 'You know, when I read the stories in the paper, I couldn't help but start laughing. You, a murderer! You genuinely couldn't kill a fly.'

'I'm still a suspect. Although, at least, I think the detective leading the investigation doesn't think I am.'

'Is that the big lanky guy I seen on TV? Grey hair, nervous type, looks like a vicar?'

Women had such strange ways of describing men sometimes. Then again, it was as good a description as any. 'Yes, him. He's called DCI Patterson. The thing is, though, even if they do find out who did these murders, I've still been in the papers the last few days. Every time I walk down the street, people will know who I am.' Daniel poured boiling water into the two teal mugs.

'No, they won't. One good thing about you not liking to get your picture taken is the only photo the papers could use was that one when you first joined Campbell & Hill about five years ago. If I didn't know you myself, I don't know if I would recognise you. Going by the newspaper photo, I mean.'

She did have a point. 'I wondered how they got that photo. Or is that a silly question?'

'It is. It was Steve, I'm afraid. Sorry. He told me. He kept going on about his newspaper interview for ages as if he was famous. I was so glad to leave him.'

With Deborah sitting at the kitchen table, leaning her elbows on its yellow-and-white-chequered tablecloth and looking up at him, it was like so many times they'd spent before. Now Daniel wanted to tell her everything. The truth was that he'd been through hell recently, yet she was part of why he had been through hell.

He began to talk and was conscious his voice was trembling a little. 'If you want to know the truth, it's been horrible these past few days, really horrible.' He coughed and blew out a deep, controlled breath as he continued to stir the teas.

'Oh, come here.' Deborah quickly stood up and walked over to him. Daniel turned around, and she held him tight in her arms. Daniel laid his head on her shoulder, smelling her perfume. It reminded him of past times – realising, despite everything, that he missed her terribly, more than he'd admitted to himself. She pushed him back to arm's length and looked at him, and Daniel hung his head. She put her hand under his chin and lifted his head up.

'Look at me, Daniel; look at me! You can't let them win. It's not fair. Don't let the papers get to you.'

Daniel turned around and went back to stirring the teas. He wasn't ready for all this. He really couldn't forgive Deborah for what she'd done, and although he missed her, the fact was that she'd left him when he needed her most. He could never forget that.

'That one's yours.' He pointed to a cup, which Deborah then lifted.

She sat back down at the table with the tea, weak as she liked it. Daniel continued to stand against the sideboard, looking down at her.

'You still haven't answered my question. Why are you here?'

'I told you. Because I wanted to see how you are. That's all. I've been worried about you. And I... miss you.'

They talked for about half an hour, and as much as Daniel tried to deny it, it felt really good having Deborah there.

Deborah looked at her watch. 'Listen, I've got to go. I just wanted to see you. I'll give you my new mobile number. I'm staying at Mum's again, so you can call me there anytime.' She got out a piece of paper and scribbled a number on it.

'Yeah, right. I bet your mum is loving this as well. "I told you so and all that."'

'You're wrong, actually. Mum's been sticking up for you ever since I left you. Seriously. You won't believe the grief I've been getting. And she knows fine well you're innocent too. As I said, just don't let the papers get to you. You need to fight this! Oh, and who's this Stone Johnson person, by the way?'

'Just some twat I shouldn't have got involved with.'

Deborah stood up and put her handbag over her shoulder. 'Yeah, well, he looks it. He seems a right creep from what I read.'

'Read?'

'No, I suppose you've probably been avoiding the papers. The papers have now turned their attention to him. You've been bumped. That's another reason you can head outside now.'

'I think I'll still be staying in for a time, thanks.'

'OK, have it your way. Listen, look after yourself. I could bring you some groceries tomorrow if you like after work. I'm working for an employment agency now. And that's another thing. Anytime you feel ready for work, there are plenty of people who are looking out for a hard-working serial killer like yourself.'

She smiled, then went up to Daniel again and held him tight. He didn't resist. He needed a hug.

They walked through to the hallway, where Daniel opened the door to the landing.

'See you, Daniel. Remember: stay positive!'

Daniel nodded as Deborah turned and walked down the stairs. He closed the door feeling better than he had in a long time.

He returned to the living room and sat on his settee. He was still thinking about how he never should have got involved with Stone Johnson when the phone rang.

'Hello?'

'Hello, Daniel? Is that you? It's me.' Me could have been anyone as at first Daniel didn't quite recognise the voice. It sounded muffled, panicky. 'It's me, Daniel,' the voice repeated. 'Me. Stone. Stone Johnson.'

Hearing that name again sent an immediate chill through Daniel's bones. 'What the hell do you want?'

'I wouldn't have called, but the fact is you're the only one who can help me right now.'

'How did you get this number?'

'You gave it to me. Don't you remember? That night…'

That night. Daniel felt sick. Everything within him told Daniel to just put the phone down. Yet this gnawing curiosity meant he couldn't help but wonder why Stone had called him and why he sounded so desperate.

'Daniel, are you still there?'

'I'm still here,' Daniel said, reminding himself he still was.

'Please, I need to talk to you,' continued Stone, as if he was trying to get back with an old girlfriend. 'I just want to meet, that's all. I'm in the Southside at the moment. There's a cafe nearby. The Glaswegian. Eglington Street, just over the bridge. Meet me there in an hour, and I'll explain everything. I promise.'

Daniel didn't need to think about anything. There was absolutely no way in the world he was going to meet Stone Johnson.

Chapter 40

A Letter Holder

Although there was no CCTV directly outside the newspaper premises, there was a small camera positioned inside the office, facing towards the door. That showed the exact time the letter was put through the letterbox: 8:22 p.m. the previous night. Other than that, it gave no clue as to who had posted it, just the letter dropping lightly onto the floor in the half darkness. However, they could now check other CCTV cameras in the wider area for anything or anyone of interest around that time.

In particular, there was CCTV outside the pub on the corner of Mansfield Street and Dumbarton Road, just down from the newspaper offices. If whoever posted the letter came from the direction of the main road, there could be a possibility of identifying the suspect. However, that was still a long shot, as that was only one direction of many the person could have approached the newspaper office from. Nevertheless, they did indeed have some luck.

At 7:20 p.m., someone turned the corner from Dumbarton Road into Mansfield Street, walking past the pub towards the direction of the newspaper office. Of course, this could have been anyone if it wasn't for one thing.

She could clearly be seen holding a letter.

Chapter 41

The Glaswegian

The Glaswegian was a traditional cafe, its long history still evident in its decor and style, which had miraculously stayed the same from the 1930s onwards to the present day. This was even more of an achievement because of all the decay and decline happening in the shops and buildings around it. As larger businesses right along the street closed down and the whole tenement fell into disrepair, the Glaswegian cafe managed to stay open thanks to a loyal following who went as much for the nostalgia as the frothy coffee.

When Daniel arrived at the cafe entrance, the area was fairly quiet. With the boarded-up shops all around, few people were walking down Eglington Street doing any window shopping. Apart from a couple of parked cars and a white van just down the road, it was clear business wasn't booming on this side of the Clyde.

Daniel pushed open the cafe door, which

gave a small tinkled welcome, to see that Stone had already arrived and was sat among a few other customers at various tables and booths. Stone looked rough. Really rough. He had a bruise on his right cheek as if he'd been punched, there were numerous scratches and cuts on his head, and his clothes looked slept in. Stone looked slept in. The super-smooth image that Daniel couldn't help noticing when he'd first met Stone was long gone. Unshaven and with his noticeably unwashed hair and dust-covered suit, Stone was almost unrecognisable. Though perhaps, thought Daniel, this was deliberate. With the newspapers turning their attention towards Stone, maybe Stone was treating every day as dress-down Friday to not be recognised.

Daniel stopped at the counter and ordered a cappuccino. He handed over his money and then sat down opposite Stone, who had a curious half-smile on his lips. It looked as if he might be in some kind of pain.

'You're looking well,' Daniel said with some pleasure.

'Really?' Stone replied, surprised. 'At least that's something. I've not had the best of times recently.'

As Daniel pondered whether to explain he was being sarcastic, the decision to keep quiet was made for him by the woman behind the counter coming round with a whipped light brown coffee in a wide cup and saucer, which she placed in front of Daniel. Stone, meanwhile, sat with a tall glass of cola in front of him, which had a long multi-coloured straw in it.

'So I assume you have an excellent reason for wanting to meet?' Daniel said.

'I have people after me.'

'People? You mean disgruntled investors? Unhappy work colleagues? Debt collectors? According to the papers, you've built up quite a loyal following over the years.'

'No, I mean I have people like… psychopath people, violent psychopaths are after me.'

'Psychopaths is it? So go to the police.'

'I can't.'

'Why?'

'Because I think the police are the ones who put them onto me. I need a place to stay.'

Paranoid as well as desperate, thought Daniel. 'Well, I hope you're not thinking you could stay at my place. Do you really think that's going to happen after all you've done to me?'

Stone straightened up and stared at Daniel with evident anger. Were those tears in his eyes? 'And what exactly have I done to you, eh?'

Stone's raised voice drew a glance from the woman behind the counter. Stone looked towards her, then lowered his voice. 'What have I actually done to you, eh?' he repeated. 'Think about it. I met you for a drink one night. That's it. Anything else was as much your fault as mine. You took me to that shithole in the West End. You're the one that introduced me to Kimberley. You're the one who fell asleep, leaving me and Kimberley to talk. Yes, I went with her to her flat. She invited me. She wasn't your girlfriend. How was I to know you had some sort of weird crush on her? In fact, it's you who owes me, Daniel. If I hadn't met you, none of this crap would ever have happened to me.'

OK, Daniel thought, maybe he could accept, to some extent at least, that Stone wasn't entirely to blame for everything that had happened. Yet, that still didn't change the fact Stone was an untrustworthy arsehole.

'I told you, there is absolutely no way you can stay with me – no chance,' Daniel said emphatically.

'Did I say I wanted to stay with you? Did I? Besides, I can't stay with you. That's what I wanted to talk to you about. I—'

Just then, Stone's mobile rang out with the theme tune to Strictly Come Dancing. He pulled the phone out of his inside pocket, looked at the number, made a confused face to a nonplussed Daniel and then put the phone to his ear. 'Hello?'

As Daniel wondered if he should just walk out of the cafe there and then, satisfied that Stone was indeed in the shit and just needed help, he watched Stone's eyes light up.

'Geneva! Hi!'

Daniel watched on as Stone said a lot of 'uh-huhs' and 'I sees' along with a few 'reallys'.

'Uh-huh, I see,' Stone continued. 'Listen, tell you what, I could come by and see you if you like. I'm just with a friend in the Southside now, as it happens. What's the address again?' Stone did a mime of a pen scribbling in mid-air to Daniel, who, out of politeness, brought out a pen from his inside pocket. Stone took it and wrote down an address on a napkin. 'That's not far. I could be there in a half hour. OK, super, see you shortly, Geneva, bye.'

Stone clicked off the phone and broke into a big smile. 'You know, Daniel, sometimes I really think there is a God.'

At that moment, Daniel was just thinking the opposite. However, he waited for Stone to give an explanation for his sudden renewed faith in a supreme being other than himself.

Stone duly obliged. 'That was Geneva.'

'Geneva?' said Daniel in an entirely

uninterested voice. 'Is that supposed to mean something?'

'Yes. Geneva's a friend, colleague, you could say; she was supposed to be a sidekick on a show I've been offered by the Beeb. I think I told you about it. But anyway, she says she wants to see me and—'

'OK,' Daniel interrupted, 'ignoring the fact that you know someone called Geneva, you can go and stay with her.'

'Exactly! I can stay with her. I could explain everything, you know, all about what's happened. She could put me up for a few days! How great is that?'

Daniel smiled sarcastically. 'Well, I'm glad that's sorted. So I best be going. Good luck with the rest of your life.'

Daniel half rose out of his chair before Stone put his hand on Daniel's shoulder, pushing him back down.

'No, wait, Daniel. You could stay with her as well.'

'Sorry?'

'You could stay with her as well,' Stone repeated.

'And why would I want to stay with her? I've already got a place to stay.'

'OK, listen... see, that's what I wanted to talk to you about.' Stone sucked some of his cola up through the straw and winced. 'Now, I don't want you to lose your temper or anything but just listen. You know how I said there are these psychopaths after me?'

'Yes.'

'Well, they're after you too.'

Daniel sipped at his coffee. It was rather nice. He wondered why he had, not once but twice against his better instincts, agreed to meet with this nutter sitting in front of him. 'Really. They're after me now, are they? And why would these psychopaths not just be after you but me too?'

Stone enthusiastically started to explain. 'See, they thought I'd killed that Susan McLaughlin, you know, the first Drainpipe Killer victim, because they believed I killed Kimberley. But now they think you killed Susan.'

Daniel continued to receive this information calmly. Nothing Stone said could surprise him anymore, and besides, he didn't entirely trust what Stone was saying in the first place. 'So these nutters think I killed Susan McLaughlin?Although, at first, they thought you'd killed her?'

'That's right. That's why I wanted to meet you.'

'I still don't get it. You're saying these people – these psychopaths – are after me now? So we need to go to the police. Right now. Get in touch with, what's his name, DCI Patterson. You need to tell him everything. He can give me, us, protection.'

'The thing is, like I said, I think it's the police who put them onto me.'

'Stone, in case you've forgotten, you were headline news in the papers, as I was. It's nothing to do with the police. You're just being paranoid.'

'I distinctly heard this psycho with red shoes mention Patterson's name.'

'So what?'

'He was talking to these two other loons with him, and I heard him talking about Patterson. Patterson said this, Patterson said that. I swear it wouldn't surprise me if he was the one who tipped them off about me. He seemed to have it in for me.'

'Like I said, you've been all over the papers. It would be nothing to do with Patterson.' Daniel then shook his head. 'OK, listen, let's just say for the sake of argument these nutters think you were responsible for Susan's murder because of what Patterson told them, then why would they be after me?'

'Because I managed to convince them you

murdered Susan McLaughlin.'

Daniel thought about this added information momentarily as he calmly took another sip of his coffee. Many questions were running through Daniel's mind, but he decided to ask the most obvious one first. 'And why did you do that?'

'Because they were going to kill me! One of them had a power drill, for Christ's sake. I had to say something to save my life, and blaming you was all I could think of. But that's why I phoned you as soon as I had the chance. Actually, I was pleased you answered the phone when I called. I thought they could have got you already.'

'So that's why you said I could stay with this Geneva?'

'Yes.'

'Because you think I can't go back to my flat?'

'I don't think that would be a good idea, no.'

'Sorry, but you really are paranoid. I'm calling the police now.' Daniel made to bring his phone out of his jacket.

'No, wait! Listen, Daniel, even if you call the police, staying with Geneva would be the perfect hideout in the meantime, even just for a few hours. For both of us. These psychos know nothing about Geneva. No one would know we're there. Don't you see? That's why it's a godsend her phoning.'

Daniel didn't know what to think. He knew he should call the police there and then. But what if Stone was right? Say these psychos did have an informant in the police. Inspector Patterson seemed all right, but could Daniel risk calling him? He was still curious about Stone's story. It didn't seem to add up, but for now, he put the phone back in his inside pocket. He wanted to know more about what Stone was saying before making a final decision. 'So tell me about these psychos. What happened exactly?'

'They kidnapped me in broad daylight. Threw me into a van and took me to this deserted cottage in the middle of nowhere. That's why I've got these bruises. They beat me with a baseball bat! I mean, these are bad people, Daniel, not like you and me. These people are really bad.'

Daniel looked at the other customers in the cafe, quietly sipping their teas and coffees, eating sandwiches and meals, and apparently living normal lives. Would Daniel ever live a normal life again? Say, for example, without ever being accused of murder or having psychos trying to kill him? He was having doubts and still had so many questions he wanted to ask Stone.

'So once you were at this cottage, did these psychos simply let you go after you told them I was the one who killed Susan?'

'No! That's the thing. Even after I said it was you who killed Susan, they were adamant it was me. It took ages to convince them it was you. I eventually told them I had proof it was you and that if they untied me, I would tell them more. I thought it would give me a chance to escape somehow. I was right. They said they would untie my legs but not my wrists. I agreed, so then I went on to explain how you confessed to me about the murders that day you came to my place and -'

'Hang on, what are you going on about? I didn't confess to anything. Where the hell did you get that from?'

'You did. I don't know why, but I distinctly remember I said something like, "You murdered Kimberley, didn't you?" and you said something like, "Oh yeah, that's right, I murdered Kimberley", I remember it clearly.'

'For God's sake, I was being sarcastic. Of course, I didn't murder her. Why would I confess to something I didn't do?'

'Well, how the hell was I supposed to know that? At the time, I thought you were going to murder me. Anyway, the fact is these psychos thankfully seemed to buy it was you who was the murderer. Then they went away for a time. Had me locked in this room, but I managed to stand on a chair and smash my way out this boarded-up window.'

'How could you do that if your hands were tied?'

'With my fucking head!' Stone frantically pointed to his head as if it was proof. 'Why do you think I have all these cuts on my fucking head? I used it as a battering ram. It hurt like hell. Then I fell outside and just ran and ran into this forest. I didn't know where I was. Turned out it was somewhere north of Kirkintilloch, I think. I eventually stopped a car, and the driver untied me. I said I'd been in a fight, but it was nothing. He wanted to take me to hospital. I told him I was fine and to just drop me near a police station. So he dropped me outside Milngavie police station. I didn't go in, though. I still had a couple of quid on me, so I got the bus back to my house, grabbed a couple of things, drove here – it seemed as good a place as any – and then phoned you.'

'I really think we should go to the police right now,' Daniel said.

Stone nodded. 'OK, I know we should, maybe, but what's the harm if we lie low for a few hours. I don't mind telling you I'm scared, Dan, and we both need a place to stay no matter what happens. Let's just go to Geneva's first, explain everything to her and then we can call the police later on.

' 'Why did this Geneva get in touch with you again?'

'I told you. She said she's interested in doing my TV show again. I always knew she would.'

'You really think the BBC would still be interested in giving you a show after what's been in the papers these last few days? Seriously Stone, give it up, that show is not going to happen. At least not with you in it.'

Stone looked back at him uncomprehending.

Daniel then thought about the whole situation. He couldn't take the chance to go home, and regardless of how he felt about Stone, going to Geneva's did seem as good a plan as any in the meantime. These psychos wouldn't know about her. 'OK, let's go to this Geneva's then. You said you have your car around the corner?'

Stone nodded, finishing his cola and eyeing the door to the street. 'In a side street.'

They both got up from the table and headed out of the cafe. Stone winced once again as he rose from the chair and was limping badly as both he and Daniel made towards Stone's car.

Daniel looked at Stone, still wondering if

what he was being told was the truth. 'Why did you call me, Stone? If you knew you couldn't stay at my place? Why did you really call me?'

'I told you, to warn you and... because, to be honest, you're actually the one person I've met in God knows how long I think I could trust. I just thought if anyone could help me in some way, you could. And besides, you're right, the truth is I don't really have any friends at the moment...'

'Let's just get to Geneva's,' Daniel said quickly, feeling slightly uncomfortable at having some sympathy for Stone.

As they turned into the side street where Stone's black BMW was parked, Daniel had one more question before getting in the car. 'Strictly Come Dancing? Really? You have the theme tune to Strictly Come Dancing as your ringtone?'

Chapter 42

Finally Identified

'That's Geneva Scott out of Castle Dangerous. I'm sure of it.'

Patterson and Simpson were on either side of Pettigrew as she excitedly pointed to the computer screen and the CCTV of the woman holding the letter walking towards the *West End Chronicle* office.

'Castle what?' Simpson asked before Patterson could.

'Castle Dangerous,' Pettigrew explained further. 'It was a reality TV show up in the Highlands where these contestants had to live in this castle and do tasks and things, and then people were voted off every week.'

'Like *Big Brother*?' Simpson asked.

'Kind of,' Pettigrew answered. 'It was more like a Scottish version of Survivor, to be exact. You know, Survivor, where contestants have to

—' Pettigrew stopped explaining Survivor on seeing the continuing incomprehension on her colleagues' faces. 'Anyway, Geneva Scott was one of the contestants who became kind of well known afterwards. You sure you've not heard of her? She even had a song out afterwards and did some appearances at supermarkets. You know the kind of stuff. She became quite a big reality TV star.' Pettigrew looked at the computer monitor again. 'Yes, I'm almost sure that's her. I mean, you can see the likeness yourselves.' Pettigrew did a Google search for a photo of Geneva. It was clear she had good reason to think it was the same woman holding the letter.

'So how come you know so much about her?' Simpson asked.

'I was a bit of a fan of the show and Geneva too. Geneva's not her real name. Her real name is Sarah Scott; she's from Banff originally, if I remember. She came across as quite stupid, but I don't think she was quite as thick as she made herself out to be. She seemed quite a nice person actually, at least compared to some of the others in that show.'

'I think we'll reserve judgement on how nice this Geneva is for the moment,' Patterson said.

Geneva's long blonde hair and striking looks were easy to recognise. She was wearing a sleeveless white top, and it was this top that made Pettigrew spot something else of interest.

'Sir, I think it's definitely her. Look.' Pettigrew pointed at the screen again. 'Geneva has a small rose tattooed on her upper-left arm.' The tattoo itself was difficult at first to make out on the CCTV, but when zoomed in, the rose shape was clear enough. They quickly found a photo of Geneva online that showed a very similar rose-shaped tattoo on the same arm. That was sufficient for Patterson.

'Okay, good work, Claire. I need you to stay here and get all the info possible on her. You seem to know more about her already than any of us do. In the meantime, Jack and myself will pay her a visit.'

No sooner had Pettigrew handed her boss a piece of paper with Geneva's address on it than Patterson and Simpson had grabbed their jackets and were heading to Patterson's car.

Chapter 43

Beechwood House

For most of the drive to Geneva's address, Daniel and Stone sat next to each other in silence, both of them lost in thought. Being in the same car brought back memories of that previous Saturday night when they'd travelled by taxi to the Fox and Hounds and the terrible event that happened later.

Daniel still didn't believe DCI Patterson had tipped off the psychos about Stone. Nevertheless, Daniel had to admit that Stone was right. Geneva's house would be as safe a place as any to stay in the meantime. Once everything was explained properly, no doubt the police could also give them protection while they found out who these people after them were and get them locked up.

'What's the address again?' Stone asked.

Daniel looked at the napkin he'd been given by Stone. 'Beechwood House, 37 Harvest

Avenue. It should be around here somewhere—There it is; we just passed it.'

Daniel had noticed a sign saying Beechwood House on a pillar next to an open front gate. Stone stopped the car, reversed a little, and turned into the curved grey-gravel driveway.

Beechwood House was as serene as it sounded. The driveway led to a pleasant-looking, detached mid-Victorian villa. Houses in this area cost a lot of money, and Geneva Scott had obviously done well for herself in the past year or so. Stone parked in front of the main door, and both men walked up to the door. Daniel pressed the authentic-looking Victorian brass doorbell, which had Press written in faded dark blue letters on it.

'I like the programme,' Stone said as they were waiting for the door to be opened.

Daniel looked across at Stone, waiting for an explanation to this random statement. 'Strictly Come Dancing,' Stone explained. 'The ringtone. I like the programme. I like the theme tune. That's why it's my ringtone.'

'You like Strictly Come Dancing?'

'Yes, I like Strictly Come Dancing. Why should that be surprising to you?' Daniel shrugged. 'Nothing, except, I dunno. I just didn't think it was the sort of thing you'd be into, that's all.'

They waited for Geneva to open the door, but she didn't. After a while, Stone rang the doorbell again. Eventually, they heard a voice call from inside, 'Come in – the door's open.'

Stone turned the dark mahogany knob, and indeed the door opened. He pushed it open a little further and made his way into the house, with Daniel following behind. Daniel closed the door behind them, and they stood waiting in the spacious hallway.

They'd both expected the interior of the home to match the elegant old-fashioned exterior. However, the hallway was decorated in a very modernist style, with a large Mondrian print taking pride of place on one of the walls.

'Hello? Geneva?' Stone called out.

'I'm in here,' a voice said from a room on the right, and Stone went towards the half-open door with Daniel dutifully following.

Walking through the open door and entering into what turned out to be the living room, surprisingly, they found there was no one there. Now both Stone and Daniel were getting confused. Where the hell was Geneva?

The room itself was barely furnished. There was a divan and a big-screen TV but not much else in the way of furniture. However, in contrast to many other homes in the city, the minimalist style here was because of a lot of money rather than too little.

Stone and Daniel looked at each other again before walking a few more steps, still wondering where Geneva could be.

Suddenly Stone felt a massive pain on the back of his head as he was thumped by some kind of heavy object. Daniel turned round in surprise but didn't have time to react as he too, was hit by the same heavy object and followed Stone in falling into a crumpled heap on the floor.

Chapter 44

Closing in on a Killer

As Patterson and Simpson drove to Geneva's address, it became clear that the Drainpipe Killer was indeed Sarah Scott. There was Geneva's link to singing and the entertainment business, plus the fact she was exceptionally fit, which meant she was more than capable of climbing the outside of Susan McLaughlin's building. No doubt some of the tasks on Castle Dangerous were the perfect training for climbing three storeys high up a tenement drainpipe. Even the rose tattoo Geneva had was another small but significant indication. Then, of course, there was the most damning evidence of all: Geneva being spotted posting the letter saying she was the 'Red Rose Strangler'.

As Patterson and Simpson drove south over the Kingston Bridge, the traffic was even more chock-a-block than usual. Only the squad car in front of them, speeding along with siren blaring, ensured they made relatively quick progress.

As they turned off the motorway into the spacious Southside suburbs, Pettigrew called with one more piece of information, which all but confirmed that Geneva was the murderer. She had attended the Natural Talent UK auditions on the same day Susan McLaughlin had.

With this final piece of information in place, Patterson turned to Simpson, ever more impatient to reach her address. 'How long till we get there?'

'Ten minutes max,' Simpson replied.

Chapter 45

Coming To Once More

Daniel gradually regained consciousness, but with such a searing headache, it made his recent hangovers seem like child's play. This was an altogether different kind of headache - a heavy-duty skull banger which throbbed with an impressive pounding bass beat. Daniel found it difficult to open his eyes, instinctively wanting to keep them shut to deal with the pain better. He tried to raise a hand to feel the back of his neck but found, to his surprise, he couldn't. His hands were bound to something.

The surprise of this made him try to open his eyes even more, and yet he still couldn't see properly, his vision blurred and cloudy. Looking down in the direction of his hands, he could just make out that he was sitting on a heavy metal chair, and it was this that he was tied to. Fear then began to grip him as he realised the position he was in. He tried to move his legs, but they, too, were immobile – each one bound to a leg of the chair. He had absolutely no idea what was going on.

He looked upwards, trying to regain his vision through the pain, but had to shut his eyes again, as the thumping headache was too much. His head also felt so heavy, his neck aching, and he frantically tried to gather his thoughts and work out where he was or what had happened.

Then some events slowly started to come back to him.

Stone. He had been travelling with Stone in a car. He remembered that. Coming to a house. Geneva – there was a woman called Geneva. Yes, definitely. Then he vaguely remembered entering the hallway of her house, but after that – nothing. Now, managing to open his eyes a little more, Daniel was conscious of a bright electric light, and that was another reason he couldn't see well because it was so bright it blinded him.

Eventually, Daniel began to slowly make out some more shapes and sounds around him. He could also hear a constant knocking, like someone chapping on a door.

Still coming to, he turned his head and to his left saw Stone, sitting next to him. He too was tied to a solid, metal chair. Stone's head was tilted forward, his eyes closed, and his broad chin resting on his chest, strands of his dark hair flopped down over his forehead. He was still out cold.

Daniel was growing more alarmed with every new thing he saw. He began to desperately tug his arms from the chair, trying to free himself, but no matter how hard he tried, he couldn't. He could still faintly hear that knocking sound coming from somewhere, and then Daniel looked to his right and saw someone else standing there.

A woman with long blonde hair.

Chapter 46

Knocking

It was with some impatience that Patterson and Simpson had reached the home of Geneva. Patterson now continued to knock loudly on the front door with a diminishing hope that it would be answered. Officers were in place all around the building. As both Simpson and himself waited outside, there was still no answer and no sign anyone was inside. Patterson tried the door handle. Locked. He knocked on the door again and rattled the letterbox as loudly as possible. Still nothing. He then opened the letterbox and looked through, but there was almost total darkness inside.

'Police, open up!' Patterson shouted, hoping that would somehow make a difference. He wondered whether there might be another way in. Yet, Geneva's home was on the second floor of this newly built apartment block, and he presumed they would need a ladder to get in the back window. The apartment block was a renovated art deco building which had once been a cinema. Now it was a stylish and exclusive residence, clearly aimed at upmarket professionals. There were two flats on each spacious landing, and through vast plate-glass windows, views stretching out northwards across to the centre of Glasgow could be seen.

'Come on – let's try the neighbours,' said Patterson.

They knocked on the door opposite, and a woman in her thirties with a short blonde bob quickly appeared. She opened the door wearing a pinny, on which were the marks of flour and jam.

'Yes?' She appeared annoyed at having her baking being interrupted.

Simpson showed his identification. 'Sorry to trouble you,' he started, 'but we're trying to locate the woman who lives in the apartment opposite.'

'Gen? Is everything all right?'

Simpson ignored the question. 'She doesn't appear to be at home. Do you have any idea where she might be?'

'No, sorry, no idea, I haven't seen her for a few days, in fact.' The woman was clearly dying to know what Gen had been up to or what had happened to her.

'It's important we contact her as soon as possible. Could she be at work, perhaps?'

The next-door neighbour shook her head. 'Possibly, but Gen works irregular hours. She's in the entertainment business, you see. I've really no idea where she could be at this time. If I do see her, I'll certainly let her know you called if you like.'

'Actually' – Simpson handed her his card – 'if you do hear her come back, just call that number immediately. We would be most grateful.'

'Certainly.' The woman smiled, studying the business card before she quietly shut the door, curiosity obviously still burning inside of her.

Simpson looked across at Patterson. 'So what do we do now?'

'Well, we'll keep a discreet car outside in case she comes back, but for now, we should head back to the station and see if Claire has found anything more on her. I assume Geneva will have an agent who could know where she is. She may well be working. We'll also get a search warrant for this place and come back as soon as.'

Simpson looked as disappointed as Patterson felt.

'We'll get her, don't worry.' It was as if Patterson was reassuring himself as much as Simpson.

They headed back to the car and began the drive back to Partick.

Twenty minutes later, as they were driving along the Clydeside Expressway, they got a call from Pettigrew. 'Sir, where are you?'

'Just coming off the Expressway; should be with you in five minutes, why?' 'There's been a new development. I'll tell you once you get back to the station.'

*

Daniel was genuinely frightened now. What the hell was happening? Where was he? This nightmare was real, and he didn't know what would happen next. He realised that the blonde woman to his right was probably this Geneva. He tried to focus more on her, but that was so difficult to do with the pain still pulsing around his skull. Yet, slowly but surely, the pain began to ease, and his vision became less blurred.

He looked towards the blonde woman again and, to his surprise, realised she wasn't standing up at all. He'd simply got that impression because of her tall stature. She was actually tied to a chair, just like Stone and himself.

It seemed as if the more conscious Daniel became, the less anything made sense. He looked at the blonde woman again, making out the features of her face now. She looked back at him as if she wanted to say something. There was such fear in her eyes.

Then, from behind her, a man came into view.

Chapter 47

Outside the Exchequer

As soon as Patterson and Simpson got back to the station and entered the main investigation room, Pettigrew motioned them both over to a computer screen, where she sat down and began to explain the new development.

'Sir, I was checking back through the CCTV that came in from the Dumbarton Road area around the time Geneva posted the letter. I traced Geneva's movements back from the time she posted the letter and came across this.' Pettigrew clicked the play button on the screen. The CCTV footage proceeded to show Geneva exiting a pub further along Dumbarton Road. 'Geneva came out of the Exchequer Bar around ten minutes before she posted the letter.'

Patterson wondered what the significance of this was. 'And?'

'Look,' Pettigrew answered.

A man came out of the pub just after Geneva did. Curiously, even though it was a warm night, he was wearing a white hooded top which was pulled up, covering his head. The man stood next to Geneva, and it was clear they knew each other as they chatted outside the bar.

However, even from the elevated view from the CCTV camera, there was a telling unease about Geneva's body language. It was as if the young man of slim build was doing all the talking, and Geneva was dying to get away from him. Every so often, she would try to edge away, but then the young man would inch closer to her again.

Geneva then looked at her watch and appeared to be explaining she had to go somewhere. It was then that the young man brought out a letter from his inside pocket. He was still talking non-stop, as if he was hyper, trying to explain something, and he pointed in the direction of the West End Chronicle office. Geneva was shaking her head and looking at her watch again. From a distance, it was as if she was miming she didn't have time.

Still, the man really seemed insistent. Uncomfortably so. Then Geneva seemed to give in, nod and took the letter off him. The man pointed along the road again, and after saying their goodbyes, Geneva turned away from him and walked in the direction of the newspaper office.

Chapter 48

Artistic Tasering

It quickly became clear that Geneva Scott may well have posted the letter on behalf of someone else, this man who she'd left the Exchequer with. Patterson also had one question he was burning to ask, more in hope than in expectation and only because Pettigrew had immediately recognised who Geneva was.

'I don't suppose there's any chance you happen to know who that guy is, do you?'

This time Pettigrew looked at the computer screen and shook her head. 'No, sir, I don't.'

Patterson sighed. 'Aye, didn't think you would.'

Pettigrew then turned back to Patterson before adding, 'But Brian does.'

Patterson looked at Pettigrew and then looked across at McKinnon. Pettigrew called him over.

McKinnon came and stood in front of Patterson and Pettigrew, suspecting what he was going to be asked, but as usual, he didn't show any excess enthusiasm or emotion at having vital information.

'So you think you know who this person is, Brian?' Patterson asked.

McKinnon nodded. 'Yeah. I knew I'd seen him from somewhere before, but I couldn't quite place him.'

'I'm surprised you can recognise him with his hood up.'

McKinnon shook his head. 'I didn't recognise him with his hood up. Claire, if you'd like to forward the tape to the relevant point...'

Pettigrew did as instructed. Now all the officers looked at the monitor again. Shortly after the man left Geneva outside the pub, walking up Byres Road, his hood was blown back by a sudden gust of wind, revealing a spiky blonde hair with purple sides.

'That's quite a distinctive haircut,' Simpson said.

'Which is why I recognised him,' said McKinnon. 'Like I said, I knew I'd seen him before but couldn't figure out where. Then I remembered. It was while I was reviewing the audition tapes for Natural Talent UK. He was one of the people from the auditions.' McKinnon then put another DVD into the player

'He's called Crack.' As Crack confidently walked onto the Natural Talent audition stage, there were some cheers from the audience and a few giggles. Crack looked nervous as he stood in the middle of the stage. After being asked who he was by the judges and indulging in some awkward small talk, he was given the go-ahead to start.

Crack looked over to the side of the stage and gave the thumbs up. Loud house music started, and Crack's arms and legs began jerking about in all directions as if he'd just been tasered. This impression of artistic tasering continued before one of the judges instructed the music to be stopped by making a gesture of cutting his throat. Crack looked confused as to why the music stopped but stood with a broad smile, fully expecting unanimous appreciation from the judges and audience.

That didn't happen.

Crack's smile faded as the judges slaughtered Crack with savage comments that made the audience almost feel sorry for him.

In one of his nicer comments, the main judge said he was entirely at a loss as to why Crack had bothered turning up and wasting everyone's time. Crack was now visibly upset and clearly raging at their disparaging comments. He walked off stage with a defiant strut which fooled no one.

'OK, apart from his dancing, has he any previous?' Patterson asked.

'None, sir. He's not on our records at all.'

'You said he's called Crack?'

'Obviously not his real name.'

'So, what is his real name?' Patterson asked with some impatience.

'His real name is Campbell – Jamie Campbell,' replied McKinnon.

Chapter 49

Special

Jamie Campbell, otherwise known as Crack, wasn't as talented as he liked to think he was. He thought of himself as the whole package, the real deal. A rare, genuine talent just waiting to be discovered. He wasn't just a dancer, he could sing, act, tell jokes and play several musical instruments. The fact he did all of these things badly and had no likeability factor whatsoever was beside the point. Crack was one hundred percent convinced that he was a star just waiting to be discovered.

In the meantime, Crack worked in various 'everyday' jobs until he was found. Call centres mostly. At night he did karaoke. Whenever he could, he went to the odd audition. He did what he called a 'contemporary dance act' which he liked to think was exceptionally good. On the rare occasion, he got a spot somewhere, usually unpaid apart from expenses, he would also invite his co-workers along to it. His co-workers often did come along, trying to give support but, at the same time, laughing to themselves at just how awful Crack was. However, instead of telling Crack the truth, they fed his ego and told him he should go on one of these talent shows. You know, on TV. They said he was much better than the rubbish usually on there. He was real talent. Special. Crack lapped up the praise because he knew deep down he was indeed something, someone really special.

The one exception to the friends that fed Jamie's ego was his best friend, Daniel McLeod. Daniel tried to support Jamie to some degree but, as a true friend, felt he wouldn't be less than truthful with Jamie about what he thought of his 'talent'. At first, this led to some ill feeling and arguments before the two friends agreed to disagree. Now, whenever they met, Daniel would simply ask how 'everything else' was going, and Jamie would give an 'all right' or 'so so' or 'not all right' without expanding further.

Deep down though, Crack deeply resented Daniel's opinion. He desperately wanted to prove Daniel wrong and become a star. Yet, apart from the odd gig here and there, Crack still wasn't being noticed. He was passing under the radar, and fame was passing him by. For Crack, this was inexplicable. He had such star quality, and yet he still had to go back to working in call centres and supermarkets and do all the other agency work he could find. With every single day that passed, his resentment at not being discovered just grew and grew.

After time it became even more than that, Crack became convinced there was a conspiracy against him. Everyone seemed to be against him. Was even his best friend Daniel against him? Jamie initially dismissed this thought. However, as more time passed, Jamie became angry against the world and everyone in it. He believed the only way to exorcise his pain was to make someone else suffer, for someone else to feel the pain he felt every day.

And then Susan came along.

Crack had met Susan McLaughlin for the first time at a karaoke night in the Five Ways, a small pub mostly known for its cheap beer. Susan was a quiet girl, but, Crack had to admit, she did have some talent. Nowhere near his own, of course, but he thought in the right hands, she certainly had some potential. It was why he would offer tips to her from his own experiences. Such as how not to let the booing put you off. Though, Susan didn't actually get any booing like Crack did. At the same time, Susan didn't seem to appreciate Crack's advice. He had the impression she always seemed to be making an excuse to get away from him. She was just like all the others, bitch.

Nevertheless, on the 19th of July, he saw

her again at the Natural Talent UK auditions. Apparently, overhearing what all the production staff were saying backstage, Susan was the 'the find' of the series so far. As for Crack, they also liked him, but it was clear that was only for his comedic value. They treated him like a clown. It turned out that for all those watching at the Clyde Auditorium that day, Susan and Crack were at opposite ends of the talent spectrum.

After the auditions had taken place, Saturday night was a bit of a blur for Crack. His anger and resentment at the way he had been treated was unlike anything he had ever felt. Yes, he had felt severe rage and resentment on many, many occasions, yet this latest humiliation brought everything to a head. He literally wanted to murder someone.

Susan.

Susan was torturing him. Jamie couldn't stop thinking about her and how she had ruined his audition. If it wasn't for Susan, perhaps he would have been adored. In a way, it was her fault. She took the limelight away from him. That fuckwit girl who, compared to him, had absolutely no talent whatsoever and yet she was considered the star turn? As Crack was getting ready to go home after the auditions, utterly depressed, he saw Susan once again across the foyer, quietly walking out the front entrance.

Susan herself was delighted at how the audition had gone that day. Yet, she was still so unsure of herself that she had kept the audition a secret from everyone else. Of course, she knew it was just a daft wee talent show, but still. This one was shown all over the UK. She planned to keep her show audition a secret until it was on the telly. Then she would watch it with her mum and, hopefully, her mum would be delighted, as well as surprised, at seeing her little girl on national TV. The secret would be revealed as she sat next to her mum she loved so much. The woman who had sacrificed so much so her daughter could have a decent life and go to university.

As Susan left the audition that day, she had to admit, she almost felt like a star. One part of her felt like celebrating, but another part of her just didn't want to get carried away. It was just a daft wee talent show, she repeated to herself once again, trying to keep her feet on the ground. So she decided she would go home and have a quiet Saturday night in. Maybe do some studying. She still had to concentrate on her studies no matter what happened. Susan headed home on the bus, but she was unable to keep the smile off her face, looking out the window, lost in her dreams. Thinking of what might be, of a million possibilities the future held. She was completely unaware Jamie Campbell was sitting

WILL CAMERON

three rows behind her.

Chapter 50

Making Friends

'Jamie? What the hell are you doing here?' As Daniel slowly regained his senses, he couldn't quite believe who was standing in front of him.

Before Jamie could answer, Geneva asked another question, calling Jamie by the name she had always known him since drama school. 'Crack, why are you doing this? You need to stop this now.'

'No, Geneva,' Jamie replied. 'The games a bogie. I know what all three of you have been up to. Laughing at me, plotting against me.'

'Plotting against you? What are you on about?' asked Daniel.

'Hang on, you all know each other?' It wasn't Geneva or Daniel asking the question but Stone, who was slowly coming to his senses.

Daniel answered first. 'Jamie's a friend of

mine.'

'You sure about that?' Stone replied, looking around, trying to get his bearings.

Daniel could understand Stone's confusion as Daniel was quite confused himself. Why was Jamie there in what seemed to be a basement? More importantly, why were Daniel, Stone, and this woman tied to chairs?

'I know all about it, Daniel,' continued Jamie, 'there's no use denying it. See, I've been following you for quite a while now.'

'Following me?' Daniel suddenly thought of Jamie outside Partick police station after his release.

'You know, at first, I thought I was being paranoid,' said Jamie, shaking his head. ' I really did. Deep down, I thought there was no way the person I considered my best friend was plotting against me. When I started following you, it was really for my own peace of mind and to make sure you really were my true friend. At first, that seemed to be the case. All you seemed to do, was go to the pub or the bookies or just walk around.'

'I am your one friend,' said Daniel, slowly realising Jamie had been on a train to psychoville, and he hadn't even noticed.

'Then I saw you go and see this one here,' Jamie nodded toward Stone. 'That's right, Daniel, I saw you go into Stone Johnson's office and then you went for a drink together. Suddenly, it all made sense. All three of you knew each other. You knew Stone, Stone knew Geneva, and all three of you were plotting against me. Making sure I failed and failed and failed! You probably had a word with those working at the natural Talent auditions, didn't you? Told them to humiliate me.'

'Jamie, if you think I somehow know this woman here, I don't; I have never seen her before now.'

'Oh, so it's just all coincidence, is it? It's just a coincidence you go drinking with Stone Johnson, who just happens to be friends with my ex-drama school friend? Yeah, right.'

'I went to see Stone about investing some money. I have no idea who this Geneva is. I had no idea, until today, that Stone Johnson knew Geneva.'

'He's right, Crack. I have never seen this man before,' said Geneva, who now had tears rolling down her face. 'You've got it all wrong. No one is plotting against you, I swear. Just untie us. We can explain everything.'

'Oh, I bet you can. No, it's too late, Geneva; I'm going to make sure all three of you pay for what you have done to me.'

Stone then spoke, looking towards Geneva. 'Hang on, so you know this guy as well?'

Geneva nodded as she spoke in a robotic voice. 'We were at drama school together. You know who him as well, in a way, or have you forgotten?' Geneva asked.

'Me? I can assure you I've never seen this guy before in my life.'

'But you have,' Geneva explained. 'That night, when we left the restaurant, the guy you thought wanted an autograph? That was Crack. This is Crack.'

Stone's eyes widened as the realisation hit him. 'Of course! That's him, that's that guy, yeah – how could I forget that haircut?'

'Yes, I'm that guy,' Jamie said slowly. 'I'm that guy you called a loser and told to fuck off. I'm not such a loser now, am I?'

Daniel looked at Jamie, still unsure what was happening but knowing it wasn't good. 'Come on, Jamie, you need to stop this now. You've had your joke. It's over now. Untie us. This is stupid.'

Jamie glared at Daniel. 'Stupid? You think being laughed at is stupid? Being insulted? Humiliated? You never really understood me, did you? You've never realised what I've gone through time and again. You may not think so, but I really do have talent, Daniel. I really do. I couldn't believe it when I saw you became a suspect for the murders I committed. It was quite funny, really. I really never figured on that happening. Maybe if you had listened to me more, you wouldn't be sitting in that chair now.'

'Jamie, I've told you I have no idea what you're on about,' Daniel said honestly, but as the seconds ticked by, he was getting increasingly worried. *Murders I committed?* What did he mean by that? 'Just let us go now, Jamie,' Daniel said once more. 'We can talk about this all you like, but you have to let us go first.'

' 'Sorry, Daniel, I can't let you go. It's too late for that. I can't let any of you go now. You all have to die.'

Chapter 51

White Street

The team quickly found Jamie's address, and as Simpson turned into White Street in Partick, a couple of squad cars followed behind. Hopefully, they would have more luck this time than they'd had with Geneva. The security door, as it was quaintly known, to 16 White Street was, like so many others, open. Damaged, to be exact, its dirty black paint scratched and scuffed, with the two narrow glass panels above it broken.

On the first floor, the dark blue door to the flat full of different bedsits had bits of paper and cards attached randomly to it with safety pins and Sellotape. J. Campbell was one of the names listed. In contrast to other scribbled names on torn bits of card or paper, J. Campbell was clearly typed out on bright white, neatly cut card.

Patterson went up and quietly lifted the letterbox flap to look inside. He could make out scruffy-looking floorboards in the hallway and three or four doors closed on either side. A fusty, damp smell wafted out and into Patterson's nostrils. Only one door inside was open, but there appeared to be no sight or sound of life inside.

Patterson gently lowered the letterbox flap back into position. The flimsy door was only slightly more secure than the main door downstairs, and with a small bump from Patterson's shoulder, the door sprang open with only a small rattling noise accompanying it. Patterson and the other officers rushed in, shouting orders to anyone inside. They knocked on the closed doors before quickly crashing into the rooms.

The first door on the left was the one that was already open, and it led to a communal kitchen. The kitchen was extremely filthy and obviously hadn't been cleaned in months. The cooker was covered in brown and black grease. There was a poster of Kasabian on the wall, its top-right-hand corner drooping down and covering a quarter of the band. One of the officers came in and said to Patterson there was only one person in the flat, and it wasn't Jamie Campbell. He pointed to one of the rooms to the side.

The room was short and narrow, like a residential alleyway. As Patterson entered, he looked down on an unshaven, haggard-looking man in his mid-fifties lying on a bed with a thin, dirty striped mattress. The man had his head slightly raised off a pillow as if the loud crashing noises had woken him, but the commotion wasn't worthy of any additional movement. The cramped space was filled with awkwardly positioned furniture. Getting from one side of the room to the other wouldn't take long, but it would still be a considerable obstacle course. A big, old-fashioned TV was balanced precariously on a couple of chairs in the corner. The room, as well as the man himself, stank of stale beer, cooking oil and traditional body odour.

'Yeah?' The man was either hungover or still half-drunk from a recent drinking session and looked up at Patterson with a bewildered expression, one eye remaining closed.

'Partick CID. What's your name?'

'Ken Thompson. How? What the fuck have I done now?'

'Mr Thompson, we're looking for Jamie Campbell, might be called Crack. Which room is he in?'

'Jamie? He's in the room next door to this one, on the right there.' He indicated this with a sideways movement of his head and then lay his head back down on the pillow and closed his eyes, correctly thinking his questioning was done for the moment.

Patterson went into the hallway and then to the room indicated by Thompson. 'It's this one,' he said to Simpson.

Inside Jamie's bedsit, in contrast to the rest of the squalid house, they found the quite spacious room was immaculately tidy. It was about twice the size of that occupied by Thompson, and there were silver-framed photos of various stars past and present on the walls: Fred Astaire, Gene Kelly, Diana Dors and Phillip Schofield. On a small table in the corner was an old-fashioned typewriter.

Patterson went back to talk to Thompson. 'When was the last time Jamie was here?'

Thompson cleared his throat before answering, the sound of regurgitated phlegm making Patterson wince.

'Dunno,' Thompson said. 'A few days back, I think; cannae mind.'

'Do you know if he stays anywhere else? Where he goes?'

'Dunno. Hardly ever see him.' Thompson yawned, a whiff of rancid breath floating across the room. 'He just comes and goes. Besides, I'm usually fucking out of it, to be honest.'

'Has he ever mentioned a workplace? Or anyone he knows? Anyone. His girlfriend, family?'

Thompson shook his head. 'Never seen a girlfriend here. He works in town. A call centre. Told me he hates it. Cannae remember the name of it. He did mention his mum one time but. Lives near the Campsies or something. Could be Torrance if I remember; aye Torrance as in Sam.'

'I'll get on to it,' Simpson said and went outside to make a call on the landing.

Patterson left Thompson and went back into Jamie's room to look around once more. There were sheets of handwritten paper. Lists of song titles and ideas of acts he could do. Elsewhere, a neat single bed was stuck in the corner, its covers immaculately folded. Officers were checking everywhere in the room as Patterson walked over to a large, imposing cupboard. On the top was a collection of magazines: *Hello, Heat, Ideal Home...*

Patterson turned the large key, which was still in the lock, and the cupboard door swung open with a loud squeak. Amongst the clothes was a white hooded top slung over the clothes rail. In the bottom corner of the wardrobe was a stack of empty glass bottles and a commando-style beanie hat.

Simpson came back in.

'Anything, Jack?'

Pettigrew phoned. Jamie worked in a call centre, but he seems to have left it last week. She's trying to find out if he has a new job or is unemployed. Good news, though. Got his mother's address; she does stay in Torrance. Mill Crescent.'

'OK, let's try there then. Let's get to Torrance.'

Patterson didn't like this running around. He just knew that every minute was vital. That they had to find Jamie as soon as possible – before he killed again.

Chapter 52

Remembering the Good Times

As Jamie stood in front of Daniel, Stone and Geneva, it reminded him of when he'd stood before the three judges at the National Talent UK auditions, only to be absolutely humiliated. The anger he'd felt that day was still raw and always there, simply intensified by flashes of remembrance that came hurtling through at random times.

With the prompt of the three seated stooges in front of him, Jamie remembered with more clarity what had happened after that audition on the 19th of July. Granted, he still couldn't quite explain why he decided to climb the drainpipe that night after following Susan home from the Natural Talent UK auditions. Maybe it was something as simple as him walking into the backcourt and observing Susan's kitchen window was wide open. Perhaps it was just the desire to do something daring, to prove to others and to remind himself he wasn't quite the failure, or loser, everyone said he was. Whatever it was, he pulled the sleeves on his jumper down over his hands and put one hand on the drainpipe, then the other. He started climbing, unsure how far he would go, but he climbed and climbed until it was quicker and easier to get to the window than to try and descend back down the pipe.

As he relived the climb, he remembered the fear he'd experienced in the early hours of what was no longer Saturday night but Sunday morning. The searing exhilaration and relief of successfully climbing into her flat came back to him. He thought about her darkened kitchen with its smell of lemon disinfectant whilst he stood there and listened to the almost silence.

He didn't even know what he was going to do to Susan if anything. Most of all, he had the idea of scaring her. Just scaring her and nothing more. Yet, once he was on top of her, something happened. He just completely lost it.

The actual murder had been surprisingly easy, and afterwards, Jamie had felt an equally surprising and delightful satisfaction. He immediately knew he would want to experience that satisfaction again. Afterwards, he didn't even have any feelings of guilt. He knew Susan deserved to be murdered. Bitch. There had been absolutely no doubt in Jamie's mind then as now:

Susan deserved to die; that was the truth of the matter.

Yet, there was a disappointing development in the days afterwards, when the local media labelled him the Drainpipe Killer. He absolutely hated that name. Hated it. Of all the soubriquets they could have chosen, they went with the Drainpipe Killer. All because he'd climbed a drainpipe? He felt insulted. He had climbed three storeys high up the outside of a tenement! Was that not worthy of a more flattering name? No, the newspapers, in all their populist wisdom, had named him the Drainpipe Killer. Jamie wasn't too pleased with that. Not one little bit.

In addition, the initial satisfaction he'd felt after he'd killed Susan slowly eased off over the coming days. Life went back to being its usual shit self. He was still being shouted at in the call centre and working other shitty jobs part-time to get by. He couldn't stand it any longer and left the call centre. He had to admit one good thing was him immediately getting a job as a house sitter. It was better than most jobs he did. They even gave him the use of a car.

Yet, one thing didn't change. All the time, Jamie knew he was pure fucking talent, and all the time, he was being ignored. He wanted to murder again. Experience the thrill he had in strangling the last breath out of Susan.

So, in the days that followed the murder of Susan McLaughlin, Jamie was just waiting for another occasion to kill. He had never experienced a high so intense as the thrill of ending someone else's life. Being told to fuck off by Stone that night just intensified his desire to kill.

Why did everyone feel the need to humiliate him? Why? Why the need to be so cruel? Then the sadness became anger, and the anger became a rage, a whirling tornado of hate for everyone and everything — especially against Stone Johnson.

Jamie still followed Daniel and had just about convinced himself Daniel was simply his friend when he saw him meet Stone Johnson. So it was true. Jamie wasn't paranoid, after all. This revelation was such a severe shock. When Daniel and Stone had met for a drink on the Saturday, Jamie had followed them all the way to the Fox and Hounds. All day, the questions and paranoia continued to fester inside Jamie, the bacteria infecting his brain with thoughts of persecution and injustice. He soon determined to murder either Daniel, Stone, Geneva, or all three. He knew he had to. He didn't have a choice.

As Jamie sat in his car outside the Fox and Hounds waiting for Daniel and Stone to reappear, to his surprise, Stone emerged, not with Daniel, but with a dark-haired beauty,

Kimberley O'Hara. So Jamie followed the taxi taking Stone and Kimberley back to her flat in Peel Street.

There he waited once more. He'd waited, looking up at the third-floor window, noting which flat they'd entered from the light that went on and then seeing Kimberley shut the curtains. Presuming Stone would be there all night, Jamie was on the verge of heading home when Stone suddenly came striding out of the stairwell. The brunette must have given him a knockback!

Jamie noticed the door to the close was still open, and it was now that Jamie spotted his chance to murder again. The lust to kill overwhelmed his senses like an intense desire he couldn't resist. Yet, this time there was no way he was climbing a drainpipe. That Drainpipe Killer name would stick with him forever if he did. So Jamie let Stone walk away into the night, then left the car, went into the close, up the stairs and knocked on Kimberley's door.

Kimberley quickly opened the door, on the verge of shouting something. She was obviously expecting it to be Stone. Jamie remembered Kimberley's surprise and confusion when she saw it wasn't Stone but Jamie standing there. Before she could react, Jamie punched her right on the jaw, and she fell back into the flat, hitting the back of her head on the floor.

This partly stunned her, meaning Jamie could sit astride her just as he did with Susan McLaughlin. It made his mouth drool when he thought about the joy of strangulation.

The killing of Kimberley O'Hara was every bit as pleasurable and satisfying as the killing of Susan McLaughlin.

Jamie carried her to the bedroom and placed her on the bed in the same position as he had done with Susan. He then noticed a single rose in a slim vase on the sideboard. It gave him an idea. Another chance to erase the name of Drainpipe Killer. He took the rose from the vase and placed it on the still-warm corpse. His thinking being that once the police found the rose and word got out to the media, the papers would have to come up with a new name for him. Something like the Red Rose Killer or, perhaps, the Red Rose Strangler? He liked that; such an improvement on the Drainpipe Killer.

However, to his extreme disappointment, the red rose was never mentioned once in the coverage of Kimberley O'Hara's murder.

So perhaps the media needed a prompt. Which is why he'd decided to send a letter to the local paper, declaring himself to be the Red Rose Strangler. He thought it would be a good idea to get someone else to post the letter directly to the offices of the local paper. That was when he thought of Geneva. He knew she would be embarrassed by Stone's behaviour and wouldn't refuse to meet him for a drink. Just as he thought, Geneva didn't refuse to meet him. However, she took some persuading to actually post the letter for him. Yet, even then, the local paper didn't mention the letter. So he was still referred to far and wide as the Drainpipe Killer. It was as if they were deliberately trying to wind Jamie up.

All those thoughts and memories of the last two weeks swirled through Jamie's mind as he now stood before these three people who had mocked, betrayed and plotted against him. He knew he now had to kill all three. To bring this chapter in his life to an end. He just had to decide who – Geneva, Stone or Daniel – to kill first.

Chapter 53

Torrance

Within half an hour, Patterson and Simpson were driving along the country roads north of the city, nearing Torrance, about eight miles away. Once they arrived in the East Dunbartonshire village, they found the house of Jamie's mother relatively quickly.

The home looked like a fairy-tale cottage. It nestled in the shadow of the high purple-and-green Campsie Hills. Its white wooden fence and well-kept garden, filled with blooming flowers, was the kind of idyllic image you'd see on the cover of *People's Friend*.

Patterson and Simpson got out of the car and looked around the building, thinking there was a chance Jamie might be there. Patterson knocked on the white door, which had a sprig of heather tied with a tartan ribbon attached to it. After a short wait, a woman in her early fifties opened the door.

'Mrs Campbell?' Patterson showed his badge. 'DCI Patterson, Glasgow CID. This is DS Simpson. Can we come in?'

Mrs Campbell's appearance kept up the image of perfection the house gave, her slightly greying hair tied back in a bun, her face at first smiling, but the smile faded as she instinctively knew these formal men arriving wasn't good news.

'Oh my, it isn't Jamie, is it? What's happened to him?'

Patterson reassured her that Jamie was fine as far as he knew. However, it was indeed because of him they were visiting.

'Do you know where your son is, Mrs Campbell? We just need to locate him. He could help us with one of our enquiries. It's very important.'

Mrs Campbell shook her head, trying to think. She just knew something was wrong – that he was in trouble. 'I haven't seen him for a few days, as a matter of fact. He's got an address in the West End of Glasgow. Just off Byres Road – White Street. You could try there.'

'Yes, we know. We've already been to that address, but Jamie isn't there. Has he a friend, girlfriend, or have you a mobile number for him?'

The smart, polite woman shook her head again, biting her lip. Patterson could tell she was holding something back.

'It's for his own good that we find him. Where does he work?'

'He hasn't a steady job at the moment – you know what the job market is like nowadays. Having said that, I believe he works in a call centre in Glasgow, the city centre somewhere, and he's just started house-sitting. He also cleans in a primary school sometimes too. And he's a musician. And a dancer. Jack of all trades is my Jamie. He's going to be on TV soon too. He's very talented. Just like his father. He—'

'You said he house-sits? Is that for an agency?' Patterson asked.

'Yes, I don't know the name. It's on Great Western Road – Kelvinbridge. City House, or it may be City Home Services, I believe, something like that, anyway.'

'Is he house-sitting now, do you know?'

'I've no idea. Maybe. I haven't seen him for a few days. So maybe.'

'Have you a phone book?' Mrs Campbell pointed to a Glasgow North phone book under the phone table in the hallway.

'May I?' Simpson went forward and picked up the directory. Searching through it, he quickly found a company called City Home Services, whose address was indeed Great Western Road at Kelvinbridge. Simpson brought out his mobile and called the number.

The woman who answered the phone listened to what Simpson had to say and confirmed that Jamie Campbell worked for them but wouldn't give out any other information over the phone. Simpson hung up, then called McKinnon and instructed him to immediately get down to the house-sitting office.

Simpson nodded to Patterson. 'Brian's on his way to the agency now.'

'OK, Mrs Campbell. Thanks for your help. If your son contacts you, please call this number.' He gave her a card. 'Like I said, it's very important. OK?'

The woman nodded; she seemed on the point of crying. She'd always worried something like this would happen. Although she'd tried to deny it to herself, deep down, she'd known it had only been a matter of time. Jamie hadn't been right these last few months. He had even gotten worse.

'Thanks for your time, Mrs Campbell.'

Outside, Patterson and Simpson walked to the car. Simpson looked over at him. 'So, what now?'

'We drive back to Glasgow and wait to see what Brian says. We'll contact the call centre just in case they know something, but this house sitting he's started could be where he is now.'

As they were driving back to the city, a call eventually came through from McKinnon. He said Jamie was working for the agency as a house-sitter. The address was Beechwood House, 37 Harvest Avenue, Giffnock.

Patterson and Simpson were still on the other side of the city but immediately headed in that direction.

Chapter 54

Disagreements

Jamie had gone upstairs, and it allowed Daniel, Stone and Geneva to figure out what they would do if there was anything they could do. First of all, they were able to properly take in their surroundings. They could see they were in a windowless basement cellar with one bare, very bright light bulb hanging overhead. Scattered around were mostly building materials, tools, some cardboard boxes filled with books and crates filled with bric-a-brac. These were positioned alongside a couple of expensive-looking BMX bikes leaning against one of the four breeze-block walls. Turning his head as far as he could behind him, Daniel saw the only way out was a slim, flimsy-looking wooden staircase which led upstairs.

All three were frightened about what was happening, but especially Geneva. She stared ahead, barely moving apart from a slight trembling that affected her whole body. Daniel then looked to his left and saw Stone staring back at him.

'We need to get out of here,' Daniel said to him firmly.

'Yes, I know that, but how?' said Stone, trying but failing to move his chair. 'I can't move an inch, and how come the chair won't even budge? I can't tip it over.'

'It's bolted to the floor,' Geneva replied in a robotic voice.

Daniel also tried to move, struggling against the thin but strong ropes tying him down. They were tied too tight for him to move at all. 'I heard a knocking earlier on. A banging sound. What was that?'

Again it was Geneva who answered. 'I think he's trying to board up the windows or something. I'm telling you he's completely crazy.'

'When he comes back down,' Daniel said, 'We need to keep him talking for as long as possible.'

'Oh yeah, that sounds like a plan,' replied Stone.

'Well, what else do you suggest?'

'I really don't know,' replied Stone, looking around before looking back at Daniel. 'Hey, is that guy really a friend of yours?'

Daniel nodded.

'And you had no idea he was off his nut?'

Daniel shrugged. 'No, no idea. Granted, I remember he once told me he hated dolphins, but he seemed relatively sane.'

'He hated dolphins? Who the hell hates dolphins?' and you didn't take that as a sign?'

'Listen,' replied Daniel, 'stop making out this is my fault somehow. I'm in just as much shit as you right now. We need to find a way of here somehow.'

Before Stone could answer, the basement door creaked open from above, and footsteps came down the wooden stairs, echoing around the cellar walls.

Jamie then stood in front of all three of his captives with a very large knife in his hand.

'Hello again.' There was a glint in Jamie's eye. He was clearly aroused by the excitement of killing again – the thrill of murdering not just one person this time, but three was intoxicating.

Daniel decided to try and get Jamie talking straight away. 'So it's true then. You're the Drainpipe Killer?'

Jamie closed his eyes and took a deep breath, trying to calm himself down. He opened his eyes again and looked back at Daniel. 'If you mean I'm the Red Rose Strangler, then yes, I am. I killed both those women in Partick. Why? Does that surprise you? Did you think I didn't have it in me to murder someone?'

The more he talked, the more it was clear Jamie was insane. Yet, Daniel really did have no idea about Jamie. He never suspected his longtime friend was mentally unstable, let alone a danger of any kind.

'Listen, I thought we were best mates. Ever since school, all I've tried to do is look out for you. How can you think differently?'

Jamie stared at Daniel and then pinched his eyes with thumb and forefinger. It was as if reality hurt whenever he tried to process it.

'Stop it, Daniel. I know what you're trying to do, but you can't stop me. You need to pay for what you have done to me. I need to do this.'

'You don't need to do anything,' replied Daniel.

'But I do. I just do. You don't understand.'

'You know what, Jamie?' said Stone. 'You're right. You're absolutely right. I actually agree with you.'

'Agree with what?' Jamie asked.

'That's it's a crime you haven't been discovered yet. I completely agree.'

'Do you?' said Jamie sarcastically, not bothering to look at Stone but continuing to look at Daniel.

'I do,' Stone continued. 'I honestly can't believe you haven't been discovered yet. I mean, it's obvious you have star quality. I'm in the business myself, as you probably know – television. I'm with the BBC at the moment, and we're always on the lookout for genuine talent.'

Jamie knew Stone was humouring him or even taking the piss. Yet, he couldn't help but be pleased with the words he heard. He looked across at Stone. 'I don't expect you to understand, but I'm really very talented. Lots of people say so. Yet, no one will give me that break. That one chance. You know, that's all I'm asking for, a chance. It's wrong.'

'It is,' Stone agreed. 'One hundred percent wrong. Listen, I know this might sound crazy, but I'm actually in a position to help you. I have an opportunity I think you'd be perfect for. You see, I've just landed a new show on the BBC. I need a sidekick, a co-presenter if you like. It needs to be someone new, different; frankly, I think you'd be perfect. I really do.'

Jamie burst out laughing. 'Seriously, you do come out with some shite, Stone Johnson.' Yet, as Jamie said this, part of him wanted to hear more.

Stone continued. 'I'm not bluffing either, honest I'm not. I can speak with the bosses at the

BBC, they think a lot of me. I think they would be delighted with you.'

'He's right, Jamie,' Geneva said. 'I can vouch for what he says. Stone does have his own show. He asked me to be the co-presenter, but I can't do it because I've got other commitments. And Stone's right, too, about you being perfect for the show, and I could also help you too, really I could. Just imagine it. It would be wonderful.'

Jamie shook his head. 'Unbelievable. Do you really believe I'm that stupid that I'm going to fall for that?' But his expression betrayed his words. As the idea turned in his mind, Jamie thought it was somehow a possibility despite all that had happened. Who knew, as crazy as it seemed, maybe this could be the break he was looking for. Finally. But was it too late? Would these three actually keep quiet about what he'd done? The thing was, if they did, Jamie could actually see himself as a co-presenter. Of course, it wasn't his ideal role, but he was sure he could make something of it if given a chance. That's all he wanted, a chance. He could—'

'What the fuck are you lot on about?' It was Daniel who stopped Jamie's thoughts of TV stardom mid-flow. 'You're offering this psycho a slot on your TV show? He's murdered two people, for Christ's sake!'

Snapping back to the reality of the

situation, Jamie was angry now. Really angry. Daniel had popped his bubble just as he'd almost been taken in by Stone's bullshit. He suddenly realised there was no way it could happen. Daniel was right. It was too late. He had murdered two people. It was over. Now he had to kill these people. This was now the best way, his only way, to achieve some kind of fame. Weren't infamy and fame simply two sides of the same coin? Jamie had to kill these three before him, and he had to get it over with ASAP.

'Listen, Jamie,' said Stone, 'forget about Daniel. He doesn't know show business like we do. You said yourself he never appreciated your talent. It's not too late. We could come to some sort of arrangement if you like. I'm sure we could. Right now. A contract. I've also got money. I've got thousands. Just tell me how much you want?' Stone was trying to retrieve the situation, but now it really was too late – the moment had gone.

Stone then turned to Daniel. 'Well done, mate, very well done. You're a real prize doughball, you know that?'

'You're as nuts as he is.' Daniel replied.

'Fuck off, Daniel.'

'That's right. You like telling people to fuck off, don't you, Stone?' Jamie said as he was brought back to reality. 'Just like that night, you told me to fuck off when you were with Geneva?'

'What can I say? You caught me at a bad moment.'

'Oh, I bet I did. And from what I've been reading in the papers, you seem to have a lot of bad moments. You're not exactly Mr Popular, are you? Anyway enough – we need to get this over with.'

'Kill Daniel first,' said Stone.

Now realising he may indeed have been too hasty with his outburst, Daniel tried in his own way to stop or at least stall Jamie from carrying out his plans. 'Listen, Jamie, you're not going to do this. For Christ's sake, I'm your friend. You know what you're going to do? You're going to let all of us go and give yourself up to the police. That's what you're going to do. It's over. You know that. Deep down, you know that. You may as well hand yourself in now.'

'Don't fucking talk to me like I'm a child. No one listens to me! No one!'

Jamie's sudden rage took them all by surprise.

'I listen to you, Jamie.' The soft voice of Geneva out of nowhere made Stone, Daniel, and Jamie turn their heads towards her once more.

'I know you think I've been working against you somehow, but I haven't. Honest, I haven't. Don't you remember, Crack, I wasn't like the others, was I? I always tried to help you. Who was the one who always stood up for you at drama school? I was always there when others were… you know, when others weren't there for you. But I was. Why would you want to hurt me, of all people? In spite of what you think now, of all people, why would you want to hurt me?'

Jamie stared at the floor as if trying to comprehend what Geneva was saying. He placed his hand on his head as if it hurt, and his wiring couldn't take another version of his own truth. Yet, a deeper part of him recognised Geneva had indeed tried to help him in the past. 'You're right, Gen. I know you were the one person at drama school who tried to help me. I do, but I have no choice now. I'm sorry. It's gone too far. I can't let you go now, even if I wanted to. I have to do this. I have to.'

The confusing and conflicting emotions within Jamie suddenly made him incredibly sad, and he walked towards Geneva with tears in his eyes. With her final kind words, Geneva had signed her own quicker death warrant. She had made Jamie realise that the sooner it was over for her, the better. He stroked her cheek and walked behind her, putting the razor-sharp edge of the knife against her neck. Geneva closed her eyes, tears still rolling down her cheeks, but she now made no noise, accepting her fate.

'Don't do it, Jamie! You can't do it! Please!' As Daniel pleaded with Jamie to stop, he was still trying to make his chair topple over, but it was to no avail. There was nothing left he could do to save Geneva. Stone looked away, hoping he wouldn't hear the parting slice of skin as Jamie slit her throat.

Jamie was breathing heavily as he steeled himself to do what he knew he had to. He closed his eyes and prepared to pull the knife across the tender skin of Geneva's throat when, from above, there was the sound of breaking glass.

Chapter 55

Footsteps

Taken by surprise, Jamie pulled the knife away from Geneva's neck. As he continued to look towards the ceiling, there was a look of fear in his eyes, and he was paralysed by indecision. Someone in fact, it sounded like more than one person had entered the house. Daniel wondered what he should do. Could he quickly kill his three captives before the unexpected intruders reached the cellar?

Still paralysed by indecision, Jamie stood posed with the knife in his hand. There was now the sound of more footsteps. It sounded like at least two people, more even, going from room to room. There were some muffled shouts, and Jamie knew he had to act now if he was to act at all. He put the knife back against the neck of Geneva. Yet he seemed mesmerised by the sounds from above. Jamie then ran up the wooden stairs and bolted the cellar door. He came back down again, his eyes wide with fear and confusion.

Both Stone and Daniel thought about shouting up towards the police but, at the same time, didn't want to provoke Jamie in any way. All four now listened to the sounds from above and could hear the hurried footsteps were getting nearer and nearer. The cellar doorknob rattled as someone tried to turn it.

There was a muffled shout of 'Kick it open' followed by the sound of a boot trying to do just that. Jamie had backed away into a corner of the basement now. The three seated captives stared at Jamie, who was crouching like a terrified child.

After a couple more kicks, the cellar door burst open, loudly slamming against the wall, and someone shouted, 'Yep, they're down here!'

Stone and Daniel looked at each other in expectation and relief while Geneva was still trembling from anticipating her death moments before.

Daniel whispered to Stone, 'Thank God. Talk about just in time!'

First, one pair, then a second pair of shoes came down the stairs into view, followed by a third pair of shoes. Red shoes which complemented green trousers.

Chapter 56

Explanations

As the three descending men came round and stood in front of the three hostages, there was a confused look from Daniel and Geneva as Stone said, 'Oh, for fuck's sake.'

'Well, well,' Davy McGregor said. 'What the fuck's going on here then?'

Instead of answering this question, Daniel had his own equally pressing question to ask. 'Who are you?'

Before McGregor could answer, Stone turned towards Daniel and said calmly, 'Daniel, remember I told you about those psychopaths?'

'Yeah?' replied Daniel.

'Well, they're the psychopaths.'

'Psychopaths? Who the fuck are you calling psychopaths?' McGregor looked at Stone and then Daniel. 'So you're Daniel McLeod then?

Ah've been looking for you. I was told Stone here killed Susan McLaughlin, but now Ah'm told you're the one who really killed her. Susan happened to be a very good friend of mine.'

'I didn't murder Susan McLaughlin,' Daniel said. 'I haven't killed anyone. It's him over there that did it.' Daniel nodded in the direction of Jamie, who had stood up again but had stayed in the corner of the basement. 'He's the one who murdered her. He not only killed Susan McLaughlin,' continued Daniel, 'but Kimberley O'Hara. Just before you arrived, he was going to kill the three of us.'

McGregor looked at Jamie and wasn't impressed by the rather pathetic-looking character in the corner. 'Is that true, big man?' he asked. 'Are you the one who murdered Susan McLaughlin?'

Jamie laughed, but it was a hollow laugh as he recognised that, although not the police, these three strangers were not good news. 'Course not! He's talking tosh. You were right the first time: it was him, Daniel, who murdered Susan, and these other two knew about it. Kimberley O'Hara was a good friend of mine, just like Susan was yours. That's why I've got them here. Fact is, we're both on the same side. Brothers from different mothers, you could say.'

McGregor nodded but didn't seem entirely

convinced by Jamie or his words. 'Brothers from different mothers? What kind of pish talk is that?'

Jamie tried again. 'I mean, I'm after who killed Kimberley O'Hara just like you're after who killed Susan McLaughlin. It's kind of ironic, really.'

McGregor walked towards Jamie. He knew something wasn't quite right about him. 'Ironic? Fucking moronic more like.'

His two sidekicks laughed. McGregor smiled, pleased at his own joke, before he looked closely at Jamie again. 'Seriously, wee man...' Everyone noticed Jamie had gone down a size in McGregor's estimations. 'What the fuck does ironic mean?'

'You don't know what ironic means?' Jamie needlessly asked.

'Naw, Ah, don't fucking know what ironic means.'

Jamie didn't know what to say. At best, he could explain what ironic meant, but he had an idea that could just make things worse, and yet if he didn't answer the question, that could be a bad move too. In the end, he decided to keep silent.

'What's your name again?' McGregor asked.

'Jamie.'

'OK, Jamie, I'll buy it for now. Let's say we do this together? It looks like we could be on the same side after all.'

Stone shouted out, 'Listen! You're making a big mistake. Jamie really is the one who murdered Susan McLaughlin. He told us all! He's the one you're after, I swear it!'

McGregor spoke to Stone while pointing to Daniel. 'But you told me before it was this cunt here, and now you're saying it's this other cunt? I'd wish you'd make your mind up; I don't know who to believe any more. It's beginning to look like both of you could have killed Susan, just like you both killed that Kimberley bird.'

McGregor then turned his attention to Geneva as if he had only now noticed her. 'And who the fuck are you, doll?'

Jamie now stepped forward from the corner and answered the question before anyone else could.

'She's called Geneva. She was in on it. She was the one who set Susan McLaughlin up, so Daniel could kill her. Stone knew all about it too. You're right, they were all in it together.'

Geneva was still wondering what the hell was going on. Weren't these three men plain-clothed police or something? Yet, they didn't seem like police, far from it. So who were they, and what was going on?

Stone then shouted at Jamie. 'You lying bastard! How—' then Stone stopped mid-shout as another thought occurred to him, and he looked back at McGregor. 'How come you knew I was here, anyway?'

McGregor indicated his two henchmen. 'These two have been following you since you went to that cafe on Eglington Street and met this one.' He indicated Daniel. 'They followed both of you after you left the café, but they lost you in the streets not far from here. Luckily they spotted your car again in the driveway here and then gave me a call to come down.'

'Well, Jamie really is the guy you're after,' Stone repeated. 'I'm telling you, that's the truth. I know I said before it was Daniel, but I was just saying that. That guy there lured us all here to do us in. He's completely nuts.'

McGregor still didn't know who to believe. Though the more he thought about it, the more he was curious and suspicious of Jamie.

Sensing McGregor's growing doubts about him, Jamie decided to try to shift events in his favour again. 'He's lying. I told you I'm here for the same reason you are. I loved Kimberley O'Hara. These three had a hand in killing her, just like they murdered Susan McLaughlin. '

Geneva then intervened by speaking in her quiet, calm voice. After not talking since McGregor and his henchmen had arrived, it made everyone turn to her in surprise. She directed her words towards McGregor. 'I don't know who you are, but you need to listen to us. You need to free us now. Why would we all be lying?' Why would we be tied up like this? He is talking nonsense. He really is completely crazy. You need to listen to me! If you want the person who killed Susan McLaughlin, you want that man there. He just admitted it all to us before you arrived.'

As Geneva seemed the most normal of anyone in the room, which, admittedly, wasn't that hard an impression to achieve, it still made McGregor inclined to believe her testimony more than anyone else's.

As everyone focused on Geneva, there was collective surprise at hearing Jamie suddenly bounding up the stairs two at a time.

'Get him,' McGregor shouted to his henchmen, but by the time they could react, Jamie was already at the open cellar door. However, to everyone's surprise, Jamie stopped at the top of the stairs, turned around and slowly started walking down the steps again. Jamie was followed down the steps by two men who stopped near the bottom of the stairs and surveyed the room. 'Hello Jamie, everyone.'

Patterson said. 'This is DS Simpson, and I'm DCI Patterson, Partick CID.'

Epilogue

As DCI Patterson walked down the steps into the basement that afternoon and took in the scene before him, he felt an instant sense of relief. For one thing, he immediately recognised Jamie Campbell and knew he'd finally captured the murderer of Susan McLaughlin and Kimberley O'Hara. As for the other characters in that basement – Stone, Daniel, Geneva, McGregor and the two henchmen –there was plenty of time to figure out later on how they all ended up in that basement.

Indeed, in the days that followed, typing up report after report, all the pieces of the puzzle gradually fitted together. Then once the photos were taken down, the files stored away, and the board literally wiped clean, Patterson could relax, at least, until the next case was put in front of him. Or, put another way, until he found himself standing in front of another murder victim.

For some reason, this case had been a little bit different for Patterson. Perhaps it was due to his anxiety continually getting worse or the situation with Stephanie not getting better. Yet, the events of the last few weeks had been far more intense for him than any murder investigation he had worked on before.

Admittedly, it wasn't the first time after a murder enquiry had ended that he felt deflated, exhausted, and not a little downhearted. He questioned whether he wanted to spend his life being the moral force in the city that chased murderer after murderer after murderer. It never seemed to stop the killings.

As Patterson tidied up the last remaining aspects of the case, he knew one thing for certain. His number one priority shouldn't be his job but his marriage. Whether with or without his help, if Stephanie didn't get better, soon she too would be on a slab. Ultimately, Patterson loved her, and the situation with Booth only highlighted that.

However, Booth was still a situation. Patterson had spent every opportunity since their encounter on the stairs trying to avoid her. She had been doing the same, avoiding manoeuvres with him, so their paths rarely crossed. He knew they both couldn't do that forever. In addition, he knew he had to get himself sorted out. His anxiety was a constant daily companion that was ever more difficult to live with, like Stephanie.

So, Patterson thought, once the case was truly over, that's to say after the trial of Jamie Campbell took place, he would take the holiday time he had built up over the past couple of years and take a step back from his job to spend more time with Stephanie.

As it turned out, the trial of Jamie Campbell never took place. Jamie was certified under the Mental Health Act and detained indefinitely at the State Hospital in Carstairs. Throughout his arrest and initial time in custody, Jamie was convinced there would be a public outcry about how he had been treated. Jamie wasn't mad. Surely the public, his fans, could see that and eventually realise how he was a human being driven to murder, an overlooked talent that deserved recognition.

Yet, there was no public outcry. Only an outrage at two young women being killed by a man who craved fame. It prompted a debate about today's society's values and whether the death penalty should be reintroduced. As for the other figures who slowly walked up the stairs from the basement that day, each had their own story to carry on.

Davy McGregor was charged with the kidnapping of Stone Johnson but given a suspended sentence. In part, the leniency was given because of his intervention, albeit accidental, that had helped save the lives of three other people. That he had planned on killing the murderer of Susan McLaughlin was quietly ignored by the procurator fiscal. Another plus for him was that he found renewed fame as a stand-up and accomplished one of his life goals. Namely to have a self-titled documentary Chuckles on Channel 5.

Stone was also able to eventually cash in on his new-found fame and role as the kidnap victim who'd just cheated death at the hands of the infamous Drainpipe Killer. After an investigation by the Financial Services Authority, he was fined and banned from operating a business for two years. Yet, after that time, he quietly started a new business, which did very well. To everyone's surprise, a satellite TV channel also gave the go-ahead for a new consumer programme starring Stone Johnson, this time without the need for a sidekick.

Geneva, too found her own success as a highly respected business correspondent, working for a large media company in Birmingham. She was delighted at finally being able to make money out of her intelligence and not her perceived stupidity. Most pleasing of all, she would also find personal happiness within a loving marriage.

As for Daniel McLeod, he found it very difficult to adapt back to normal life after the shock of finding out his friend was a murderer, a murderer who had also planned to kill Daniel. Still, after time passed, the trauma he had experienced lessened, and he slowly began to get on with his life again. He found a job as a parking attendant in Glasgow city centre. At night he went to college and studied accounting, eventually having his own accounting business. He also reconciled with Deborah, who first became a regular visitor to his flat in Broomhill before moving back in with him.

The last piece of the puzzle which fell into place was Daniel finally finding out what was in the little plastic bag Deborah had paraded in front of Steve outside the butcher's that Saturday morning.

Sausages.

Printed in Great Britain
by Amazon